The Plastic Rosary on the Mirror

Michael C. Mergler

D0963799

St. Michael Records, Inc.
Dayton, Ohio

Published by: St. Michael Records, Inc.
PO Box 2912, Dayton, Ohio 45401-2912
www.stmichaelrecords.com

*This book is a work of fiction. The names,
characters, places and incidents are used fictitiously.*

Cover Design & Artwork: Gary Hartman Design
Cover Photos: Richard P. Kallas Photography
Typesetting by: Seth Sampson
Executive Producer: Tony Ciani

Printed in the United States of America

Works of non-fiction by Michael C. Mergler:

*Long Night's Journey Into Day -
a rock 'n' roll Faith Witness*

2 CD's with 90 minutes of music and a 100 page book
that tells the true story of one man's journey to God.
Order Blank in rear of this book, or Order at our website:

www.stmichaelrecords.com

CONTENTS

This book is dedicated to the sanctity of marriage and the pursuit of Wisdom by those who desire to be more Christ-like, and to my wife, who not only puts up with me but loves me, too.

May our children and descendants always have faith in Jesus Christ and his one, holy, catholic and apostolic Church.

May we all work for Christian Unity by our obedience to the teachings of Christ, and our love for each other.

ACKNOWLEDGEMENTS

I don't believe in Forewords. I go straight for the story. But I must thank: *Deborah Trimborn*, one of my opticians, for encouraging me to write a book to amuse her; *Bud Macfarlane, Jr.* for encouragement, discouragement and good advice; and my draft readers - *Laurence Bonhaus, Tony Ciani, John Johnson, Ann & Mel Maron, Robert McGuire, Mark Minardi, Kristina Perkins, Wayne Post,* and especially, my de facto editor *Thomas Steigerwald*, for their constructive criticism. Special thanks to our apostolate's suffering soul and prayer warrior, *Hazel Thirkield*, and our ever faithful Executive Producer, *Tony Ciani*. Most of all, thanks to our *God*, who answered my prayers for help with this book by sending the *Holy Spirit*, and the recession of 2002, for just enough time away from my real job to write it.

With Our Lord,

Mike Mergler
On the Assumption of the Blessed Virgin Mary
August 15, 2002

Chapter 1 - *It Was All Just an Accident, Really*

Bam! The steering wheel exploded and what seemed like baby powder and glitter blew into his eyes. Tony put his forearm out just in time to take the brunt of the blow from the airbag, a laceration he would only become aware of later on when he noticed the scab.

He had been standing on the brakes trying to push them through the floor to stop the van but too little, too late. He had caught sight of the other car speeding off the ramp across his path out of the corner of his eye, but not soon enough to avoid the crash. The lady next to him had been luckier. She was half a car length behind Tony. Enough to avoid the whole mess.

The speeding car grazed across the front of Tony's van, hit the median and spun. Traffic came to a standstill in every direction as stunned drivers gawked at the carnage. Tony was the first one out, hacking and blinking from the airbag explosion but otherwise unhurt. He had his seatbelt on and the only pain he felt was across his chest where the shoulder belt had dug in. He dropped his plastic rosary between the seats. One minute ago he was calmly on the third decade, the birth of Jesus. Now he was in shock as he ran toward the other car to see if the people inside were alright. Quickly he peered inside.

It was empty.

He spun around desperately searching for the occupants. "What the ...?" he thought. Then he saw him. Lying face up on the median was a young man with his eyes open unmoving. "Get up!" he thought, "Get up!" He just lay there, staring right into the glaring sun. Tony reached down and felt his neck. Then he saw the blood. It slowly began to run down the concrete behind his head, disconnectedly, as if it wasn't really from the victim at all. But he knew better. He stood up and faced the stunned traffic, threw his arms in the air and began screaming hysterically, "Get an ambulance! Get an ambulance!"

He saw dumbfounded faces in cars and trucks everywhere, staring back at him. "Do something!" he screamed frantically as he waved his arms at them all. Then suddenly every hand went up, cell phones to the ear. It would have been comical if it had not been so tragic. People began to get out of their cars and comfort him. Tony was crying, "We have to pray for him. We have to pray for him," to total strangers. A big black woman hugged him while he sobbed uncontrollably. "Oh, God, Oh, God, Oh, God," he cried hysterically. He was totally, depressingly helpless. All he could think of was, "What if this was one of my own kids?" And then he thought, "It *is* just like one of my own kids. We're all responsible for taking care of God's children." And this made it even more horrific.

He knew it wasn't his fault. The boy had run the light. But it didn't matter except to the cops. It seemed like it took forever for them to get there but in reality it was only about 90 seconds before the first cruiser showed up. Care Flight landed within ten minutes. They were back in the air in less time than that. "We don't think he'll make it," the cop told him. "We have to investigate it as a possible homicide. Would you like to go to the hospital?" he asked. "We'll need to confiscate your license until the investigation is completed."

Tony was thinking how the rosary had saved him, again. He was going fairly slowly when the accident had happened because he was praying, something he did in the car everyday. If he hadn't been praying he would have been going faster, and the boy would have hit him broadside, and possibly killed him. "The rosary saved my life," he thought, in a practical, matter-of-fact kind of way. But he didn't dwell on it. He was too depressed about the dying young man he had hit. "How many times have I driven like an idiot," he thought, "when it could have been me? Why wasn't he wearing his seatbelt? What was he thinking, running the light?!?"

All day, Tony prayed for him. He lit candles. He asked everyone he saw to pray for him. All to no avail. Or was it? The boy stayed alive until late that night. The nurses were amazed that he lasted that long. Long enough for his parents to see him and approve transplanting his organs to save the lives of 3 other people. The doctors said if he had lived he would have been a total vegetable from the brain injuries. Good comes out of bad. Isn't that just like God! Then why did Tony feel so horrible?

"Tony" was Anthony Joseph Mirakul, who appeared to the rest of the world to be nothing more than an average Joe with a wife and kids, a mortgage and a job he sometimes hated. His supervisors only saw the world on its own terms so they were unappreciative of his wise, spiritually-based insights about business. Usually by the time reality had proved Tony correct his bosses had forgotten what Tony had said. So they didn't pay any attention the next time either. And why should they? Tony himself was unaware of the depth of his own wisdom because he had no benchmark to measure it by.

Tony had carried baggage most of his adult life. His family and his teachers had concentrated on his flaws, hoping to improve him. But what they had done instead was make him feel like he could never be good enough to please them.

It was surprising then that Tony managed to inculcate most of the true Catholic values he was taught from the *Catechism* and the *Bible* into his character. Many times these truths conflicted with the messages Catholic kids received about trying to be accepted by the larger world of post-war America. Tony would sum up his educational experience with this statement: "Be a radical Christian willing to live and die for the love of God and your neighbor no matter what the cost, but make sure you get a good job, make a good living and don't rock any boats and embarrass us."

From the bishops on down, the word was "blend in and be acceptable" to protect the immigrants from anti-Catholicism in America. It had the unintended effect of teaching America's 60+ million Catholics to avoid standing up for their faith so they wouldn't be labeled as "different."

As a sinner Tony had failed to live as a true Christian many, many times. But even when he tried to live by these principles he found he often did not "blend in." He had gradually come to realize that a true Catholic would never be able to blend in enough to be accepted by the world. "You cannot serve both God and mammon" was still true. There would always be tension between these opposing forces.

As a youngster he had believed he was inadequate and it was his own fault. It had taken a long time for him to gain the wisdom that taught him his own self-worth was not based on his success or failure in worldly terms or even in terms of other's expectations. It was only on God's terms that real judgment occurred, or even mattered. This gift of wisdom he had been receiving little by little his entire adult life led him to understand that it was only his faith and servanthood to the Lord that would save him. As a result, Tony just chugged along like the tortoise in the fable, looking like a loser to the rest of the world but growing steadily in wisdom and faith and blessings the world could not see and did not value.

This car accident was one more paradox of blessing. Tony made himself go right back through that same intersection the next day to get back up on that horse and ride. He would recover from the trauma both physically and emotionally. He would have a few sleepless nights and a few crying jags but there would be no post-traumatic stress. He would, however, forever see the face of that dying young man lying there with his eyes wide open but not seeing anything. And his wisdom and appreciation for the gift of life would continue to increase.

Tony would be blamed by his boss for totaling his vehicle at the next sales meeting. It wouldn't matter that it wasn't his fault or that the other guy died. All his boss, Carson Penney, would think of was the hassle of replacing the company car Tony had totaled. This was odd since Carson, who had nothing better to do, actually loved to buy used cars and trucks. He prided himself on buying old vans with 100,000+ miles on them and running them out to 200-300,000 miles. If an ad said, "Runs good, needs engine," he would buy it. And when the vehicle broke down it was always his employee's fault for being too hard on it, never the fact that they were old heaps that needed maintenance once in a while. "Why are you so hard on cars?" he would ask Tony.

Tony would just shrug. No use protesting. Tony had a nasty penchant for telling the truth, one of the aforementioned principles that always seemed to cause him trouble. He would tell his boss the truth about his junk car buying and his boss would tell him, "Nobody else complains." Of course, other people did complain but Carson ignored it. He really didn't want to hear the truth. Tony finally gave up and started joking about how he would destroy anything the company gave him. So he was branded as the man who destroyed cars. He could be driving down the road at 25 mph and shrapnel would fall out of the transmission onto the street. Of course, it was Tony's fault.

If a muffler fell off on the freeway you could bet Tony was right behind it getting one of his tires shredded. When it came to cars, Tony had a cloud over his head, like *Joe Btfsplk*, the cartoon character in the old *Li'l Abner* comic strip.

Tony didn't care. He would go on being Tony. He even picked up hitchhikers. Sometimes he would do this with his kids in the car. He would teach them little life-lessons this way. This really angered his wife, Amana. She thought it was unsafe and he was irresponsible for doing this. And maybe he was, but then so was the Good Samaritan. Tony didn't think it was right to pass someone on the road who needed a ride, unless there was some circumstance that precluded it. Tony believed that God only put people in his path at a time when Tony had the time to give them a ride, and his help or advice. If Tony really needed to be somewhere at a particular time God made sure there was no one on the road hitchhiking. At least that's what Tony believed.

Still there had been problems. Like the time he had picked up a black man near his parish who claimed he hadn't been able to find Tony's church after being sent there for help by another Catholic church downtown. When Tony took him to find their pastor and couldn't, he ended up giving the man a check for part of his rent so he wouldn't be homeless. A week later Fr. Studer chewed him out for supposedly telling this man he could go around and collect money in the priest's name in the neighborhood.

The man, it turned out, was a scam artist and had used the priest's name and Tony's check as an entree to scam money out of others. Fr. Studer was livid that someone had used his name and insisted that Tony must have told him to do it. Of course, Tony was oblivious to all of this. It took him a while to figure out what the priest was even talking about.

Fr. Studer told Tony he "better never use his name again to help any homeless people," and Tony just scratched his head. No good deed goes unpunished. At first Tony was angry. What he had done seemed like a perfect example of what Catholics were *supposed* to do but it didn't seem like Fr. Studer got it.

Then Tony remembered some of the times his own actions didn't line up with what the Church taught and decided to cut him some slack. After all, the devil went after the priests more than the lay people because everyone expected priests to be holier. If the devil could turn a priest he got a bad example bonus. Tony knew that the priests were just as faulty as everyone else. They just had a different job description. Every Christian was called to help make disciples of all nations, not just the priests.

Tony had not always been so wise. It had taken Tony over 40 years to learn these simple truths. And it had been a wild ride getting there. But now he knew.

This was Tony's world the day of the fatal accident when praying his rosary had probably saved his life, for the second time. It was late 1999 and the millennium was about to turn. America and the world were anxious about their computers possibly shutting down on 01-01-00 but Tony was following the lead of the Pope, who, instead of storing bottled water in the basement of the Vatican, was planning a huge Jubilee year of celebration. Tony did absolutely nothing to prepare for Chicken Little. Such was the wisdom he was growing in. And, of course, he would be right. But there were still a few times when he wondered if the Ark might leave without him because he didn't prepare anything.

The road he was traveling along with his wife, Amana, and their kids was curvy, steep and rocky. But they were making slow, steady progress on the road far less traveled by. Where they would go in the next few years is probably best understood by starting at the beginning for all concerned.

It was early 1951. Anthony Joseph Mirakul was the first and only baby boom baby for his parents. Apparently there was some complication that precluded his mom from having any more babies but his parents never told him what it was. People in his parents' generation didn't tell their kids such things.

It didn't matter anyway. The baby boom generation was like one big extended family. There were always kids over at someone else's house and vice versa. The fact that Tony didn't have any brothers or sisters never bothered Tony. It never even crossed his mind.

Tony went to Catholic grade school then played with all his Protestant and Jewish friends after school. When polio was being attacked Tony went with everyone else and swallowed the sugar cube they gave him in the gym at Leggett public school. St. Hedwig's Catholic school where Tony went also used the same public school gym for basketball practice because they didn't have a gym. And there weren't any nasty protests about it. That's just the way things were growing up in Akron.

Anthony Joseph "Tony" Mirakul had talent. His parents were sure of it. They just hadn't figured out exactly what it was yet. A good example of this was music. Tony took accordion classes at Zinner's in downtown Akron. His parents had enrolled him there because they had been sold on "the richness of music being necessary to the complete education of any child" by an itinerant music man who sold accordion lessons for Zinner's, and also Tupperware.

Tony had been to about 5 classes and had picked it up pretty well. Well enough that he didn't squeak. He also understood the beginnings of music theory that they were teaching him. It all seemed natural to him, just like math. And he was good at math.

Tony was eleven and in the 5th grade at St. Hedwig's, the Polish parish just north of downtown Akron. He was a good student but a bit hyperactive. With 55 kids in his class it moved too slow, so he was always lipping off.

Today his lip would get him in more trouble at Zinner's. Classes were only a half hour in a group (Tony's parents couldn't afford private lessons), and the class usually ended with some type of game that was actually a review of what they had learned. Today was no exception. The instructor divided the group into two teams and they had a competition with points. Tony was a competitor and liked this part of class best.

As the competition wound down it was a tight contest. Tony's group had one kid in it who wasn't particularly quick. Naturally, the final question that would decide the contest came down to this poor kid.

Tony knew the answer. It was a "G clef." Everyone on his team was anxiously waiting for the kid to answer it right so they could win. Tony was edged forward on his folding chair hanging his accordion down in front. "F" the kid said, as if it was a note.

"No!" Tony shouted, "It's a G clef!" As he yelled this he swung back violently in his chair. The accordion flew up over his head and the straps pulled it backward over the top of him. Tony panicked knowing that he had lost control of his instrument. For a split second he tottered on the two back legs of the folding chair, then the momentum of the accordion swung him back and over. The chair collapsed and flew out from under him all at once. Tony stuck out his hands and took two other kids down with him. The accordion went over his head and hit the back wall, then bounced back and landed on Tony's chest as he hit the floor. Everything just seemed to explode all around him. "Ooof!" He just lay there with the accordion pinning him to the ground. The hard commercial asbestos tile hurt his back, and it was cold. Books and papers were scattered everywhere. Tony knew he was in trouble.

The instructor helped everyone up and didn't yell too much at Tony. But when his parents came to pick him up, they received a check for their remaining prepaid lessons and were told that Tony was unwelcome to come back.

So there it was. Tony had been expelled from accordion school. Myron Floren had nothing to fear from Tony now. Neither did the Yankovics. Tony's parents were upset but didn't punish Tony because he was an only child and basically was spoiled. But after that they stopped looking for extracurricular activities involving music for Tony's personal growth, preferring to support more benign activities like radio DX'ing or potholder weaving on sick days when Tony had to stay home from school.

With so many baby boom children Tony was middle to above average in most things and totally forgettable to most everyone, although if he ever wanted to play rock 'n' roll music getting kicked out of accordion school would look good on his resume.

Tony came from good East European family stock on his dad's side, what used to be Prussia and also some Romanian. That's why they were in St. Hedwig's, a Polish parish. It was the closest to Prussian and Romanian they could get. Two of the three Masses on Sunday were still said in Polish. His father, Lawrence, worked the line at Goodyear, or Goodrich, Tony could never keep them straight. Eventually his dad moved to Firestone and became a foreman. His mom, Virginia, was Sicilian, and she stayed at home to cook and clean but took in sewing for extra cash.

Tony's father didn't like his wife having to work, even this little bit. His pride was hurt as head of the household because they needed the money. Tony's father was happier working the line than as a foreman, but he took the job to earn more money to provide for his family and so his wife wouldn't have to work. But Tony's mom kept working anyway, using the money for things they wouldn't have had otherwise.

Tony had a less than perfect relationship with his mother. She came down on the side of "blend in and be acceptable" to the exclusion of all else. She was a dichotomy of personal piety and indifference to anyone different from her. This moral dissonance irritated Tony no end, and caused him to love/hate his mom.

Instead of appreciating the sacrifices they made for him he concentrated on their imperfections the same as they did with him. Consequently, it was not a pleasant household to be in. Most of the time his parents were either ragging him or he was ragging them.

Tony would have to grow up before he finally appreciated the many sacrifices his parents had made. It would not be until he had his own family years later that he would see all that they had done, especially his mom, despite their inconsistencies.

Then he would realize how much responsibility it was to lead a family. And how expensive. In fact, the only way Tony was granted this wisdom was when he came to understand that his real mother, spiritually, of course, was the Blessed Virgin Mary.

Once, when one of Tony's black friends' momma died, he couldn't understand why his friend was so hurt, owing to the distance he felt from his own mother. But something changed for him in his late 30's. The Mother Mary he had always taken for granted while growing up - the May crownings, the rosary mysteries, the great songs he still would hum at odd moments - all became real to him as wisdom was granted him by God. And as Mary became real to him he slowly began to develop a relationship with his earthly mother, in fits and starts, of course.

His earth mother was still an odd mixture of ritual prayer and disdain for everyone else. But as Tony became more understanding of our human failings, including his own, his relationship with his mom improved. Mother Mary had given him the mother's love he had been missing. As they say in the news business, "If a guy says he has a mom, check it out!" If Tony had been asked he would have said, "I'm just now getting a mom. Check it out!"

But that was in the late 1990's. Aside from his relationship with his mom, growing up in Akron in the 50's and 60's had been blissfully ignorant fun for Tony. He played virtually every sport, if not organized, then pickup. There were always kids to get up a game with. He learned valuable social skills by having to organize the daily games. His father built him an indoor basketball court in their garage, and they played wiffle ball or baseball with a tennis ball in the backyard using a broom handle for a bat. This made it a real challenge to hit the ball and kept it from going too far when it was struck. Of course, all the mothers on the block complained that their brooms were always missing. Whenever someone needed a bat, no broom was safe from having its head sawed off.

Tony always had money in his pocket for a double cheeseburger or some fries, not because his parents spoiled him but because he had a paper route. He delivered in an old ramshackle apartment complex just a bike ride away from his house. It was easy to deliver but hard to collect because the residents were transient and poor.

Once Tony's lip actually came in handy on his route. There was a severely retarded boy, actually a teenager, whose family lived in one of the apartments. The boy's father made him a giant tricycle with three 26" wheels from old bikes. This made an enormous tricycle that was very stable to ride. It was almost impossible to tip it over. The boy would ride everywhere on his trike, drooling and making unintelligible moaning sounds as he rode.

His family was incredibly poor. Too poor to afford the 58 cents per week for the paper or even just Sunday only. It would be nice to say that Tony occasionally left them a free paper but no such idea ever crossed his mind. The Beacon Journal kept close tabs on every paper and so did Tony, since Tony had to pay for every one, no freebies. Consequently, Tony had little or no contact with this family other than seeing their son riding around the neighborhood. He knew they were poor, however, not only because they didn't take the paper but because the boy would often ride around shirtless in his underwear. Tony felt sorry for him but didn't know what he could do about it.

One hot summer afternoon Tony rounded the corner on his route to see a pack of 6 or 7 boys in a ring around the retarded boy on his trike. They were yelling and taunting him and wouldn't let him pass. Several of them were pelting him with pea gravel from the gutter. The poor child was totally bewildered, obviously frightened, and moaning and drooling in a panic because he couldn't escape.

Tony saw this, jumped off his bike and started screaming at the pack to let him go. Startled, the group turned around to see a furious Tony swinging his shoulder bag full of papers in a circle over his head like he was going to decapitate them all. Tony was screaming to get away from the boy and never bother him again.

As Tony began to advance the pack began to scatter. Even though several of them were bigger than Tony, Tony was angrier. He looked like a crazy man, spinning that bag and yelling at them. As they ran off in every direction Tony kept screaming at them to never come near the boy again, or they would have to answer to him.

The retarded boy wasted no time and rode off the minute the other boys began to scatter. In less than two minutes there wasn't a soul left on the street as far as the eye could see. Tony stood there fuming for a few minutes and then went on with his route, slamming every screen door after he threw the paper in because he was so mad.

Word got around the apartment complex about what had happened and after that no one picked on the retarded boy again. The neighborhood bullies and street urchins were terrified of Tony, and that was just fine with him. Sometimes his lip came in handy.

The only time Tony ever got into any real trouble himself was when he and his best friend Lenny Apsimov went nuts over slot car racing. Unfortunately, they didn't have enough money to pay to use the slot car track at a local hobby shop as often as they wanted to. So they had to find some dough.

Lenny came up with the bright idea of forging one of his father's checks by making it out to Tony. Tony didn't think it would work but against his better judgment went along with it. Lenny made out the check for $10 for "yard work", which was a lot of money back then, and Tony cashed it at the neighborhood pharmacy and gave the money to Lenny. Lenny then spent it all on himself at the track. Tony didn't even get to enjoy it.

This whole thing didn't make sense to Tony and he started worrying about it. Lenny assured him that he would just steal the check when his dad's statement came and he would never know about it. Tony didn't think this would work and so he worried for weeks. Finally Mr. Apsimov's statement came and Lenny stole the check.

Unbeknownst to Lenny or Tony, Mr. Apsimov contacted the bank for the missing check. After a few weeks the bank sent a photocopy, and low and behold, it was made out to Tony. Mr. Apsimov called Tony's dad, and then Tony caved and told his dad about what they had done and how Lenny had instigated it and taken all the money. Tony was sure he would be sent to the federal penitentiary for check forgery. "It's at least 10 years in the pen for that, isn't it?" he worried. Tony was miserable.

Tony's dad met with Mr. Apsimov and when he came home Tony thought for sure he was going to get a beating, or be grounded for life, or both. But it turned out his father was more angry with Mr. Apsimov, who made Tony's dad buy back the check, as if the money was the most important point of the episode and after his own son, Lenny, had actually spent all the money. Tony got only a minor punishment and swore to himself he would never do anything illegal, or that stupid again. The anguish for 6 weeks had been far worse than the moment's pleasure. It just wasn't worth it. Tony was relieved it was over and very thankful for his father's love and protection.

Tony didn't run around with Lenny much after that. And when he did he never let Lenny suck him into any of his schemes again. Tony made up his mind he wasn't going to be weak-willed like that again. What a horrible feeling it was, waiting to be caught.

By the end of Tony's freshman year at St. Vincent High School he no longer saw Lenny at all. Their paths had just diverged in the woods of life. The last he heard of Lenny he was running his own moving company specializing in moving elderly people from anywhere in Ohio to anywhere in Florida when they retired, and dodging the Better Business Bureau and the Ohio State Attorney General over customer complaints.

Tony couldn't seem to make up his mind in high school if he was a jock or an intellectual. His school, St. Vincent's, had a complex about trying to be like the University of Notre Dame in sports. They were the *Fighting Irish*, too. Everything was green. Sometimes athletics overpowered everything else, including academics. There was tremendous pressure to excel at sports. That's probably why Tony stuck it out to play football. That, and his hero, Jim Brown, legendary running back for the Cleveland Browns. Many considered Brown the greatest back to ever play the game, not just because of his stats but because of his desire. Defenders didn't tackle Brown. They jumped on him and held on until there were enough of them to ride him down. Tony learned what desire and determination were from watching Jim Brown carry 3 men on his back until he gained enough yards for a first down.

Every Sunday during the season Tony sat on the floor eating his mom's cold roast beef sandwiches with lettuce and mayo while his dad sat in his easy chair and enjoyed a Carling Black Label beer ('*Hey Mabel, Black Label,*' the ad whistled), and Jim Brown carried the other team on his back. It was awe-inspiring to watch. Tony was a step too slow for football but he made it up with determination because of Jim Brown.

On the other end of the spectrum, Tony loved to debate. He enjoyed the mental competition, and he loved to travel to the tournaments in other cities. He may have been the only kid in the school's history to letter in both Football and Debate. He loved to scratch out the yards, and he loved to win debates. He just didn't make such a big thing out of being a debater to avoid potential ridicule.

The highlight his junior year of Debate, besides winning the tournament at Carnegie-Mellon in Pittsburgh, was picking up one of the earliest copies of Jimi Hendrix' *Are You Experienced?* that he found in a North Pittsburgh record store long before it was available in Akron, and also going down to the very point at the confluence of the Monongahela and Allegheny Rivers where the Ohio started and peeing into the river in the dark. It was actually kind of scary, the black water swirling everywhere. Tony didn't want to fall in there. He would drown for sure.

"I wonder how long that'll take to get to Cincinnati?" He asked his teammates, rhetorically. His brainier teammates thought he was serious and started calculating average current flow per hour divided into 408 nautical miles to Cincinnati and came up with either 136 hours or 102 hours depending on whether the average speed of the current was 3 or 4 nautical miles per hour. Tony was sure he didn't want to be around these guys when he got out of school.

Just for fun he asked them what it would be if the average speed was Pi per hour. "That should keep them busy," he thought, and he scurried up the bank to get away from the swirling black water while a shudder ran up his back.

Tony had a girl his Junior and Senior years of high school. His schoolboy crushes before that were never very deep nor very painful when they didn't amount to anything. But this time was for real. She was a strikingly tall brunette with imploring brown eyes. Her name was Mary Ann Fulloder, and he loved the way she smelled. It must have been the pheromones that gave her a natural scent that drove Tony wild. He found her unbelievably attractive physically. It was his first real love.

She wasn't dumb but she would sometimes mix up words. For example, once Tony pulled into a parking garage with her on a double date, and she pointed at the brand new car in front of them and said, "Oh, look, a Vulva!" meaning a Volvo. Tony, and the couple they were with, burst into laughter, which Mary Ann did not understand, being blissfully ignorant of what she had just said. Tony loved her anyway.

Tony's bubble of love burst not long after they graduated from high school. He went to Kent State, and Mary Ann went to work. Before Tony finished his freshman year she was married and pregnant. Or pregnant and married. Tony wasn't sure which came first. He was heartbroken. There would be no more romantic late night dances in the dark in her daddy's den. He just wasn't ready and she was. An older guy had moved in. Tony petulantly wondered if he had a Volvo.

Tony became a field player from then on. He was always dating somebody new. He may have been comparing everyone he dated to his old flame. Or he may have just decided to be aloof. Either way, nothing serious was happening on the love front from then on through the rest of his college days, although he learned from many a coed that he had a certain amount of hidden sex appeal. This would come in handy in the real world.

And the real world was coming.

Chapter 3 - *Clerical Error*

John Davenport wasn't much for religion but he wanted to marry Lucy Bartini enough to not only be married in the church but agree to raise their kids Catholic. By this John meant that Lucy could raise them Catholic. He wasn't going to do anything. Nevertheless, here he was at St. Raphael's for his second daughter's christening. He was holding Donna, their first born, while Lucy was holding newly born Amanda.

John handed the birth certificate to Father Urban Hoecht, a no-nonsense German priest, in what was a largely Italian parish. "Father Sauerkraut," as he was known behind his back, proceeded to read the paper over, only to find that they had misspelled Amanda. "They left the 'd' out," he told John. "Besides, there's no Saint Amanda, so I can't name her this."

Lucy offered that her middle name was Maria, which surely qualified her because she was named after the Blessed Mother. "I guess I can just ignore that her first name is Amana, as far as church tradition is concerned. But I've got to follow the birth certificate for the records to match up," Father said. "So I guess her name is Amana Maria Davenport." John protested that her name was Amanda but to no avail. "Neither one's a saint," Father said. "Heathen," Father thought. "Nazi," John wanted to call him but didn't. "O.K.," Lucy said, "We'll call her Amana then." You don't buck the priest.

And so Amana Maria Davenport began her life as a Catholic at
St. Raphael's on High St. in Springfield, Ohio in June, 1954.
Second daughter of John & Lucy Davenport (Bartini) she was
a distant relative of Henry Flagler, the Buckeye who made it
rich with Rockefeller in Standard Oil and later built the railroad
so his rich friends could ride it all the way down to Key West,
and come stay at Flagler's hotels in St. Augustine for lavish
parties. Flagler disliked Catholics, notwithstanding that he
loved St. Augustine, the city, named for the great Catholic
saint. Now his grand niece was one. A Catholic, that is, not
necessarily a saint. And none of his money ever made it into
Amana's hands because he tried to extend the railroad across
the Straits of Florida to Havana only to have it blown away in
a hurricane, and along with it all his wealth. Amana would be
a normal middle class baby boom kid with the only thing
keeping her from a world of WASPness being her mother's
Italian immigrant parents.

"Tha-doon-yah-nah-mush-a-thod-the!" her grandmother
would snap when Amana would do something stupid, like
take a spoonful of food out of a bowl and drip it across the
tablecloth, rather than put the bowl next to her plate. That
meant, "You need a good hit on the head!" in Sicilian, which
was hillbilly Italian. "Aw-thayed-ee!" meant "would you just
look at that!" when someone did something idiotic. It was the
closest thing in Sicilian to "oy-vay!"

Amana would be a teenager before she knew what some words
meant. "Bastha" was really pasta, or spaghetti. And "Bastha with
Soogoo" was spaghetti with meat sauce. The "Gocka-roonee"
was what you got if you ate too much fruit. "Bootatoonie" was
a ski cap, something Amana learned when she lost it at Elder-
Beerman's department store on Siebenthaler when she was a
budding thirteen and asked the clerk "Mister, have you seen my
bootatoonie?" which the man took to mean something obscene
and yelled at her.

The family had moved to Dayton a few years after Amana's birth, so all she really remembered of growing up was Dayton. And even that she was trying to forget, Dayton in the 50's and 60's being about as far removed from anything happening as one could possibly get. Dayton was the tool & die machine shop beer drive-thru capital of the world. It's nickname was "Little Detroit" because it had over 30 auto plants, more than any other city in the world except Detroit. It was said that when Detroit sneezed, Dayton caught pneumonia. And John Davenport worked for GM, the area's largest employer.

This meant alternating good times and bad, lots of overtime and lots of downtime for strikes. Feast or famine. It bred a certain selfishness and frustration in everybody, union or management, and *everybody* was in union or management, except the federal workers at Wright Patterson Air Force Base, which had its own boom-bust cycle. The latter was dependent on the winds of Washington, rising and falling with defense spending in Congress.

The whole town was manic-depressive when it came to work. At any given time one person could be working himself to death while his neighbor was starving to death. If defense was hot, autos were not, and vice versa.

Geniuses and giants had roamed the environs of Dayton at the turn of the 20th century. The Wright Brothers taught the world how to fly, and as spoils received effective control of the Air Force. Wright-Patterson AFB stood as testament to that. At the same time, Boss Kettering had invented the electric starter, which GM had to have to make its autos run, so to get the patents they bought Dayton Electric and built the parts factories in Dayton. Then John Patterson bought the cash register patent and built National Cash Register, creating thousands more manufacturing jobs. This all happened in the early 1900's and the town had been coasting ever since.

This was Dayton's curse. It hadn't produced an original idea or a strong leader in half a century. The community couldn't seem to find any shared purpose for its existence. Eventually this devolved into a civic inferiority complex that would produce comments like "That's a great idea but they'll never let us do that here." "They" being this mysterious group of somebody-elses who kept all good ideas from happening in town. And that's why everyone was so frustrated and self-centered. They were all fighting over the scraps that fell off the table.

Into this world ventured Amana Davenport along with her older sister Donna. Donna was the beautiful one. When Donna was little everyone thought she should be a movie star, like Shirley Temple. Then when Donna became a teenager everyone compared her to Natalie Wood in *Rebel Without a Cause*. She definitely had Natalie's features but what was unusual was her vivid red hair with dark complexion rather than freckles. The result was a unique and mysterious look that only Donna possessed. This eventually led her to modeling.

Amana on the other hand was not as gifted with looks. She was a strawberry blond with very little of the Sicilian in her, except for one thing, she was built for babies. She had full breasts and full hips and men were instinctively attracted to her without realizing why. So despite forever being in Donna's shadow, and definitely feeling inferior to her sister, Amana had the gifts men really wanted in a wife and mother. Amana didn't understand any of this, thinking especially that her hips were a drawback to attracting men. She wished she could look like Donna who was thinner overall and less hippy.

As a child Amana was impish. For example, she loved berries of all kinds but particularly strawberries. Once when she was 3 or 4 years old her mother Lucy found her sitting in their small strawberry patch grinning from ear to ear. She had stripped the plants of every piece of fruit and happily eaten them all. From then on she was known as "Strawberry" because of both her hair color and her penchant for eating every strawberry in the house and garden.

In early adolescence Amana took to playing with a number of the boys in the neighborhood. This was quite unusual since the boys usually hung with the boys and the girls with the girls. Amana did her share of playing with the girls but she also liked sports and other games the boys would play. Her favorite was "Sky King," which the boys loved to play, fighting over who would get to be the hero, Sky King. Amana loved to play this because she always got to be "Penny," the damsel in distress. For some reason this appealed to Amana's budding sexuality, although she had no idea that was what was going on. Most girls like the idea of being saved by the handsome prince but Amana's fantasy was more realistic, since "Sky King" was in a more contemporary setting.

This was how Amana achieved her first kiss. It was just after Butch Conn had saved her in the desert mountains of San Gabriel. That is, he had carried Amana down from the loft her dad had built in the back of the garage, which served as the San Gabriel Mountains during that day's game of "Sky King."

Poor Butch didn't have a chance. Amana just reached up and kissed him while he had his hands full carrying her. All the boys went "Ecch!" and made fun of Butch, which ended the game immediately. But later Butch snuck back and cornered Amana by the side of the garage and stole another kiss now that he knew Amana liked him. It wasn't a bad first kiss at all.

As Amana and her sister Donna grew older they both attended Julienne High School, an all-girls Catholic school just north of downtown. Amana tended to be shy in her sister's shadow. To protect herself she joined the Service Club. This allowed her to go to social events she would otherwise be too shy to attend.

The Service Club would set the tables for banquets and otherwise do all the support work for events both at her high school and the Catholic boys' high school as well.

The biggest advantage of this was Amana got to go to every dance without feeling a need to have a date. She could be there and observe without being out on a limb socially. She would work furiously to check everyone's shoes before a sockhop and then wander in and enjoy the dance knowing that she had a safe place to run back to if she needed to.

These dances were her favorite, especially the summer dances outside in the courtyard behind Chaminade, the boys' school. Amana knew what "sweet summer sweat" meant long before it was used to describe the dance in the song "Hotel California." The humid Ohio night was sensual. The music pulsated under the stars. She would imagine herself in the arms of one of the older boys, dancing so tightly. Her imagination never went beyond this point because just to be wanted was all she wanted. It was a fantastic adolescence, pining away for Mr. Right.

Soon some of the mystique surrounding the two schools, and especially the courtyard, would disappear. Declining enrollment would force the merger of the two institutions and something would be lost forever, that daily distance from going to two separate schools that made coming together for a dance, and especially a dance in the courtyard, so special. Now girls and boys both would walk through the courtyard 4 times a day, robbing it of its special status as a rare, almost secret, meeting place. Many of these children were products of romances that began in that courtyard and ended in marriage. Some families had seen 3 or 4 generations get their start from a dance in that very courtyard.

Attending a dance there was a little like walking an emotional high wire without a net. Raging hormones threatened to throw you to your death but happiness waited for you at the other end of the wire. It was always a chore for the Brothers of Mary to control. It was not Catholic to be too sensual, yet it was perfectly Catholic for love to bloom. It was why boys and girls, soon to be men and women, came together at the dance. It was modern courtship, threatening to spin out of control at any second, thereby making it so fantastical. The brothers were alternately amused and offended by what went on, occasionally intervening to pull some couple back from the edge of perdition. They were, of course, far more lenient than the sisters at Julienne, since they were men. The sisters would tell you so, given the chance.

Amana didn't understand any of this. All she felt was the taut tension of adolescent desire. But she was far too inhibited for it to turn disastrous at that place and at that age. For her it was sweet deprivation.

Amana would be part of the last graduating class before Julienne merged with Chaminade, and the Julienne property sold off. The usual sadness of graduating from high school would be heightened by the sense of the end of the school itself. There would be nothing to come back to. And the new arrangement would never be the same. The courtyard would soon be nothing more than a well-traveled thoroughfare for students. Amana felt like she was getting out just before the door slammed her from behind.

Donna had graduated a year earlier and gone off to New York to become a regular old model, the term "supermodel" not having been coined yet. Amana went to college because she had more brains. Goodbye, Dayton, Hello, Columbus. Ohio State beckoned. With 40,000 + students the top 100 adjectives to describe OSU would never include the word "intimate."

It wasn't long after Amana matriculated to OSU that John Davenport took a job with Firestone Tire & Rubber in Akron. Akron and Dayton both were about to embark on the same long 30+ year decline that would decimate them both. Akron's decline would be milder only by comparison. The Davenports would long for the good old days in Dayton not knowing that they were actually better off than if they had stayed. The Dayton they knew was gone forever, victim of the racial cold war that broke out in the late 60's when the whites abandoned the center city to a black powerbase that would exploit its own people even worse than the whites had. It was sad but the Davenports were too busy getting on with their own lives to notice what had happened to their old hometown. They got to experience Akron's version of the same thing instead.

Ohio State was dramatically different from Julienne. All the wraps had been taken off. Amana tried beer and booze and pot. She even tried a little cocaine, which she declared, "incredible but too expensive." She hadn't yet found that special guy to gift her virginity to although she was getting anxious to find out what sex was like. It was this latter ambivalence that bothered her. She wanted to try sex but she also wanted to find the love of her life.

The good nuns had placed so much emphasis on sex being bad that she never thought of it as something good to give to the man she would share her life with. The idea that it was something you were supposed to do that wasn't evil had never come up at home or in school. In fact, it had been made more attractive by the forbidden nature her teachers had associated with it. Their attitudes didn't make sense. If sex was so bad why was it supposed to be saved for the love of your life? So even though she wanted to find that special guy she wasn't sure she would be able to wait for that one, true love before she had sex.

This went on for the first two years Amana was at OSU. At the beginning of her Junior year she met a business student named

Simon Wasp. Simon came complete with a reputation. He was handsome and brash. He performed with his own band around campus. Amana was impressed when she saw him perform on stage. When she told him between sets how impressed she was with his singing, Simon asked her out. Soon he was seeing her regularly. Amana was smitten. For Amana this solved her dilemma. She had met the man of her dreams, she thought.

Wasp was classy. He took her to real restaurants not just campus dives. He bought her roses. Flaming red roses. He took her on picnics in the woods where they ate on his huge blanket and then they kissed, for hours. Amana was deliriously in love.

She and Simon talked about making love but Simon held off, telling her it had to be "really special." Wasp told her they should make love for the first time on the 50 yard line at "The Horseshoe," OSU's football stadium. Amana was aghast. "Someone might see," she told him. Simon assured her it would be at a time and place when no one would see them. Amana thought this meant in the middle of the night but Simon had other plans.

Amana didn't really know it but it was every OSU male's fantasy to have sex on the 50 in the "*shoe*." Anyone who loved Ohio State football was used to either being in the stands or watching the game on TV on Saturday afternoons in autumn. The sea of red was an awesome sight. To make love there would surely make them legends if they weren't caught. There had been many attempts, many arrests and many expulsions but no one had ever managed to elude the security staff and actually make love on the field. But Simon Wasp knew he would be the one to actually do it.

His only problem had been getting the right girl. Of his hundreds of conquests every one had balked at the idea because they didn't want to be expelled. The girls around campus said an escape from Alcatraz was more likely to be successful than making love at midfield.

Unbeknownst to Amana Simon Wasp had been wooing her with this one thing in mind. He had noted that she wasn't afraid of affection in public places and had decided that she was worth the effort because this was absolutely essential to his plan. That's why he had paid so much attention to her. Amana had no way of knowing about this diabolic plan of Simon's. She thought they were in love. She would do whatever Simon wanted.

Simon had it planned this way. When winter came there was less security at the stadium. Simon got a small tent and then he waited. As luck would have it the first snow of the year didn't come for months but when it did it was a blizzard. This was exactly what Wasp wanted.

At the very worst part of the storm he grabbed his tent and Amana and made it down to the stadium. The "*shoe*" was almost a whiteout. The security staff had fled for home. Simon and Amana could barely find the center of the field. Amana was scared. She was having second thoughts about the whole thing. But Simon persisted. "You'll never forget this," he told her. Wasp counted off yards and scraped away enough snow to put up the pup tent. He dragged Amana in.

It was a wonder they could find each other at all under all the layers of clothing they had on. They looked like a sale table of winter coats at Value City or the Goodwill store. Underneath all this it didn't take Simon long. It was cold and it wasn't very pleasurable for either of them. Amana held him close despite this and told him, "I don't imagine we'll ever tell our kids about this one, will we, sweetheart?" Wasp was turned off completely by this remark. He told her. "There'll never be any kids to tell." "What do you mean?" Amana begged him. "I mean you and I are never going to have any kids or be anything. I'm done with you now." Amana was crushed. Her chest felt like it was being bent in two it hurt so bad.

The storm had slowed enough that the stands were now visible from the entrance to the tent. Wasp pulled a Super 8 camera out of his bag, flung off the coats and started filming the naked Amana and himself, then he swung out the entrance of the tent and panned the stadium. "Proof," he said. Amana yelled at both the chill and the violation of her privacy.

Wasp ignored her and kept filming. Then without offering any help to Amana he dressed and began to take the tent down. Amana had to scurry to get her clothes on in time. Wasp seemed oblivious to her even being there. She began to cry. At this he turned and told her, "C'mon. We don't want to get caught." And he began to hustle off the field with Amana dragging up the rear.

The word spread like wildfire. Wasp was a hero. Amana was devastated. It wasn't long before Amana's picture was being bandied about by the frat boys. Amana's misguided love for Wasp made her the campus fool. Wasp's many other conquests were the only ones who had any sympathy for Amana. They knew it could have been one of them.

The school couldn't really prove anything but they didn't need to expel her. She withdrew within the week. Wasp was never disciplined. He was so proud of himself. He had made off scot-free. Simon Wasp had become an OSU legend, and with a virgin, no less. But as befits such a legend, he arrogantly considered it par for the course. His next stop was the world. Hello, Life, Goodbye, Columbus! Wasp was going to be a star someday soon. He was already starting to forget Amana.

Amana returned home and holed up in her room. She was in despair. Her parents were embarrassed and ashamed of her. Amana was ashamed of herself. She decided to swear off men. "If this is the way it's going to be, why bother?" she thought. Her depression would continue for months. She was traumatized. She was terrified of "love" and sex and men.

Since then she had been drifting with no real direction in life. She had gotten lazy about going to Mass while at OSU and now she stopped entirely, although she still prayed occasionally, mostly for an end to the way she felt. She finished up college at the University of Akron but her heart wasn't in it. She worked but without any passion for it. It was like she was waiting on something or somebody. Her parents wondered if she was ever going to leave home again.

What little contact she had with men was never one-on-one dating. It would be years before she went out on a full-fledged "date" again. Then when she did go out on a few dates all of them wanted sex right away, which had continued to discourage her. She had pretty much decided that in the future she would "give'em what they wanted," she was so cynical. "At least I'll get out of the house once in a while," she thought. Reluctantly, she agreed to go on a "blind date" to please her sister, Donna. She wondered what kind of pathetic loser Donna had come up with this time.

That's when she met Tony. And she would soon realize that her prayers were heard and answered.

Simon Wasp was the pride of Wooster, Ohio. Just ask him. He would tell you. His ego was as large as a Mail Pouch ad on the side of a barn. You could see it coming from miles around. Wasp was strikingly handsome with a Jay Leno chin that women loved (should "lenochin" be an adjective?). In fact, Wasp always got the girl, if not for good, then at least pregnant. And he had more public talents, too.

Wasp's family were nominal Christians, like so many Americans. Simon thought they were Presbyterians but they hadn't gone to church in so long that they might have been Methodists, for all he knew. He did know they weren't Pentecostals or Catholics. Simon thought those people were weird.

Simon's dad was a middle executive at Firestone and his mom was an interior decorator, something she could combine with raising Simon. Like Tony Mirakul, Simon was an only child. But unlike Tony's parents who were limited in how much they could spoil Tony by their smaller income, Simon's parents had the wherewithal to buy off Simon at every whim. Simon was more a badge than anything else. He rarely saw his Dad. But it didn't matter to Wasp. He learned to connive by watching his mom. Even the good things that she did, like collecting for cancer research or providing something for a potluck dinner at school, Simon saw with an ulterior motive on her part.

As a teenager his mom even gave subtle encouragement to his conquest of girls by being proud of "what a man" he was becoming. Even when he got his first cheerleader pregnant she considered it "her problem," not Simon's. She didn't even tell Simon's father. Simon never paid the consequences for anything.

Just about the time Simon's adolescence started, Simon's father left his mother for a younger woman in Medina in a case of classic mid-life crisis. Simon's dad made enough money for alimony so it was almost like he wasn't even gone, having been basically absent all along. If Simon's mom was hurt it didn't show much. She was able to maintain her lifestyle, so life went on virtually unchanged in the Wasp household.

For some reason Wasp decided to pick up the guitar his Junior year of high school. It just seemed cool to him. It was also a great addition to his good looks, giving him a double whammy with the ladies. He got used to sampling whatever he liked on the school menu. He also found out he could sing, and even write. What's more, he realized that girls liked ballads and pop tunes, not hard rock. "Trite stuff works the best," he would say. His hero was Paul McCartney.

Egged on by his mother, Wasp became more and more of a performer as time went on. Always the front man, he went through many lineups of various musicians, always abusing his players but also trading up in talent with every replacement. Wasp had the cold-edged blade to be successful. By halfway through college he had become an accomplished entertainer, a pro. He knew all the right moves and had his act down, like a mini Tom Jones. He wouldn't have minded if girls threw panties at him, like Tom, but he preferred taking them off himself.

Shortly after college he drew the attention of one John Joules, rock concert promoter *par excellence*. "Jewels" as he called himself, was smart and wily enough to know what to do with the mercenary Wasp. Simon, meanwhile, had acquired a sugar daddy named Jesse Green, a naive, mild-mannered, part-time disk jockey who saw Wasp's talent but failed to judge his character. Green had sunk his life savings into demo recordings of Wasp and had even signed a management/producer deal with Wasp.

Of course, all deals in the entertainment business are made to be broken. And that's just what Wasp and Jewels did. Jewels promised to cut Green in on a quarter of the management fees that he received, in return for assigning Wasp's contract to him. Green didn't know that Jewels wasn't intending to actually manage Wasp, either. Jewels knew he couldn't handle him. Jewels had other plans for Wasp. He would sell his contract off to a major management team and take a finder's fee residual to do nothing, and then promote all Wasp's concerts where he could make some serious money. Green would end up with a pittance, if anything.

First off, Jewels talked Wasp into changing his name. "Nobody is attracted to a Wasp," Jewels told him. So one night they tossed down a few beers and tossed out a few names. "What's your middle name?" Jewels asked. "Douglas," Simon said. "Simon says, *Douglas*," Jewels announced. "So Douglas it is. But let's make it friendlier. How about *Doug*?" "O.K." Simon said. "Now what about a last name? It probably should start with a *D*," Jewels mused. "How about *Dean*?" Simon suggested. "I've always liked James Dean." "Well, that's good but down South they'll think you're a sausage. How about *Dineen*?" Jewels threw back. "Hmmm. *Doug Dineen*. Not bad," Simon responded.

And so Simon Wasp became Doug Dineen, superstar to be. Or so they planned.

Tony Mirakul had done some stupid things in his life. In fact, far more stupid things than smart ones. And so it was no surprise when he dropped out of college one quarter short of his degree, picked up a guitar, which he had learned a few chords on, and hitchhiked to LA.

He answered an ad to help drive across country with a thick-headed guy who was going to learn to be a welder in San Francisco. Tony would kid him, "Yoost got off dee bote, vant to be velder," he would say, Swedish style. Andy, the would-be-welder, told him, "I'm going to weld the cables on the Golden Gate Bridge. When we finish them we start all over again. I'll never be out of work."

So they drove around the clock with no sleep, 33 hours to Boulder. Then they rested 2 days. Tony broke his rule against drinking to try the local beers that weren't available east of the Mississippi. He couldn't understand why Coors was so popular. He thought Olympia tasted better. Then they drove another 28 hours straight to SF. Tony almost ran the van off the road in Donner Pass because he nodded off.

When they arrived in San Francisco all Tony could do was walk around all afternoon staring up at the skyscrapers in awe. He stood under the Transamerica Pyramid for 15 minutes alone, shifting his weight back and forth from one foot to the other. He had never seen anything like this back in the Midwest. His neck hurt from looking up. He knew he looked like a rube but he didn't care. This was awesome!

San Francisco was an odd combination of scale. Some things were too big, like the Bay Bridges or the Pyramid. The houses were just a little too small. The hills were just a little too steep. There were bizarre things like Lombard St., the "crookedest street in the world," which snaked back and forth down the hill like a perverse wheel chair ramp made of brick. Every few blocks you were in a different town. Cable cars seemed more dangerous than quaint as he watched the brakeman in the back struggle ferociously to pull back on the handle to stop the car. It was foggy and cold far more than he ever thought it would be. He hadn't brought enough warm clothes. And when it was warm, say 70 degrees, half the streets were blocked by film crews trying to shoot a movie or TV show.

As long as he had money in his pocket, Tony loved it. Except for the earthquakes. Tony could feel these. Even the small ones. For some reason Tony was more sensitive than most. Anyone could feel a 5 on the Richter scale. Tony could feel the 4's and sometimes even the 3's. He would be walking down the street and say, "Did you feel that?" to whomever he was with. "No," they would say. Later he would hear on the news that there had been a slight tremor just about the time he had felt it. "I don't think I could live here permanently," Tony thought.

Tony moved in with some friends he had known at Kent State and who were living in the Sunset district. This was handy enough with the city's bus system. Tony went everywhere on sort of an extended vacation. His friends had decent jobs so they would pay for anything major, like a big meal out or *Grateful Dead* tickets at Kezar Stadium.

"Boring," Tony thought after a few hours of the *Dead*. "You mean they're going to play for 8 hours? Now I understand why you take drugs before these things," he told his roommates, who were doing acid and having a great time. "I'll come back and get you in 6 hours," Tony said as he left.

Tony started to frequent the club scene down on Union St. and other areas near Fisherman's Wharf. Once he caught a glimpse of Clint Eastwood heading into a jazz club. His favorite club was called the *Drinkin' Gourd*. The performers they booked there usually played an acoustic folk or light pop type of music. Tony soon befriended one of the regulars who usually performed on Friday or Saturday night, or both. His name was Jim Post and he hailed from Chicago. He and his late wife had performed together as *Friend and Lover* and had a hit record years before called "Reach Out In The Darkness." Once Tony had befriended Jim he asked him, "Which one were you? *Friend* or *Lover*?" Jim just rolled his eyes.

Tony had heard some singers before but never anyone like Jim Post. Jim needed no microphone. He was the loudest singer on the planet. And he had a beautiful tenor voice with as close to perfect pitch as Tony's ears could tell. None of Jim's recordings ever did justice to his live performances. In the studio they had to compress his volume just to get him on tape. None of the equipment could handle him. He always sounded squashed on his records. But not so in concert. The tourists would come into the *Drinkin' Gourd* and get their ears pinned back.

Tony enjoyed kidding around with Post. And Post took him under his wing like a little brother. Jim would invite Tony to visit some interesting places. Once he got to sit in the control room of the studio where *Creedence* recorded all their hits while Jim recorded there, too. Post would often try out new songs on Tony to see what he thought of them. Tony was just brash enough to tell him what he actually thought, too.

In Post's act he used to do a song called "Buzzy and Jimmy."
It was one of Tony's favorites. There was one point in the song
where Jim would stop playing guitar for a moment while he
repeated the refrain. He would sing, "This is the bush where
the wild roses grow, where Buzzy and Jimmy could see..." and
the song would go on. One night while listening to this Tony
had an idea. So he enlisted one of the waitresses he was dating
who worked at the club in his scheme. They went downtown
together a couple of afternoons and collected the rose petals
that all the flower vendors discarded on the street in the flower
district. It was a great cheap date, too.

They put all the petals they collected into two enormous bags.
Then when Friday night rolled around they stashed them
behind the bar and waited. When Post started up the song, Tony
and the waitress grabbed the bags of rose petals and slipped
behind the stage on opposite sides from each other. When Jim
got to the part of the song when he stopped playing and sang,
"This is the bush..." Tony and his friend unleashed the bags of
rose petals, throwing the contents as hard as they could over
Post's head. The two giant globs met right over Jim's head and
exploded everywhere, showering him with rose petals.

At first, Post was angry, thinking someone had thrown
something at him to attack him but then he saw the rose petals
everywhere and got a tremendous rush of energy. The
audience meanwhile gasped at the crash of rose petals over his
head, then, getting over their astonishment, began to clap and
cheer wildly. There were rose petals everywhere in the small
club, the ceiling fans distributing them to the farthest corners
of the room.

As Post finished up, "Dancin' the old time Lindy Hop, they
were lookin' each other in the eye, and they were dreamin'
about those funny little babies, comin' by and by," the crowd
went nuts. The tourists wondered if they did this every show.

Post was beaming. Tony was hiding. The club no longer smelled like cigarettes and beer. There was an overpowering perfume of roses everywhere. And Post was on a natural adrenaline high finishing his set like it was a command performance for the queen. It may have been his best ever.

"Don't you ever do that again, you crazy person," Post told Tony after the show, as Jim grinned from ear to ear. "I never repeat myself," Tony promised him, giggling. It was great to be young and goofy and in San Francisco.

Chapter 6 - Hollywoodland

After wearing out his welcome with the friends he was staying with in San Francisco, Tony decided to continue on his quest by hitchhiking down to Los Angeles to become a big star. He bid them and his friend, Jim Post, farewell. He stopped in Carmel for a few days, staying with an old girlfriend until her boyfriend came home. "So that's what 'Back Door Man' was about," he thought to himself as he left, understanding the song for the first time. Then he thumbed his way down through Big Sur and past San Simeon ("Big castle," he thought, "wonder who lives there?") until he reached Los Angeles.

Having nowhere to stay, Tony took over a couch in the lounge on the second floor of a guy's dorm at UCLA. No one seemed to notice him since he only slept there. In fact the only time anyone ever spoke to him was once when he was microwaving a whole pound of bacon to make bacon, tomato, avocado and alfalfa sprouts sandwiches, something he had been introduced to in San Francisco. They didn't have any weird food like this back home in Akron. Tony felt "hip."

Tony began going from office to office in Hollywood trying to play guitar and sing. Tony had heard that James Taylor had walked in to Columbia Records, sat down and played "Fire & Rain," and they signed him on the spot. But that story must have been apocryphal because secretaries would look at him like he was nuts. No one auditioned live in an L.A. record office!

Tony was wandering around with his guitar in Lawrence
Welk's building one day when he shared an elevator ride with
Dick Clark. He decided to ask him how a person got a break.
Clark told him, "You make your own breaks." Tony thought
about this as he walked from record office to record office
trying to audition.

No one ever seemed to be in their office in L.A. They didn't
seem to do business in business places. Tony was not a brilliant
thinker when it came to figuring out the duplicitous ways of
man. He was too straightforward, too Midwestern. How things
worked had to be explained to him. But once he understood he
was very versatile. He could refine an idea or a way of doing
things to make it better, he just couldn't invent it.

One day he actually met someone in the music business at a
business office. His name was Peter McCood. Peter had just
written several hit songs and was at the top of his game. Peter
undertook educating Tony in "Hollywood 101."

Peter explained that all meaningful business in Hollywood was
done on an informal social basis. He explained that everyone in
Hollywood had some talent. In fact, there were far more
talented people on the street than the average Hollywood star.
That's because talent was a given. What really mattered was
who you knew, or who you were sleeping with. Who was
backing you determined whether you would have a chance to
be successful. Powerful individuals, either individually or in
constantly shifting groups, took certain people under their
wing and did what was necessary to make their protégés' stars.
Even this could not guarantee success but it was impossible to
be successful without it.

Usually large sums of capital were necessary to make someone
a star, something that most artists did not have. The money and
the connections were the power in Hollywood as in any

business. It just seemed more bizarre the way Hollywood did it. And it was only money. A couple extra zeros at the end didn't matter in Hollywood. It just meant a couple extra zeros on the payout end.

The second thing Peter told Tony was that he wouldn't make any money until he had made other people a lot of money. He would be last on the list to cash out.

Tony listened to all this with resentment in check. Part of him was ego-driven or he wouldn't be there. This made him want to be first, not last. The other part of him was the rational side that told him it was logical that the investors would want payback and control. The artist was secondary.

Finally, Peter explained to Tony that he had to find the informal places to hang out where he could meet people and start making connections. It was a networking job.

Tony appreciated "learning the ropes" from Peter. Peter was a prince. "He must be from the Midwest," Tony thought to himself.

Tony decided he needed to dig in if he was going to work this game. So he set out to find himself an apartment. He moved to the *Y* for a few weeks and then answered an ad for a roommate with a female. This was L.A. so coed apartment sharing was no big deal. Once she was convinced that Tony was harmless she took him in.

Her name was Violet Blue, "JAP", or Jewish American Princess, as she called herself, and she was in L.A. to become a star just like everyone else in Hollywood. Tony thought "JAP" was supposed to be a term of derision but Violet gloried in it. She dressed only in iridescent clothing, even her underwear. She was extremely busty but refused to use her feminine pulchritude to advance her career, insisting that she be accepted for her talent. After Tony's "class" with Peter he figured Violet was going nowhere. But she would do fine as a roommate. He would just never be able to look at anything iridescent again without thinking of Violet parading around the house half-naked. Eeeee!

To thank her for sharing her place he offered to make her dinner. Tony thought it would be nice to sauté some of the fresh peppers he had snagged at the grocery and make omelets. Tony cut up what he thought were some sweet banana peppers and threw them into the skillet to cook. Within a minute or two Tony's face began to burn. He rubbed at the spot. Within no time Tony's entire face was on fire from ear to ear. Tony began to panic. His skin was burning like he had never experienced in the worst sunburn of his life. His eyes began to burn. Even his eyelids. He wiped his face even more.

He started yelling for Violet to help. She rushed in. "What's the matter?" "My face feels like it's on fire!" Tony screamed. Violet dithered for a moment, then ran to the sink. She grabbed a pot, filled it with water, turned and threw it at Tony's face. "Sploosh!" "Hey!" Tony was suddenly soaked.

As the water ran down his clothes and dripped to the floor, the pain returned. Now it was spreading down his chest. "Aiyeeee!" Tony yelled. He started running around trying to air dry himself. His eyes were burning and he could hardly see. "What's happening?" he cried.

Finally, Tony calmed down enough for Violet to ask, "What were you doing?" "I just cut up some peppers and threw them into the skillet. That's all," Tony replied. Violet looked in the skillet. Now Violet was from Maryland but she had been on the West Coast long enough to know that the peppers in the skillet were hot peppers. "These are hot peppers," she told him. "Did you rub your face or your eyes after you cut them up?"

Tony thought for a second. "I might have," he told her. "Well, that's what it is then. Pepper juice on your skin." "What?" Tony said. He had never handled a hot pepper before and he had rubbed his face, blown his nose and wiped off sweat from his forehead and cheeks. Then he had rubbed all over trying to stop the burn. He was still on fire but at least he now knew why. "I'll never touch another hot pepper again!" Tony exclaimed. Now he felt stupid. Violet began laughing.

It turned out to be a great icebreaker since Violet told everyone the story when she introduced him as her new roommate. How could anyone not like such a rube? "So you're from the Midwest? Got any hot peppers out there?" people would ask him at parties and then laugh.

Tony tried hitting on Violet a few times in the first few weeks he was there but finally decided she wasn't his type. Then they settled in to just being roommates as if they were the same sex. Tony would put on his best falsetto voice and kid Violet, "Are you wearing that little shimmery paisley thing tonight? If not, I'd like to borrow it." Violet would answer, "Only if I can wear those slacks you've got on, dearie."

This went on for about two months, both of them commiserating with each other about the doors slammed in their faces. Then one day Violet told him that she had another girl friend she would like to have move in with her and asked Tony to leave. Tony was not so much hurt as irritated at the inevitable hassle of finding another place to live.

This time he vowed to get a place of his own and get a roommate who would sublet from him. His apartment with Violet had been in Pasadena. Now he moved to West Hollywood to be closer to the business. He found a little bungalow on a side street between Fountain and Santa Monica, just right for two. Then by accident he ran into a fellow musician he had met in

San Francisco named Randy Angel and invited him to share his digs. Randy was happy to find a place to live with someone he knew.

Randy's real name was Randy Gladstone, from Boston. Randy had wanted to be a star himself but he was so obnoxious that he had worn out his welcome with virtually every major player in the music industry. None of them would speak to him anymore. So Randy supported himself by selling heavy machinery off a small flatbed truck. He would travel around the West Coast with large machines he bought from a supplier at wholesale and sell them at a discount to factories. "I'm here, today, with the machine!" he would say, shaking his head. "Fantastic deal. No waiting!" And he sold them. He actually made more money doing this than all but the highest paid stars and managers made in Hollywood.

Tony would ask him, "Why don't you just sell equipment? You're far better off." "I'm an artist!" Randy would tell him. "I'm just putting together a stake!"

Randy sunk all his profits back into demos of his songs. Finally Randy grew tired of this dead end and decided he would become a record producer instead. "Anybody can press a record," he told Tony.

The next thing Tony knew, Randy came home with a record he had produced for a girl he had discovered named Diane Warren. Tony thought it stunk, and told Randy so. Randy was unfazed. "She's great," he told Tony. "Well, not as a singer," Tony replied. "But her songs are great!" Randy told him. Randy kept at it anyway with absolutely no success.

About ten years later Tony would discover that a girl named Diane Warren had just won her first of many Grammy Awards. Eventually she would become a legend in the industry with hit after hit after hit - as a songwriter! Tony would be faintly amused that his old friend Randy had discovered her but never made a dime because he tried to make her a recording artist instead of concentrating on her songwriting. Such are the vagaries of the business.

In the meantime, Tony was hanging out occasionally at the "Improv" nightclub, trying to meet people, dating the hostess, laughing at the comedians like Jay Leno and Richard Belzer and Gilbert Gottfried and Freddie Prinze. It was fun to hear them take risks with new routines. Once in a while someone hit a home run. And it was just fun being around such an odd bunch.

For example, one night Tony was sitting in the audience and he noticed that the guy behind him was staring intently at the back of his head. This went on through several acts, for more than an hour, with Tony turning around every once in a while to find him still staring at the back of his head. Finally he decided to say something, but when he turned around he realized that the guy was comedian Stanley Myron Handleman. Stanley spoke up before Tony could say anything. "You've got a nice head," Stanley told him. "I'd keep it." Not knowing what to say, Tony just offered, "I'll do that." Then Stanley calmly got up and left the club, leaving Tony scratching his "nice head."

There was one time when it wasn't particularly fun, however. One night he caught Elayne Boosler's act. In it she did a bit about being Jewish and sneaking into Mass and "taking the wafer," as she put it. Tony wasn't a particularly good Catholic but Catholic he still was. There wasn't anything more sacred than Holy Communion, the Body of Christ, God in the flesh. When Boosler did her bit it wasn't funny. It was just offensive, and it made him angry. He didn't go around making jokes about that awful Passover food he had to eat every year at his friend Lenny Apsimov's house when he was growing up. He expected the same in return for something as sacred as the Eucharist.

This incident set him to thinking. It was the first time in his life that someone Jewish had been disrespectful to Catholics. Growing up his best friend had been Lenny Apsimov. They used to sleep out together in Lenny's back yard. They loved to listen to WBZ in Boston and WLS in Chicago late at night because they would hear all the newest records 3 or 4 months before they played them in Akron. It was romantic to listen to far away places and imagine what they were like. It made Tony want to travel.

Tony was almost like a second son to the Apsimovs. He was always invited for Passover, although he didn't quite understand what it all meant. And, of course, he was part of Lenny's Bar Mitzvah, which he realized was kind of like the Sacrament of Confirmation, when Tony became an adult in the Church.

Tony remembered two things from Lenny's Bar Mitzvah. First, his mom had bought a *Bas* Mitvah card, which apparently was for girls, so everyone had a good laugh about the silly gentile kid who brought the wrong card. All day, Tony kept saying, "My Mom bought it," or "I didn't even know girls had Bas Mitzvahs," because he was embarrassed at the mistake. Second, he was amazed that the first half of the ceremony was almost exactly like the first half of the Mass. "So that's where it comes from," he thought. When he got older he would know this as the Liturgy of the Word, and it made perfect sense that it would be directly from Jewish practice. The early Christians simply added the Last Supper from Jesus, and *Voila!,* they had the Mass.

Growing up in Akron Tony had played Little League ball where most of the kids were Jewish. He had always hung around with Jewish kids, although they all seemed to be better off than his family was. Tony grew up thinking being Jewish was synonymous with being rich. It wasn't until he went to college that he learned there were Jews who were poor. He was honestly surprised by this.

They had been so innocent in those days that he could remember returning from playing in a Little League State Championship game in a station wagon where half the kids were Jewish and the other half were Protestant and Catholic, when the Beatles' "Baby, Your A Rich Man, Too" came on the radio. The Jewish kids all started singing "Baby, You're a Rich, Fat, Baby, You're a Rich, Fat, Baby, You're a Rich, Fat Jew." But when the gentile kids joined in the Jewish kids all stopped and told them they weren't allowed to sing it because they weren't Jewish. None of the gentile kids knew what to make of this. "Touch-eee," Tony thought.

They were all too young yet. They hadn't learned about all the baggage everyone was carrying. They hadn't been taught to be prejudiced. They were just kids goofing around. But when Tony got older and wiser he learned that Jews and Blacks were both off limits for criticism, even if it was true, because someone would label you "anti-Semitic" or "racist" if you said something and you weren't from that group. As an adult Tony understood why it would offend people the same way he was offended by Boosler's routine. If Boosler had been one of the kids in his neighborhood he probably wouldn't have taken it so seriously. But now he did.

Luckily, Boosler's bit of bad taste was an anomaly. The rest of the time Tony was perfectly comfortable being the token "goy" with his Jewish friends. His sense of identity as a Catholic actually grew from this experience. In many ways being Catholic was an extension of being Jewish. If Jesus hadn't come, Tony figured he would have to be Jewish himself. It was more of a shared tradition than he realized.

Of course, Hollywood was more an ethnically Jewish town than a religious one. Tony realized early on that being Jewish had nothing to do with religion in Hollywood. Virtually no one practiced Judaism. He did remember his friend Tommy Ventz once had a yarmulke on for Shabbat but that was the only time he ever saw one. Eventually, Tommy left the entertainment business. The last Tony had heard Tommy had become a rabbi and moved to the Holy Land, although he wasn't absolutely sure if that was true. But it certainly sounded in character for Tommy.

Tony, who felt like he must be the only Catholic for miles, loved living in his cute West Hollywood bungalow. He used to shop at the Alpha Beta grocery just around the corner from his house. There he would occasionally see an attractive girl that he soon realized lived down the block from him. He would watch her in the Produce department, squeezing the avocados. He had just about screwed up enough courage to introduce himself and ask her for a date when he happened to see her onstage at the "Improv."

He not only didn't know that she was a comedienne but he wasn't prepared at all for her act. Her name was Sandra Bernhardt, although for some reason whenever he saw her on TV after that the talk-show hosts always wanted to call her Sarah. In her act she portrayed herself as something that Tony didn't learn the word for until years later, a "Dominatrix."

What Tony did know was that she terrified him. He never did introduce himself and kept to his own side of the street from then on. Los Angeles was a whole lot different from Akron. So much for that crush.

One day Tony and his roommate Randy were out riding around town when they noticed a pretty girl struggling outside an apartment with a couch. They stopped to help, and ended up carrying the sofa up two flights of steps and down a corridor for the girl. Both of them were attracted to her. Of the two it appeared she was more interested in Tony, striking up a conversation with him. Tony asked her out but she told him she had a boyfriend she lived with. But she asked for Tony's number and told him she might call him sometime.

Her name was Janelle Coventry but she went by Jan. She told Tony she was apprenticing at RCA as a sound engineer, and also worked the road as a sound mixer for live shows by an all-girl's group, the *Moist Towelettes*. She asked Tony for a ride so he took her down to RCA, and she gave Randy and him a quick tour.

Randy was smacking his lips at all the equipment, while Tony was tuned in to Jan. But after the tour they parted company and Tony figured he would never hear from her again.

Not so, however. She called two days later and asked if he wanted to go to the beach on Saturday. Tony readily agreed. So that Saturday he picked her up, and they headed for Santa Monica. They sat and talked all afternoon but there was one thing Tony was puzzled about despite all the talk. She kept telling him that she could have made $500 that afternoon but she had chosen to be with him instead. Five Hundred Dollars was a whole lot of money when the minimum wage was only about 3 bucks an hour!

At first, Tony was flattered but he couldn't figure out what she could have been doing that paid that much, and why she had blown it off. She also told him that she was having boyfriend problems and that her boyfriend was violent. She was sometimes too terrified to go back to her apartment. Tony, trying to be chivalrous, offered that if she ever needed help she could come to him. She thanked him and told him she would remember that.

After dinner, Tony deposited her at her apartment, got up the courage to kiss her goodbye, and headed home. He wasn't sure if he would see her again, or if he even wanted to. He called her once or twice over the next week but she was never in.

Then one night about 3 AM Tony was awakened by a banging on his front door. He ran to it and asked who it was. "Jan," he heard back. Throwing open the door, there she stood, looking terrified. "I needed somewhere I could go where he could never find me," she panted. Tony took her in and tried to calm her down. She was in tears. "He tore up our apartment," she cried. Soothing her, Tony told her she was safe there, and they would deal with it in the morning. Then, just to be safe, while she went into the bathroom, Tony went out front to make sure there wasn't someone following her. He made it back in and locked up just before she came out of the bath.

He hugged her some more and finally she calmed down. They were both tired. Tony suggested they get some sleep, thinking she would crawl up on the couch. Instead she marched over to Tony's bed and got on top of it. Tony went to get his pillow and head for the couch but instead she grabbed his arm and pulled him toward the bed. Tony got in. She sat up, pulled all her clothes off, threw them on the floor and cuddled up to Tony.

The next thing Tony knew she was fast asleep on his chest. Tony stared at the ceiling thinking, "How do I get myself into these things?" and couldn't sleep a wink.

The next morning, bleary-eyed, Tony took Janelle back to her apartment. When they walked in she started to get teary again. Tony was shocked. When she had said her boyfriend tore up the apartment Tony thought she meant that he had thrown a few things around in anger. But this was like something out of a movie. The entire apartment was destroyed.

There were holes in the walls. It smelled like someone had tried to start a fire. The furniture had been chopped up like kindling. They walked gingerly toward the bedroom, Jan calling out to see if anyone was there. There wasn't. Tony was frightened but didn't let on to Jan.

The bedroom was even worse. There were huge holes in the walls like they had been struck with a large blunt object. There were smaller holes that looked to Tony like bullets had gone through, or else a shotgun blast, he wasn't sure, not being much on guns. The mattress was slashed. The picture tube in the large TV in the corner had either been shot out or smashed with a blunt object. And there were little white index cards strewn everywhere about the floor. Janelle started picking them up. Tony went to help.

As he did so he began to read the index cards. They seemed to be people's names, all men, it appeared. Some of them were prominent names he had heard of. Every card had a description below it of something that seemed sexual to Tony, although many of the terms he had never heard of. But there were enough he had heard of to get the picture.

He turned to Jan and innocently asked her what they were. She sat cross-legged on the floor in front of him and explained that there were many men from all over the country who came to L.A. on business and would pay lots of money for certain things they wanted, and that's how she made her living. Tony was starting to figure out why it cost Jan $500 in lost income to go out with him.

She went on to explain that she had promised her boyfriend when they moved in together that she would give up the business but she just couldn't because the money was so good. So she had continued to service her clients when they called. And that's why her boyfriend had gone berserk. Apparently this was not the first time she had promised to quit but then gone back for the money.

Tony listened and quickly helped her pick up the rest of the cards, averting his eyes so he wouldn't have to read them. He was now terrified. "What if her boyfriend comes back?" he thought. "He'll think I'm a trick."

As quickly as he could, Tony excused himself and skedaddled. He hit his car and didn't look back. Once he had put some distance between himself and Janelle he thought, "I could have been killed and not even known why." He also thought, "She really liked you to give up $500 just to sit on the beach with you." Tony was flattered. But not so much that he ever wanted to see her again. He kept thinking over and over again, "The wages of sin is death. The wages of sin is death."

Several years later, back in Ohio, Tony would read a story about a high-priced call girl they found hacked to death in the Hollywood Hills. The article would say that her name was Lisa Murtrie, also known professionally as Jan or Janelle Coventry. Originally from Seattle, she had been associated for a time with the *Moist Towelettes* all-girl rock group as a sound engineer on their tours but most recently was believed to have been the girlfriend of a well-known multi-millionaire playboy, who had inherited a fortune from a swimming pool solar panel company. The authorities were questioning her boyfriend.

Tony would shudder, and then begin to cry. He had held her in his arms and felt her tears on his skin like a lost little girl. He must be the only man in her life she ever slept with that she didn't have sex with. He might be the only man who had never used her. So why did he feel guilty? Because he felt like he had abandoned her. He didn't know how to save her. He had discarded her like the men who had used her.

He wouldn't allow himself to say it was none of his business, or that he had been in danger. No, he would feel like he had abandoned her knowing she might be killed. "But you didn't make her choices for her," he would tell himself. "Still, I should have been smarter, I should have had the wisdom to somehow turn her away from death." He would take out his rosary and begin to pray for Janelle, beautiful Janelle who was no more, and he would ask for wisdom to know when to speak in the future.

But all this would take place a few years from now. Today Tony just needed some distance. "L.A. is dangerous," he thought.

Not everything in Hollywood was this serious. Tony had taken a job delivering a local entertainment paper on a route from La Cienega out to Santa Monica. UCLA was on the route. He began delivering to a used record store called Rhino Records. Befriending the boys who worked there he overheard one day that they needed a 3rd baseman for their softball team. "I used to play 3rd base," Tony piped up, interrupting the conversation.

The next thing Tony knew he was starting in the Hollywood Celebrity Softball league. And he must have been the missing link because the team began winning. In fact, they played so well that they made it to the championship vs. "Happy Days."

There they would have to face the most feared pitcher in the league, Henry Winkler.

Rhino Records was the visiting team, batting first. It was a see-saw battle with each team mustering just enough to take the lead before the other side got its back up and held them. Coming up in the top of the seventh and final inning, Rhino scored two runs to go ahead 7-6. In the bottom of the inning, "Happy Days" loaded them up with one out. Then Donny ("Ralph") popped out, making it two down. Anson Williams came up next. This was it. "Potsie" had the chance to be the hero or the goat.

He drew a ball, then fouled one off. Then he drew another ball. Somehow everyone knew the next pitch was it. It headed down the pipe. "Potsie" swung.

Up to this point Tony had been a minor factor in the game with one double and a run scored. There had only been a few routine balls at third all day. Now Anson's big swing resulted in a dribbler down the third base line, almost like a bunt.

Tony took off full blast toward home, and in one beautiful motion swooped up the ball barehanded and threw a bullet sidearmed to first. "Potsie" was out by a half-step. Even Tony knew it was an awesome play. It was almost like someone else, not Tony, had appeared and made the play. The "Happy Days" team was stunned. The Rhino team went nuts, tackling Tony like they had just won the World Series.

Ever the gentleman, Henry Winkler, "The Fonz" himself, went out of his way to shake Tony's hand. "That was a major league play," he told Tony. "Thanks. Sorry it had to be a nice guy like 'Potsie'," Tony told him. "I'm not. If he'd have won the game we'd have never heard the end of it," Henry said. "You did us a favor. Of course, I never said that," and Henry Winkler winked.

"I'm hanging up my spikes," Tony told the team at the end of their victory celebration of hot dogs and soda at "Tail o' the Pup." "I'll never make another play like that one. Time to go out on top." Tony had only played six games in a Rhino uniform, and he was retiring. Somehow the Rhino folks thought it was perfectly appropriate. It was almost mythical. Perhaps someday they would look back and wonder if it had actually happened, or was only a dream - the year that Midwestern boy strode into town and helped them win the pennant, only to vanish as if he had never even been there.

The Rhino boys would go on to international fame and fortune by purchasing the rights to old records that no one else wanted and repackaging them and selling them on TV and the Internet. But there would never be another summer like the one when they won the Hollywood Celebrity League.

At home after the game, Tony found Randy seasoning a brand new giant cast iron skillet so he could cook up some millet. Randy was a vegetarian who wouldn't use the same pans that meat had been cooked in even after they had been washed. "Coodies," he said.

Now that Tony was established in his own place Violet Blue came over to visit, along with her new roommate, Angi, who had taken Tony's place. Angi promptly fell in love with Randy and moved in with him a few weeks later.

Tony called Violet and told her, "You know, this is the second time in a year that I have somehow created a matchup with one of my roommates. When I was in San Francisco I picked up a girl on the cable car who was vacationing from New York. She said she would come home for dinner with me as long as I understood she wasn't going to sleep with me. So I took her home for dinner, and she ended up staying for a week, with one of my roommates. Then she flew back to Syracuse, gathered her clothes and flew back out a week later and moved in with us. Then we had to get a bigger place to live."

"You could make some money as a 'shadkhin'," Violet suggested. "What the heck is that?" Tony asked her. "A matchmaker!" she told him. "You could make a fortune putting people together." She was actually beginning to sound serious. Tony put on his best Billy Crystal voice, "What am I, chopped liver?" Then he broke into Crystal imitating Brando, "You know you broke my heart, Violet. You broke my heart. I must be meshugg to listen to you." Violet wasn't getting it. "What? I broke your heart?" Violet sounded alarmed. Tony started laughing. Finally, she figured out Tony was kidding her.

Then Tony suggested that either he should move back in with her and leave the place to Randy and Angi, or Randy and Angi should take Violet's apartment and she should move in with Tony. Eventually, Randy and Angi moved into their own place and both Tony and Violet had to find new roommates because they were each stuck with leases. "He was *your* roommate," Violet complained. "Well, *you* brought her over," Tony fired back. They both thought it was funny, and a pain in the neck, at the same time.

Eventually, a cable guy named "Fred" moved in with Tony. Fred got lots of mail but none ever addressed to "Fred." But he paid his rent and half the time he didn't come home at night, so Tony just let it go. He figured the cops would show up at his door or he would read about it in the papers if anything serious happened.

Tony was dating the hostess at "The Improv" so he never paid to get in. On Monday nights he went to Open Mike Night at the "Troubadour," another famous nightclub, because it was free also. One week he happened to visit "The Troub" on a Friday night. This was unusual for Tony because they charged admission for the show on the weekends. Normally he would be doing something free somewhere else. The marquee said that the weekend act was "Steve Martin."

Now Tony had never heard of this Steve Martin, this being the mid-70's and Steve not being very well-known outside L.A. at that point. So Tony went in and sat at the bar. He ordered a Shirley Temple, because that was all the money he had, and he liked them. Tony was minding his own business, deep in thought, when the guy next to him tried to strike up a conversation. The bar was dark, and Tony wasn't paying much attention.

"What brings *you* here tonight?" the stranger asked. "Oh, just hanging out. How about you?" Tony answered. "I came to see my friend, Steve Martin." "Oh, what's he do?" Tony asked only slightly interested. "He's a banjo player," the stranger answered. Tony was not interested for sure now. "Oh, well, what do you do?" Tony asked, trying to be polite. "Oh, I'm a musician, too." Tony asked him, "Well, where've you played lately?" The stranger answered, "Oh, let me see, Chicago, Minneapolis, Fargo, Bismarck, Pocatello, Boise, Seattle..." Tony interrupted, "Well, who's your booking agent?" The stranger answered, "William Morris." Tony knew that William Morris was the biggest and most prestigious booking agency in the world. Intrigued, Tony asked, "Well, who the hell are you?" "Martin Mull, you ever heard of me?"

Tony began laughing, "Of course I have. *Living and Dying in Three Quarter Time!*" Tony exclaimed, naming an album he thought was Mull's but which was actually by Jimmy Buffett. "Oh, really?" Mull asked incredulously.

Tony became more animated now talking with Mull who overlooked the faux pas and encouraged Tony to go in and see the show. "He's a great banjo player," Marty insisted, "You should see him." "Thanks, I'll do that."

There was only one problem. Tony didn't have the price of a ticket. So he followed the unwritten Troubadour rule for all starving musicians. He snuck into the showroom by saying he was going to the bathroom, which could only be accessed from the showroom. Many a star had snuck in this way during their scuffling days, and the Troubadour was well loved because of it. It was almost a communal rite of passage, to sneak into the Troubadour when you were poor, then come back and play for the club when you made it. Never mind that not everybody made it. It was still a tradition.

So Tony sat on the steps to the second floor and watched the show, not wanting to take up a paying customer's seat. Expecting a banjo player, what he got was 2 1/2 hours of the funniest stuff he had ever seen or heard. Mull had played a practical joke on him but Tony certainly didn't mind. Tony was certain Martin was going to be a huge star someday as word of his antics spread. But he didn't know that his path would cross Martin's again back east.

Life in Hollywoodland seemed to be nothing but a series of bizarre incidents separated by short stints of calm. It was surreal to go to the grocery and run into a star who asked you how the tomatoes were, as if you were any more of an expert than they were at picking them.

"Why, yes, I think the Romas are edible but the Beefsteaks are hydroponic and lack flavor."

"Thank you, normal person."

"And, oh, yes, buy the avocados green and let them ripen for a few days at home. If you buy them ripe they'll be bruised in transit."

"Why, thank you, fawning fan."

Chapter 8 - *Then Hire Me*

After about a year and a half Tony began to grow weary of the Hollywood scene. His mentor, Peter McCood, offered that Tony had two options. One, he could hang around Hollywood for another 3 or 4 years and possibly make it, or he could go someplace else and either try to crack the entertainment field in an easier location, or do something different than performing.

Tony mulled this over for a few weeks and then decided Peter was right. The last straw was when some one-hit-wonder from Reseda told Tony he had no talent and should get out of the business. Tony knew he had some talent. The guy was just an arrogant jerk from the Valley. But he had an A & R job and Tony didn't.

Tony decided that if that was what he was up against he'd probably be happier doing something else back home. So he sold off or gave away all his belongings, except a few clothes, and hit the highway in his old blue Plymouth Duster. He took along a spacey guy, a friend of Randy Angel's, who called himself Berkeley Bob. Bob didn't really need to go anywhere but he enjoyed sharing expenses. Tony never did learn his real name.

They decided they would take their time going back so they headed South on the 405 to San Diego, crossed over at Tijuana and headed across the mountains toward Mexicali. Tony didn't know that the mountains were notorious for *banditos* until they got almost to the outskirts of Mexicali and Bob said, "You know, I've heard that you're not supposed to drive up in the mountains around here because they'll put rocks across the road and ambush your car." Berkeley Bob was a walking, talking anti-drug commercial.

Tony had wondered why there was so much debris on the road in certain places. Now he knew. He shuddered at the thought of being kidnapped by *banditos*. He wondered what they would have done with Berkeley Bob. Torturing him would have been no fun since he wouldn't have realized he was being tortured. Killing him would have been just as unsatisfying. Tony concluded that they would either keep him around for comic relief or set him free in the village as fast as they could get him there.

After eating dinner in town and buying a set of handmade placemats and matching tablecloth for his mother, Tony pointed the Duster toward the border, only to be stopped by a cop. Apparently, Tony, who couldn't read or understand a bit of Spanish, had gone the wrong way down a one way street. The cop spoke enough English for Tony to plead with him to let him go. He could see the border station two blocks away but all Tony could imagine was rotting in a Mexicali jail cell, writing home asking for toilet paper. The cop was getting tired of this stupid gringo and had just started to wave Tony off on his way when the cop's supervisor pulled up and told him he would take over from there.

The super didn't waste any time. "Give me twenty-five bucks," he demanded. Tony felt oddly relieved. Despite being terrified a minute ago his chutzpah kicked in. "O.K. now we're haggling," he thought. "Twenty-five dollars! I've only got five," he told him. Tony took a fiver out of his wallet and waved it at the super. "Twenty dollar," the cop shot back. Tony held his ground. "I've only got five!" The cop stuck his head inside the car and said, "C'mon, there. How much you got?" Tony held out the five. Exasperated the cop said, "O.K. You got ten? Gimme ten." Tony figured this was as good a deal as he was going to get so he said "O.K." and handed him a ten. The cop stuck the ten in his shirt pocket, turned to see if anyone was looking, then waved Tony away and walked off.

Tony was still headed the wrong way on the one way street so he hit the gas and headed right for the border station. "They don't play by the same rules down here, do they?" he commented to Bob. Bob said, "I think that was a fair price."

The customs people at the border asked Tony what country he was from. After what Tony had just been through he answered, "Ours." The agent didn't like this. So he decided to have some fun with them. He asked them how long they had been in Mexico. "Just a few hours," Tony answered truthfully. "Hmmm," the agent said. "Do you have anything to declare?" "No, nothing." Tony didn't know that Berkeley Bob had stuck a bottle of Mezcal up into the heating duct of the car. It was probably best that he didn't.

The agent continued, toying with them just for fun, "Did you get the black wrought iron lanterns?" "No." "The onyx chessboard?" "No." "B.F. Goodrich sandals?" "No!" "Pismo clam cocktails?" "What?" "Please, sir, I have to ask these marketing questions," the agent said, sternly. "Well, then, no," Tony told him. "Did you have any women?" he asked. "No!!" Tony answered indignantly. "I didn't think so," the agent answered. "Alright, you can go." He waved them on.

Tony and Bob didn't see the smirk on the Border Patrol agent's face as they sped away. They were just happy to be back in the Land of the Free. Berkeley Bob said, "Good thing he didn't ask if we bought any Mezcal." Tony said, "You mean you're smuggling in booze!?!" "Smuggling is such a strong word," Bob answered. "I only brought enough for my own personal use." Tony looked at him and figured it was useless so he just drove.

The rest of the trip was fairly uneventful except for lunch in Juarez. Somehow Tony let Bob talk him into going across the bridge over the Rio Grande to eat. Tony must have had rocks in his head to go back into Mexico with Bob.

At the restaurant they met two beautiful young school girls and Bob, who spoke a few words of Spanish, tried to strike up a conversation. After a certain amount of gazing back and forth the girls finally got up to leave. Bob was asking them where they were going, and they were trying to tell Bob something but Tony couldn't figure it out.

After enough gibberish Tony took Bob's arm and pulled him along back toward the bridge to El Paso. They waved goodbye to the girls and then Bob decided he wanted a pair of sandals. They went into a storefront and Bob asked "How much?" The clerk said, "Seven dole-lars." Tony grabbed Bob's arm and pulled him away for a minute.

Tony explained to Bob that in Mexico they expected you to haggle with them over price. Tony told Bob to try to beat the price down by offering him less than Bob wanted to spend. Bob nodded.

He turned to the clerk and said, "O.K., now. I'm gonna offer you less to try and beat you down on the price." The clerk looked puzzled while Tony's mouth dropped open. "How about 2 dollars?" Bob offered. The clerk looked at Bob and said, "No, seven dole-lars." "You mean you won't take less?" Bob asked him. The clerk shook his head. "O.K." Bob said. "I'll take 'em."

Tony couldn't believe it. As they left the store Tony scolded him, "You could have bought those for $1.75!" "That's O.K." Bob said, "$7 was a good price."

Tony was sure now he would never do drugs.

In the car back out on the road they were about an hour out of El Paso, headed east on I-10, when Bob started mumbling, "Mi casa, Mi casa...You know, I think those girls wanted us to go home with them!" Of course, all the girls really meant was that they were going home. But even Berkeley Bob had dreams. Tony just looked at him and then back at the road and sighed.

Aside from Bob's inanities nothing happened from then on back across Texas, Arkansas, Tennessee, Kentucky and into Ohio. When they finally got to Akron Bob got out on Market St. downtown, thanked Tony for the ride, turned around and headed back toward California. "I think I'll go back through Chicago," he said as he wandered off. Tony watched him go, shaking his head. "Dear God, watch over Berkeley Bob. Because you know he can't do it himself," Tony prayed.

Tony moved back in with his parents for a while. He decided to call on a guy named Rob Gullett. Thomas Robert Gullett, actually, but he hated the name Tom. Tony had known him in high school, and he had heard that Rob was now a booking agent. Tony approached him to become his agent. Gullett said he was too busy. He was now working as production manager for John Joules, a regional concert promoter based out of Akron, and he told Tony he just had too much work to be booking anyone. Tony thought about it and went back again in a few days and tried again. Gullett told him emphatically that he had too much concert work to be booking anyone. So Tony then told him, "If you've got that much work you need help, so hire me!" Gullett told him he'd think about it and let him know.

Figuring this was a kissoff, Tony turned his attention to other things. But two days later Rob called him and told him "Jewels" wanted to meet with him. "Who's Jewels?" Tony asked. "You'll see. He's my boss," Gullett told him.

John "Jewels" Joules interviewed Tony from the couch of his living room, which also doubled as his office. Tony asked him about this and Jewels told him that his rent was a business write-off so he lived for free. Jewels asked Tony how good he was with numbers. "Pretty good," Tony told him. "Minor in Statistics, Kent State." He didn't tell Jewels that he had dropped out short of his degree. "Do you think you could manage more than one set of numbers at a time?" Jewels asked. "Sure," Tony assured him. Tony got the feeling that Jewels was always looking for an angle.

And so began Anthony Joseph Mirakul's somewhat remarkable career as a rock concert promoter. He needed a job. This would do.

Tony would later describe these times as his "scufflin' days" working as a promoter. Or more accurately a promoter's assistant. Tony wasn't flamboyant enough to be a real promoter, out front. He was always behind the scenes taking care of business. This both shielded him somewhat, and also meant he wasn't taken seriously, either. He didn't mind the first part but sometimes it bugged him that people didn't recognize his talent. To most of the cool people who hung around the scene he was just a gopher.

Some people were downright malicious, like a singer named Doug Dineen that his boss Jewels had managed for a short while. Dineen hung around the office a lot when he was in town. Jewels had sold Dineen's contract to some high-powered New York manager-attorneys for a finder's fee, a residual, and the understanding that Jewels would be Dineen's national promoter. They, in turn, inked a big record deal for Dineen with Clay Davids at Agravista Records, and ever after that Dineen had loved to torment Tony by making Tony carry his guitar for him. Only it was more than just carry his guitar. Tony had to carry it while Dineen taunted him. Tony would deliver it where Dineen wanted it and then Dineen would change his mind and make him move it somewhere else. Dineen would yell, "You're not even fit to carry my guitar, Meer-a-*not*-cool!" or "Herrrrrre's, Tony!" as if he was a late night talk show host performing for Dineen's amusement.

Despite all this Tony put up with it for the good of the organization because it might mean some business if Dineen really made it someday. His record producer said that Dineen had a "voice like a god." Tony had dealt with many a prima donna in the business so Dineen's abuse was not without precedent. Judging from his attitude, Dineen already thought he was a big star instead of the unknown that he really was.

Despite a few mean people like this, most people hanging around the business simply ignored Tony, unless they wanted something. They would ask him to do things behind the scenes, like make sure their drunken girlfriend got home safely because they knew Tony wouldn't take advantage of her, or bail them out of jail for non-support so none of the "cool people" would know they were bums to their kids.

Many a time Tony was the only sober soul standing at the end of the night. He didn't do drugs, so everyone counted on him to pay the groups, settle the bills, lock up and see that everyone got home safely. He was the designated straight person. And his reputation was actually so solid that the big booking agents and group managers in LA & NY would take his word without a contract because they knew he would make good on whatever he promised.

Once Jewels talked him into cosigning a car loan for him because he had bad credit. It wasn't that Jewels didn't have any money. He was just too disorganized to pay his bills on time.

Nor was Tony without his sinful side. Tony didn't think of himself as particularly attractive but in his college days after his high school sweetheart had broken his heart, he had learned that some of the most attractive women, and often the hardest ones to get, would gravitate to him. Sometimes they would wake him up in the middle of the night, banging on his door because they wanted to sleep with him. He was reticent about chasing women and this only made him all the more attractive to them.

He would overhear guys at meetings or parties talking with great bravado about a particular woman they would like to bed, and realize that he was the only one in the room who had. This was something he would never disclose, certainly not to any bunch of losers who had to talk about it. Tony hated locker room talk. It made him squirm because it was degrading to women and exalted only the basest instincts of man as an animal. Only scum talked like that.

When it came to women Tony never talked. He just did. He was not interested in showing off to other men. It was his own private business. He was not completely comfortable with his own attractiveness or his own sinfulness in this regard. Most men would have loved to have women chase them. Tony was ambivalent.

Tony also "ran the pad." No, not the apartment. Tony cut the deals, did the numbers, ran the "pad," as it was called in the business. He had a phony set of books for the performers and their accountants, a less phony set for the backers who put up the money to promote the concerts, and a real set for the IRS so no one would go to jail, least of all him.

Tony was superb with numbers. He would figure the expenses, estimate the costs and then tell his boss, Jewels, how much they could afford to pay the groups. Sometimes Tony would make the numbers too high to be profitable because he thought the group would be a losing concert. He had an enormous amount of influence this way. Then Jewels, armed with the information Tony supplied, would negotiate with the agents and book the shows.

This always involved a "pad" because every group thought they were a sure thing (they weren't), and so the groups and their managers wanted all the money. But such a high risk business had to pay off pretty handsomely or no one would risk their money promoting it, so the pad made up the real profit on the show.

Tony had this down to a science. He had stationery from every hall and every supplier in the eastern half of the U.S., and before each show he would type out bogus bills in the amounts he wanted to show the groups' accountants and then pocket the real bills so they never saw them.

Sometimes he would change the numbers around so they didn't match the budgeted categories the groups expected but they would still total out pretty much the same overall. It looked more real that way. Or he would even come in a little under budget and throw the groups a little extra money to make them think he was just a backwoods rube. All the while he had every imaginable category padded for profit. He was even so bold that he padded the hall rent, something no one ever suspected because anyone could call and check a rent figure. So no one ever did.

Now everybody in the business knew about the "pad." Entertainment had its own weird form of morality. As long as you didn't get caught it wasn't lying, it was expected business practice. And Tony was so good at it because the big coastal accountants and managers thought he was just a low-rung schlep; they never suspected he was one of the finest numbers men in the country.

Tony, for his part, was actually guileless. He had simply learned that the "truth" in show business was whatever *you* presented that was believable to anyone else in the business. Tony knew that they knew that he was lying to them, and he knew that they were lying back. So it didn't seem like lying. At least back then.

Oh, there were complaints sometimes. Because of his experience with Martin Mull in Hollywood, Tony convinced Jewels they should book Steve Martin just about the time he was getting "hot." Jewels was reluctant to do this at first because Martin didn't have a hit music record, and Jewels didn't have a good feel for the comedy market so Tony convinced one of his friends to bankroll the show. Tony was sure there was a cult following out there for Martin, and he was right. Martin sold out two shows on Halloween night.

For his effort Martin was only paid $18,000, the "pad" being so large. Tony's share of the profits alone was enough to pay for Tony's house. Actually it was only a $10,000 shell he had to rehab but it still sounded good when he told people that "Steve Martin paid for my house."

Martin, for his part, never toured again. Tony overheard him calling his manager from backstage, livid with the high expenses Tony was claiming. "Why make diddly squat for all this work when I can get a million bucks for a picture!?!" he heard Martin screaming into the phone. Why, indeed.

Chapter 10 - *Jewels*

John "Jewels" Joules was a piece of work. A short, wiry guy of French ancestry who liked to twist an imaginary handlebar mustache, he seemed to live for the glory of fame, cocaine, elbow rubbing with celebrity, and the conquest of women. Most of all, he loved the scam. Jewels would pull off anything, just for the sheer rush of fooling someone. It was always best if money was involved but even that didn't matter, if he could pull it off. His favorite movie was *The Sting*.

Tony was the perfect second for Jewels. Tony preferred working behind the scenes rather than being the point man. He saw how people bugged Jewels for free tickets. How they woke him up in the middle of the night looking for coke. And he wanted no part of it. Everybody knew Jewels. Nobody knew Tony, or at least only a handful of people in the business, enough for Tony to function.

They spent millions making Jewels' name a household word in the markets they worked. They adopted the name "A Family Jewels Production." And everybody thought "Jewels" was their best buddy or long lost friend. Tony for his part, actually ran most of the business.

Jewels depended on Tony to do all the nuts and bolts work - figure out the expenses and hold the profit margins, run the shows, deal with the acts and the managers and the

suppliers and the facilities and the stagehands at the gigs.
Jewels would take Tony's numbers and cut the deals with the
booking agents and managers, find the backers to finance the
shows, and show up at the gig with the girls and the cocaine
where necessary. And even where unnecessary.

Their relationship was almost love/hate. They always fought
tooth and nail about what shows to do, what to pay and every
other detail of the business. They would even throw phone
receivers at each other. Litanies of obscenities often were
exchanged between them. Tony would regularly quit, storming
out of the office, usually late in the day when he'd had about
all he could take of Jewels. Then Jewels would call him late
that night and ask him some mundane question like "What's
the rent at Vet's Auditorium? I'm trying to get these numbers
you gave me down." And Tony would tell him "$1750 flat" or
"$500 vs. 10%", and Jewels would say, "O.K. See you in the
morning," and Tony would say, "O.K." And the next morning
(actually noon) they'd go to work and never even mention the
day before. It was kind of like the cartoon where the coyote
and the sheep dog go at it all day over the sheep, and then at 5
o'clock the whistle blows, they clock out, and walk home
together. "See you tomorrow, Ralph."

There were times, however, when Jewels would give Tony a
heart attack. He would disappear for days only to show up an
hour before show time with a load of cocaine and large sums
of cash to pay everyone. Tony would scold him and Jewels
would whisper something like, "Jocko had to fly me in from
Miami. I had to raise enough cash to pay all the groups by
doing a deal. I told Jocko I had to get back. But Olivia was
there, and he didn't want to leave." "Olivia?" Tony would say.
"Yeah, he's her boyfriend." "As long as he's got coke!" Tony
would say. "Well, you know what they say, 'Things go better
with Coke!'" And Jewels would twirl his imaginary handlebar
mustache like Snidely Whiplash and grin like a stoned

Cheshire cat. Jewels, unfortunately, had a sense of humor that most folks recognized as OFWH, only funny when high.

This type of thing had happened so many times that Tony almost began to take it in stride. "He'll be here," he would tell people frantically looking for him. "I hope," he would say to himself.

One time Tony had to hold off paying everybody all night. *Sha Na Na*'s manager was having a snit fit demanding payment before they would go on and it was 5 minutes to show time. Tony finally said, "Look. We've always paid you before, and we have a whole string of dates yet to go. You're going to get paid. Besides, you know, 'The show must go on.' We can argue about things later." Amazingly, he bought it. Tony actually had no idea how he was going to pay everyone. Then he got a hand delivered message from one of Jewels' party buddies. Jewels was in the county jail. Tony needed to come right away.

Quickly Tony told everyone he would be right back, and while the show went on, Tony rushed to the jail. He was sure Jewels had been busted for drugs this time. When he got there he found Jewels calmly sitting in the waiting room. "What are you doing out here?" Tony asked. "Shouldn't you be in the slammer?" "Parking tickets," Jewels replied. "They don't put you in the slammer for not paying parking tickets, they just want the money."

"Well, why didn't you pay them?" "I registered them for court then forgot about it because we had some dates out of town. So they put out a habeas on me. I need $250 per ticket." "How many tickets do you have?" Tony exclaimed. "Eight." Jewels replied. "Don't you have any money? How are we gonna pay everybody?" Tony was really unnerved at this point. "I can't open the trunk." Jewels told him. "Why not? Did you lose your key?" Tony couldn't figure this one out. "No, you maroon. I can't open the trunk. There's *other* stuff in it." Now

Tony understood. Tony walked up, plunked down his personal credit cards for $2000 and bailed Jewels out. "C'mon. We gotta get back before anyone misses us," Tony yelled at Jewels.

On the way back Tony asked Jewels why he didn't have one of his good time buddies put up bail. "Don't be silly. You can't trust them," Jewels said. "You're welcome," Tony said back. Jewels looked at him funny. "Oh, yeah. Thanks." Of course, Tony had to bug Jewels every day for a month to get back his 2 grand. "It can wait for your statement," Jewels said.

Jewels had hammered it into Tony, "Always use other people's money." And "Money is the easiest thing in the world to get." Holding on to it was the hard part.

Jewels was a piece of work alright.

Jewels was always up to something slightly shady, if not downright illegal. Tony was always jawboning him from the other side. He would appeal to Jewels' sense of right and wrong or his desire to stay out of jail. Usually Tony had more success appealing to Jewels desire to maintain his freedom than his conscience.

One dark episode involved forming a partnership with Cosmo Bartini from Detroit. Reputedly Cosmo was connected to the Chicago mob, although he seemed to run a number of legitimate businesses. Tony's mother was Sicilian so Tony had always thought of himself as mostly Italian even though his surname wasn't. So Cosmo and Tony seemed to get along well. If Cosmo wanted facts he always went to Tony for them.

They started out with a huge outdoor concert at Kent State about 5 years after the shootings. Tony had been a student at Kent during the riots but had enough sense to stay in the dorm that ill-fated day, although he didn't do much studying. It appealed to him to do a big concert there. It was sort of a "back to normal" thing he wanted to do for his alma mater. Jewels had come up with the idea of putting on a huge show with 8 to 10 well-known acts who weren't big enough to headline a stadium on their own. This was brilliant because they were all booked on a flat fee basis, no overage. So if the concert did well, all the profits went to the promoter, not the groups. They decided to name their outdoor concerts after local rivers or bodies of water just for a hoot, so they called it the "Breakneck Creek Music Festival" after Breakneck Creek just outside of town.

The show did so well that Dix stadium was jammed. Several of the groups began to demand more money insisting that their fees were based on an expected attendance of 40,000 people and there were more than that in the stadium. But Jewels had the Ticketron statement that showed only 35,000 tickets sold. "Count the drop," they demanded.

The "drop" was the actual ticket collection of torn stubs. Jewels had Tony round up all the drop and bring it under the stadium to the locker room. He then began to negotiate with the various managers and ended up paying them all an extra $10 grand because "We did so well," as Jewels put it. Everyone seemed happy with that, and they decided the show could finish now without a hitch. Except there was one problem they hadn't counted on. It rained and the final group couldn't go on. After a two hour rain delay it was impossible to restart the concert because part of the temporary electrical panel built for the show was under water. The fans rioted and burned down the stadium press box.

Jewels and Tony stared helplessly from across the street at the hotel as the flames shot up into an already black sky from the storm. "I don't think they're going to invite us back," Tony offered. "Sure they will," Jewels said, ever the optimist, or fool.

"It's just money. But just to be safe I think we should leave town as soon as possible. It will be easier to settle things at a distance by phone." So Jewels had Tony drive him over the state line into Pennsylvania and down to the Pittsburgh airport where he caught a flight to Los Angeles for some "R & R," as he put it.

"Isn't this interstate flight to avoid prosecution?" Tony asked Jewels, half-seriously. "I haven't been charged with anything yet." "Yet," Tony noted. "Actually," Jewels continued, "I don't think anyone at the state or federal level is interested in anything hitting the papers that combines the words 'Kent State' and 'prosecution'. They're all still laying low from 1970."

Tony changed the subject and began haranguing Jewels about paying all 8 groups an extra $10 grand. "That's $80,000 we should have pocketed," Tony told him. Jewels finally explained to shut Tony up. "Look. I couldn't let them count that drop. We put 75,000 people in that stadium, not 35,000." "What?" Tony exclaimed. Jewels elaborated. "I talked Skinny at Ticketron into setting up two show codes on the computer that were identical in every way except for one digit. Then I only showed the groups one of the two reports. We sold 40,000 tickets at $9 a pop over and above what we made on the first 35,000 tickets. That's $360,000 pure profit. Of course we can afford $80,000 to shut everybody up." Jewels was right. This even shut Tony up. He just whistled.

Bartini loved it, too. In fact, it spoiled him. It made him think this kind of money could be made on every show. Unfortunately, some shows lose money. Take Cincinnati.

They tried the same thing at Nippert Stadium at the University of Cincinnati at the "Mill Creek Music Festival." But this time Jewels decided to headline an up and coming group named *Aerosmith*, for political reasons. *Aerosmith* had the same New

York agents as his protégé, Doug Dineen. Jewels liked to call the group "Arrowhead" but Tony referred to them as "Tippecanoe" which Jewels didn't understand. Tony explained, "Tippecanoe and Tyler, too. The lead singer's name is Steve Tyler. I hate it when I have to explain the jokes." "It has to be funny to be a joke," Jewels said. "If you were a history major like me it would be funny," Tony offered. "If I was a history major like you, I'd hang myself," Jewels countered.

This was to be *Aerosmith*'s first ever gig as a headliner, and it was a huge outdoor concert with 8 other groups. This would allow their agent to start booking them as headliners everywhere. Jewels did a similar favor for the *Eagles*, except he was the first to ever pay them $100,000 for a show, which skyrocketed their asking price everywhere. But that's another story.

For the Nippert show Tony had to run around to a bunch of small towns in Ohio, Indiana and Kentucky collecting money for ticket sales from all the little "head shops." Jewels borrowed a souped up Mustang for him and gave him an oriental bodyguard named So Wat to ride along with him for protection. Tony took one look at So Wat and thought "inscrutable." So off they went on a wild ride across three states at speeds over 110 mph on all kinds of back roads, Tony driving like a madman and So Wat meditating in the passenger seat unperturbed. They collected over $150,000 in small bills which he and So Wat stuffed into their pants. And they did it all in one day. When they got back they stuffed the wads of bills into a safe, Tony turned in his paperwork, and thought that was the end of it.

The next day, however, the money was short. Everyone with access to the safe got called on the carpet, and it was such a muddle of lost details because everyone was scurrying around getting ready for the show, and using the cash, that it never was determined if anyone had pocketed the cash or if it went out for bills or was simply lost. The remainder of the cash Jewels pocketed. "Always get your hands on the money. If it's short, you can always fight to get more later," Jewels would tell Tony.

Tony had other things to do. *Aerosmith*, now thinking they really *were* headliners, had demanded 20 rack of lamb dinners which Tony dutifully had ordered and went to pick up from Chester's Road House way out in Montgomery. He then delivered them and set up the feast in their main dressing room. When he came back in later, one rack of lamb had been nibbled on and the rest of the repast sat untouched and cold. Meanwhile the walls and floor were covered with shattered glass, mayonnaise, ketchup and mustard. Tony was pissed. Bad form. He made a mental note - no glass in *Aerosmith*'s dressing rooms from now on. A few minutes later, Steve Tyler walked in, looked around and started helping Tony pick up the glass. "Sorry," he said. "That's O.K. I'll clean it up," Tony told him. Tony never did find out what happened or who did what. But Tyler was always nice to him after that.

At another big outdoor show at Indiana University that summer, this one called the "Jordan River Music Festival," named after a creek than ran through campus, Jewels headlined *Aerosmith* again. About an hour before the show was to start Tony couldn't find his date, a girl named Tina Bracken, only to see Tyler walking across the stadium bringing her back from *Aerosmith*'s trailer. Apparently, he had found out she was with Tony and had whisked her out of there before anything could happen to her. Tony almost said "Thanks, Tallarico," his real name, but thought better of it, sticking with "Steve." Tyler made small talk, "We're all going to see John Cougar at the Bluebird downtown tonight." "I can't take the pink suits," Tony offered. "That's the only reason we go," Tyler replied, sauntering off. "Be good," Tony yelled after him. "And if you can't be good, be loud!"

"They've got great toot," Tina told Tony, once he was out of earshot. "It's a shame you don't use it." "Someone's got to drive," Tony reminded her, not wishing to get into it for the umpteenth time why he really didn't use drugs...

Back at Jewels' apartment after "Jordan River" they were brainstorming other ideas for outdoor concerts. Rob Gullett had an outrageous idea that Jewels started to run with. It was called "200 Years of Rock 'n' Roll" and the dates were to be July 2, 3 and 4, 1976, at Indianapolis Motor Speedway, America's Bicentennial Birthday.

Rob had the idea of doing a massive outdoor concert, ala *Woodstock*, to celebrate the Bicentennial. He wanted to book every major act in the business on the show. Promoters were always dreaming of creating a one-of-a-kind event that would go down in history but only Bill Graham and his cronies had pulled anything close to it off when they organized *Woodstock* back in 1969.

That's when Jewels' imagination took over. First, he came up with the name - "200 Years of Rock 'n' Roll." Then he and Tony and Rob made a list of every major act that should be on it, from the *Eagles* to *Fleetwood Mac* to *Pink Floyd* to *Led Zepplin* to *The Who* and the *Rolling Stones*, plus everyone in between. But the three of them were perplexed at who the headliner should be. "They're all going to fight over who headlines just like Woodstock," Tony said. "And Hendrix is dead." Jewels was pacing back and forth in the apartment, staring out the window. The radio was on in the background just barely audible. It was a rock station playing "Come Together" by the *Beatles*. All of a sudden, Jewels yelled, "That's it! That's it!!" "What's it?" Tony and Rob answered in unison.

"A *Beatles* Reunion!" Jewels exclaimed. "You're nuts!" Tony shouted back. "Yeah!" Rob chimed in. "That's got a snowball's chance of happening."

"No," Jewels began. "Here's what we do. The key is to get all four of them in the same place at the same time. Gravity will take over from there." "You mean momentum?" Tony asked. "Whatever," Jewels continued. "We book all four of them individually with their own bands. Then when they get there, we'll schedule them so all four sets follow each other back to back at the end of the show. Then they'll have to come back on for an encore together!" "And I can play keyboards!" Gullett said, sarcastically. "That's interesting," Tony chimed in. "You never could before." "I'm a genus!" Jewels exclaimed, leaving out the "*i*"on purpose as if he was his own separate specie. He was so proud of himself.

"What about their agents?" Tony asked. "We'll buy them off," Jewels told him. "Everyone has his price. In fact, we'll offer them whatever their greatest fantasy is, within reason, of course." Rob jumped in, "Can you arrange a date for me with Linda Ronstadt?" "Of course!" Jewels said egotistically. "Well, you'll have just about as much chance of booking a Beatles reunion as getting me that date," Rob told him.

So they argued. Finally Tony and Rob shrugged their shoulders and gave up trying to dissuade Jewels. "We'll book all the most famous acts in the world and then advertise 'plus a special headliner to close the show.' Even a moron will be able to figure that out," Jewels told them. "What a maroon!" Tony repeated, ala Bugs Bunny. They all laughed, and Tony drifted off in a daydream.

He thought about how it could be done. It would probably be easier than anyone thought. His mind wandered, imagining them booking each of the four Beatles with their own bands, and Jewels assuring their agents that they would not even advertise them. It was to be a special surprise. Each of the four was to think that they were the secret headliner for the greatest rock 'n' roll show ever. Naturally, they would want to be there for that. Tony drifted further off, not hearing Jewels or Rob talking or getting on the phone. In his mind he saw it all unfold...

Secretly Jewels bought off each agent by offering them something they would normally never be able to find, those things having to remain secret because in many cases the statute of limitations would take years to run out. Jewels told the booking agents that if any of the groups complained after the show the agent could plead ignorance. After all, they were doing just what the contract said they would do.

Cosmo Bartini loved it. He supplied them with mega-millions to fund the event. No one at Family Jewels knew where the money came from but they weren't asking.

Jewels booked everyone on a flat fee basis. Once the biggest acts were booked everyone else they wanted worked cheap, not wanting to miss the event. Everyone except *Aerosmith*, who were demanding to headline. Jewels said he would put them on as the final act on the first night, July 2nd. Jewels was smacking his lips. He could see how much money was to be made.

Tony was frenetically trying to put together the ads and was buying advertising right and left. "Get Larry Lujack to do the radio spots again," Jewels was screaming at him. "What about Imus?" Tony screamed back. It was promoter's heaven. Putting on a huge event was a constant natural high. It was manic. There was nothing else like it in the natural world. No drugs. Just adrenaline non-stop for weeks, even months, before the show happened. It was addictive.

Every time they did one of these exhausting events they would be frazzled and almost zombie-like for the last few weeks before it happened. Jewels would swear that this was going to be his last show ever. It wasn't worth the aggravation. "Just one more hit and I'm through," he would say. Then after the show was over, just like an addict, he would start to plan the next one. Tony knew he would never give it up. The only way Jewels would stop would be if he got sent to jail or died on the job.

An artist friend had drawn a caricature of Jewels which adorned their office apartment wall. It was a picture of Jewels with a phone cord wrapped around his neck several times, twirling a real handlebar mustache while he tells an agent on the line, "I'll give you $10K vs. 60% of the gross." It was perfect.

Although they figured that the Speedway could easily hold the 500,000 it held for races, they weren't sure how many more they could cram in for a concert. They set the tickets up on Ticketron to max out at 750,000, figuring that would be more than they would ever sell. Then they sold that out a week in advance. Jewels had them re-program it for a million without any idea where they were going to put everyone. By showtime the first day they had sold 910,000. Luckily, not everyone came all three days. The crowd varied from 600,000 to 700,000 the first two days, which was manageable. They also learned enough from the first day to make adjustments in preparation for the second and third days. Security was excellent because the Speedway was used to handling crowds of a half-million people. Tony was pleased because no one had been seriously hurt, so far. But crunch day was yet to come.

When July 4th dawned it wasn't long before the individual *Beatles'* trucks began arriving. Then it wasn't long before the roadies began to figure it out. Most of them thought it was cool. A few came and complained to Jewels. He told them each one was just booked to play their own set of music. It wasn't until all the equipment was unloaded and all 4 *Beatles* had arrived, each with their own private retinue, that they began to realize all four of them were there with their groups, and all four thought each of them was the headliner.

They all tried to reach their agents and managers but they were all conveniently unavailable, it being a holiday. Then they descended on the main trailer demanding to see the promoter. Normally they would have had underlings do such dirty work but they were all so mad, feeling tricked, that they went looking for Jewels themselves.

Tony was slightly in awe to see all of them there together. However, the awe quickly dissolved when they started screaming at him, "Are you the promoter?" "Uh, no. Here, let me take you to him," he told them.

Jewels was now on. This was to be his finest moment. After being severely upbraided for booking them all together and being told in no uncertain terms that either they weren't going to play, contract or not, or at the very least they weren't going to play together, Jewels calmly explained that he had booked all four of them just as each of their contracts said, and that he didn't do anything wrong or deceitful. After all, they had wanted to be on the show or they wouldn't have been there.

Then he told them that he knew they were all honorable men and would do the right thing. This seemed to calm everyone down as they realized they were stuck. Everybody knew they were there now. It would be bad to refuse to play. It would look arrogant and petty. Everyone agreed that they could put up

with it somehow. But who would play first? Jewels had a simple suggestion. He had Tony get a hat, place four pieces of
paper in it, each with a different number from 1 to 4, and had
each of the Beatles draw a number. "It's a Christmas gift
exchange!" Ringo playfully suggested. Everybody laughed at
the absurdity of what they were doing. John drew one, Ringo
two, then came Paul with number three, and finally George
was fourth.

And so they went on stage in that order, each playing 30-40
minutes. The crowd went nuts. There were now over 950,000
people, counting gatecrashers, crammed into the Speedway,
all of them craning their necks. They had already seen a
Yardbirds "reunion" with Clapton, Beck and Page all playing
together for the first time, and during Harrison's set Clapton
would return to play the solos on "My Guitar Gently Weeps"
live, for the first time ever. The excitement had reached a fever
pitch even before McCartney and Harrison played their
respective sets.

The only thing Jewels and company had not thought of was
the riot that would be on their hands if an actual reunion
didn't happen now. No matter that they had never promised
any such thing publicly. All four were there and anything less
would be disastrous now.

Tony found himself performing a kind of shuttle diplomacy
back and forth between Lennon's and McCartney's dressing
rooms. Ringo didn't really care, George would probably go
along. It was up to John and Paul. Tony was sweating bullets
as he went back and forth with missives from both men plus
whatever Jewels interjected. Paul had wanted Linda to sing
but Linda, bless her heart, was wise enough to tell him that she
really didn't want to sing, she wanted to take pictures, which
was both true and helpful, given the divisiveness such a

demand would have created. The major sticking points came down to money and rights to the video and recording of the performance. After all, a *Beatles* reunion was worth millions.

Tony could hear George finishing up his set as he ran back and forth. He knew he had to do something. Finally he decided there was only one thing to do, beg. He got down on his hands and knees and asked John to please have mercy on him and on the poor schleps who were out in the audience. There were surely going to be people hurt if they didn't play. There were just too many people. This seemed to get through to John. "I'll do it if he does, anything else we'll argue about later," he told Tony.

Tony was up off his knees like a shot and headed back to Paul's trailer. Paul was tired of seeing him. He wouldn't let him in. Tony beat on the door. "Please, Mr. McCartney," he pleaded. Then he started crying from the sheer frustration. Finally, Tony sobbed, "Have mercy. I didn't even like you guys!"

A few seconds later the door opened. There stood McCartney with a smirk on his face. "What do you mean, I never even liked you guys?" Tony had collapsed on the metal footstep in front of the trailer door. "I had curly hair, and everybody made fun of it because you guys had long straight hair. None of the girls liked curly hair anymore. I tried straightening it but it didn't work. It just burned my scalp."

"You mean you conked your hair because of us?" McCartney asked with a chuckle. "Yeah," Tony said. "And so that's why I didn't like you guys, even though you were pretty good." At this, Paul burst out laughing. "Pretty good, huh?" he said. "O.K. Let's do it." Tony just sat there. "O.K.," he said. "You go on, I'll catch up." "I think he just said he was going to play," Tony thought.

And play they did. Jewels had taken the time after Harrison's set to have the equipment moved. Somehow the road crews had figured out what gear to use where and everything was ready. The back of the stage was jammed with what seemed like every rock star on the planet, jockeying for position like schoolgirls to see and hear themselves. It was surreal. Tony dragged himself back from Paul's trailer but before he could get up the steps to the stage Jewels came running and grabbed him. "Get up there!" he yelled. "They want you to introduce them." "What?" Tony thought. He raced up the steps excusing himself past famous people right and left. Paul saw him and grabbed him. "Lead us on, mate!" he said.

Tony took the microphone and waved at the crowd which drew a thunderous reaction. Then he made a motion to quiet down. When the crowd settled down enough to hear he simply said, "Ladies and Gentlemen, *THE BEATLES!*" Behind him the opening notes of "Daytripper" rolled off George's fingers as if he had been practicing for the last six years just for this moment. The crowd went wild. The noise was deafening. It was enough to make the band lose time. But they didn't. They fell in like they had just rehearsed yesterday.

Within 16 bars there were smiles on every face in the band. This wasn't so bad after all, they were all thinking. Forty-five minutes into the set they started pulling in players from behind them on stage. It was a party in the garage now. An hour and fifteen minutes after that they finished with "Hey, Jude," recruiting everyone on stage to sing. There were over 50 stars on stage at once, singing their hearts out, along with almost a million other voices joining in.

Tony joined in, too, on one of the background mikes in a group of about a dozen stars who were having too much fun to notice he was nobody. Rob Gullett was on another mike next to Linda Ronstadt, grinning from ear to ear. He was playing Air Keyboard while Linda laughed at him affectionately.

Tony wondered if they could be heard all the way to Terre Haute. Then a bizarre thought crossed his mind. "This is only a million people. Imagine what it must be like when God mounts his throne to shouts of joy, and it's *billions* of people! Now that would be loud!" The thought hurt his head.

It was all over too soon. Everyone milled around on stage not knowing what to do. Everyone was hugging everyone else. There was so much energy that no one knew how to discharge it. Jewels' insane idea had worked. Everyone knew they had just been a part of something they would remember and cherish and retell for the rest of their lives, complete with embellishment.

Tony got some water and went back to work. Time to clean up and move out. There were stagehands on the clock. This show was over. Then he stopped for a second. "Yeah, but wasn't it great?" he told himself, smiling. Someone was calling "Tony!" Then again, "Tony!!" He realized he had been drifting along in a pipe dream.

Jewels yelled at him, "Tony! Hey, earth to Tony!" "What?" Tony said, half-asleep. "We can't get the venue," Jewels told him. "What?" Tony asked again. What Jewels had said wasn't registering. "We can't get the Speedway. It's not available. That idea's dead."

"Oh," said Tony. And he yawned, got up and went to the kitchen and poured a glass of OJ. "So what's next?" he said.

Chapter 12 - *Scams*

After the "Jordan River" show Cosmo Bartini called Tony and wanted the rundown on what happened to the money. Jewels meanwhile was stonewalling handing over the money to Cosmo. Tony figured Jewels was either using it as a bargaining chip in some negotiation with Cosmo, or using it to pay off creditors the business owed. So Tony wasn't very forthcoming with Cosmo about where the money was. Cosmo started screaming at Tony that he was going to send someone down there to "take care of him" if he didn't cough up the money or the details. Tony was more terrified than he had ever been in his life. But he told Cosmo, "I'm Italian (even though he was only half-Sicilian). And I don't work for you. I work for Jewels. You'll have to speak with him." And surprisingly, Cosmo got very calm. Somehow he understood that Tony was saying he was loyal to who he worked for, even when threatened. Cosmo admired this.

From then on, Cosmo always treated Tony with respect, and never threatened him again. And Tony remained scared to death of Cosmo. Especially when he had to explain to Cosmo why certain shows lost money. Jewels never quite replicated that first big show that made tons of money. Eventually, Cosmo got tired of losing money in the concert business and went on to more profitable things. And Tony breathed a sigh of relief. "Let's stick to backers who've inherited money and won't kill us if they lose it," he told Jewels. And for once Jewels was immediately agreeable.

But Jewels was still the *scam king*. Sometimes he would confound Tony by booking a string of shows that Tony told him was a loser. "Jewels, we're going to lose our shirts!" Tony would scream at him. "Let me worry about it," Jewels would say. After this happened on a few isolated dates, Jewels pulled it on a whole tour with *Styx*. Jewels had the idiotic idea that they could book them into high school auditoriums in small towns around Ohio and the shows would sell out because the kids would be so impressed.

"I did this once with *Herman's Hermits*," Jewels said. "Actually, it wasn't really *Herman's Hermits*. What we did is we found some guys in Youngstown in a garage band, and we paid them a grand a week to dress up and cover all the *Herman's Hermits* records. We found this one kid who looked just like Peter Noone. We sold out every little town across the upper Midwest from Wilkes-Barre all the way to Sheboygan."

"How could you do that??" Tony asked indignantly. "Well, I felt guilty at first. But then I saw all those little girls screaming at what they thought was the real thing, and I realized that as far as they were concerned it *was* the real thing. They loved it. Now why ruin their fun ? Those little girls would have never had a chance to see the real band up close like that," Jewels explained. There was almost some logic to this. After all, they screamed so loud anyway, you couldn't hear the music. Nevertheless, Tony knew there was something wrong with it somewhere, if only that it was probably illegal, not to mention dishonest. But that was Jewels. He honestly thought of himself as a benefactor. "It's our job to relieve their hum-drum existence!" he said, in a self-congratulatory way.

Now he proposed that they mount a small town tour with an up and coming group from Chicago named *Styx*. "That's great except for two things," Tony said, "First off, the kids are used to going to concerts in the bigger cities now so they won't pay the higher prices we'll have to charge to see them close to home, and second, *Styx* won't draw flies." "They're only $1500 a night and I'm doing their manager a favor," Jewels replied, overruling Tony's objections.

Sure enough, though, Tony was right. The "Small Cities Tour" was a huge flop. They didn't draw more than 125 people in any city they played - Van Wert, Napoleon, Jackson, Rio Grande, Galion, Hillsboro, all little burgs in Ohio. Squat. Nada.

Jewels used Doug Dineen for the opening act, sans band. Since Doug was from Wooster, Ohio, Jewels didn't want to introduce him as being from so small a town. Jewels thought about it. "Hey, Dineen, weren't you just out in L.A. on vacation?" "Yeah." Doug told him. So Jewels introduced him as "Direct from Los Angeles, California - Doug Dineen!" Jewels was dreaming of all those profits Dineen was going to make for him on tour when his record was a big success. Unfortunately, it wasn't going to be on this tour.

After this bloodbath, Tony couldn't understand why Jewels seemed so pleased. He kept bugging Jewels. Something didn't seem right to Tony. Finally Jewels told him. "I sold 200% of the tour." "What do you mean ?" Tony asked. It didn't make any sense. "How could you sell 200% of something? There's only 100% to sell." "Not so," said Jewels. "I found backers for the tour to put up the money and I sold 200% of it." Tony scratched his head. "But we lost money," he said, dumbfounded. "Exactly. I knew you were right. It was a stinker of a tour. So I sold 200% of it. Whatever we lost we got twice that amount from the backers. So we made whatever we lost."

Tony couldn't believe it. "Just like *The Producers*, except it worked," Tony mused out loud, scratching his chin. "What's that?" Jewels asked. Tony explained the plot of the movie to Jewels. Jewels laughed. "I'm a genus!" Jewels exclaimed, Mrs. Malapropishly. Except he knew what he was saying.

Tony thought Jewels had gone over the top with this one. Tony didn't know the backers so he wasn't sure what to do about them losing their money. Why did Jewels have to be so incredibly brilliant at being dishonest? Why couldn't he come up with some legitimate ideas? After ragging Jewels long enough, Jewels finally promised to make it up to the backers who had lost money by including them in a future moneymaking tour.

Jewels agreed to this not so much because it was the right thing to do as he was just tired of Tony bugging him. Tony knew it wasn't perfect but he knew the backers would probably prefer getting their money back over just knowing they had been scammed and the money was gone. Tony also knew he'd probably end up doing most of the work to make it right, too. Such was life with Jewels.

It had taken Tony awhile to figure it out when he had first entered the business because he was so guileless, but a good portion of his income was expected to be money from scams pulled in the line of work. The *scam* is ever present in the entertainment business. If someone cannot stomach the *scam,* they don't belong in the business.

The scam could be anything - selling complimentary record albums the promoter receives to the second hand record store, selling a few comp tickets for concerts and pocketing the cash, charging people to get backstage, you name it, it happens.

Everybody scams whenever they can. Not just the promoters. Everyone. The agents, the show workers, the ticket sellers, the radio and TV station personnel, the stagehands, the booking agents, the managers, even the groups. Sex and drugs and money are the main forms of currency, and scams produced the "coin of the realm." That's why it's called *sex and drugs and rock 'n' roll!*

Oddly enough, within this decadent world there was still a set of rules. It was perfectly alright to run a scam on your own employer for sex, drugs or money. If you were caught, rather than being fired, your boss was more likely to ask to be cut in on the action. He would actually credit you for being industrious. Nor was there likely to be any long term repercussion from attempting a scam on someone else in the business.

First off, no one wanted to admit they had been fooled, and second, it was a matter of pride to be an insider pulling off the scam, rather than being "the mark." Consequently, attempting a scam was a low risk proposition because there was very little potential downside. Even a failed scam was likely to be a source of pride just for the "Chutzpah" of trying to pull it off. The mark might even brag about having been able to figure it out. Anything that needed to be resolved would be negotiated between the parties. Everyone negotiated everything. And skillful negotiators were revered in the business.

On the other side of the coin it was never alright to turn anyone within "the club" in to the police or authorities. It was much like the mob in this regard. You never betrayed a member of "the family" to an outsider. And despite the entertainment business being made up of every low-life in the world who was attracted to fame and fortune, these rules seemed to hold. It was coast to coast news for anyone to "turn over" on someone else in the business. Even a local yokel would be shunned forever if he did that. "You'll never work in this town again" actually meant something.

Tony had learned "the ropes" from Jewels, who was one of the best in the business. It hadn't been long before Tony was cooking up minor scams that made Jewels proud. For example, once he caught some guys charging admission to a private party upstairs at Richfield Coliseum during a Family Jewels concert and rather than throw them out, he simply charged them all admission and pocketed the cash. When Rob Gullett, their stage manager, found out, Tony bought him off with $100, and when Jewels got wind of it, Tony "split 50/50" with Jewels, giving him 20% of the take. Everybody was happy, except the guys who thought they were pulling a scam in the first place by charging for a party with a free show, and not paying for the tickets for their patrons. Everybody got into the act. Even people no one would ever suspect. Take, for example, Jackson Browne.

Jewels was a great friend and supporter of Jackson Browne. Jewels had been one of the first to book Jackson for small clubs at a grand a night and took major risks helping him build his career. Jackson was loyal to Jewels and would always play dates for him when touring the East and Midwest.

As Jackson's fame grew his entourage and equipment grew in size also. But rather than let this go to his head he was known for his empathy for those around him. This culminated in Jackson taking the old standard, "Stay" and turning it into an ode to all the workers behind the scenes. The roadies, the stagehands, the promoters and everyone else involved in support all loved the fact that Jackson had re-written the song to acknowledge their existence and importance to the music business. Consequently, Jackson was admired and respected by the many thousands of people who actually made the business go. There was great industry joy when Jackson's *Running On Empty* live album and tour made him a superstar.

When Jackson toured the Midwest with *Running on Empty* Jewels had to fight for the dates because so many promoters wanted the *Empty* tour. Only personal intervention by Jackson with his booking agent kept the dates for Jewels. "Payback," Jackson told him.

Jackson had added an odd hospitality request in his contract rider for this tour. It was the first ever tour with a wine list. Each night of the tour Tony had to find 4 expensive wines listed on a wine list in Jackson's contract. Unfortunately the wines listed weren't available in the midwest, so Tony had to substitute expensive European wines, hoping Jackson wouldn't be upset. The bill was running hundreds of dollars per night for this wine.

After a while Tony realized that he never found any empty wine bottles after the shows. In fact, he never saw anyone drinking any of the fancy wines he worked so hard to find, not even Jackson. Then one night he had to go onto one of Jackson's tour buses to get something while the group was on stage. He just happened to notice a huge instrument-type case on rollers, the hard shell type with steel reinforced corners. It was the largest instrument case he had ever seen.

Curious as to what kind of instrument it could possibly house he opened it. Inside, instead of instruments, he found wine. Every bottle from every stop on the tour was inside, all carefully laid sideways in foam rubber cutouts. Four bottles a night for 100 nights at $100 a pop was $40,000 of wine. An average person was lucky to make half that for a year's work! Tony worked his tail off and only made $18K, above the table, that is.

Jackson, Tony was told by one of his roadies, was taking the vino home to stock his wine cellar in California, all for free. Jewels was impressed when Tony told him about the elaborate protective case and its contents. "No recognized income, no income taxes. It's all just *hospitality*," Jewels whistled. "Brilliant! What a great scam! I knew there was something about that boy I liked!!"

Jackson had a reputation that Tony would best describe as "the troubadour philosopher" due to his introspective songs.

Jackson was about as deep as most folks got. Consequently, a scam seemed out of character for such a "serious artist." Tony felt a little like Dorothy when she saw the man behind the curtain. He was disappointed. And a little hurt. He felt like the innocent bystander. For the first time he realized that scams were not harmless.

Jewels reminded Tony that the hospitality belonged to Jackson, and he could do with it whatever he wanted. If he wanted to save the wine it was his prerogative. "He's out for himself like everyone else in the business is," Jewels told Tony. "Wouldn't you be upset if he was disloyal to you and played for another promoter?" Tony asked. "Yeah. But that would be bad business because he owes me. Still, I wouldn't be surprised. It's a dirty business," Jewels explained. Tony thought about it. "Well, I guess it's his wine alright. But it still seems petty to me. Hospitality is supposed to take care of the needs of the group backstage so they can concentrate on doing a good show," Tony answered. "Not be a scam to beat the taxman." "You're just jealous because you didn't think of it yourself," Jewels chided him. "O.K., then. *You* find the wine for the rest of the dates," Tony threatened him. "Forget it, *notcool*! That's your job!" Jewels told him, laughing. Tony was angry, and disappointed. "I guess I just expected more. That's all," he told Jewels. He clammed up and began to roll it around in his mind trying to put the best face on it for Jackson's sake.

At the next concert date Tony dutifully supplied 4 more rare and expensive bottles of wine. For a moment he was tempted to hold an impromptu wine tasting backstage for everyone but he thought better of it. Instead he decided to save someone the trouble of carrying the bottles from the dressing room to the bus and did it himself. He left them standing on top of the large anvil carrying case ready for their trip back to California and went back in to put on the show.

As Jewels' right hand man, Tony was often nothing more than a "gopher." But he had taken that title to a new level. Tony had a reputation for being able to find any thing at any time in any place. He could find scaffolding at midnight in Podunk if he had to. He once climbed a barbed wire fence into a lumberyard at 3 AM to get a bucket of latex floor leveler that they needed to repair a stage for an outdoor show and left a note with a personal check in the door to cover the cost so when they came in the next morning the yard people wouldn't think they had been robbed. They cashed the check, too.

He could find guitar strings at midnight, blueberry pie in winter, fix a dead hair dryer five minutes before showtime, produce a band-aid, valium, fuse or 12AX7 tube in the middle of a set onstage, even find ice in the desert. Tony would say, "If I was a (fill in the blank), where would I be?" and then come up with it in even the most extreme cases. What's more, no one could ever remember him failing to come up with the item needed, or a work-around to solve the problem. His problem-solving capabilities were truly astounding, and legendary within a small circle of friends and business acquaintances.

In spite of this, Jewels would denigrate Tony in front of others because he was afraid the people he wanted to impress would not be impressed with Tony. So Jewels made fun of him. Tony wasn't "cool." In fact, Dineen's nickname of "Meer-a-*not*-cool" had stuck, and Tony was often called "*Not-cool*" when people phoned in or saw him somewhere. Tony only resented this when it was someone like Dineen using it because it was done maliciously. Other folks who used it playfully he didn't mind.

In spite of this lack of respect, Tony was a loyal, dedicated employee of Jewels, and a better friend than Jewels gave him credit for. Tony would never leave Jewels in the lurch like most of his good-time buddies would.

In this context, Jewels would often have Tony handle secret or delicate matters for him. Tony often didn't know if he was handling a business matter or a personal one for Jewels. The only thing Tony wouldn't handle was anything related to drugs. "If you ever involve me in that you'll never see me again," Tony told Jewels. And Jewels knew he meant it.

A few weeks after he had handled one such matter for Jewels he overheard him talking on the phone with Dineen about it. Tony had been given the assignment of meeting up with Charlie Fehr, the Cleveland Indians' almost certain hall-of-fame left-fielder. Tony had picked up an envelope with a large sum of cash from Charlie and delivered it to Jewels. Jewels had assured Tony it was not drug money. Tony had delivered it to Jewels and hadn't thought anything more about it.

Now he overheard Jewels talking with Dineen about "Charlie's money" and "Donna." Donna who? Donna Davenport? Lately he had seen Dineen hanging out with Davenport, and he knew Dineen was cheating on his wife back home in Wooster. He knew this because he had come in to the office late one night and wandered by Dineen's car parked in front of Jewel's apartment only to see Donna and Dineen amorously engaged in the back seat. "Tacky," he thought at the time. "Get a motel."

So after Jewels hung up Tony pressed him for an explanation. "What does Charlie's money have to do with Donna Davenport?" Tony queried.

At first, Jewels wouldn't tell him. But this only made Tony more adamant. Finally, Jewels caved in. "Alright, I'll tell you but you can never repeat it." "O.K.," Tony promised.

"Donna had an abortion and Charlie paid for it." "What ?!?" Tony snapped. "Donna didn't want her modeling career to be ruined so she had an abortion. She could never get her figure back after that," Jewels offered. "I can't believe it!" Tony cried. "She killed her own kid for her modeling career, and you had me get the money for it?" Tony was livid. Jewels was backing away from Tony. "Dineen handled it. I was just the middle man," Jewels protested. "What is wrong with you?" Tony demanded. "Oh, you think it's so easy, do you?" Jewels retorted. "Donna's modeling career is all she has. It's her whole life, AND her only hope to make it!" Jewels justified it.

"O.K. Let me see, now. If Donna had a manager who was standing in the way of her career and she killed him, it would be murder, but since it's a baby, it's alright??? Is that the way it works??" Tony screamed at Jewels. "It's not the same thing!" Jewels yelled back. "The hell it isn't. It's exactly the same," Tony screamed back. "How could you do this... and drag me into it?" Tony demanded. Jewels made no answer, and Tony stormed out.

Tony had quit Jewels many a time before but had always showed up for work the next day after he cooled off. Now he thought about quitting for real. But he didn't have anything else to do or be right that instant... Besides, he knew he hadn't done anything wrong himself. He just couldn't believe anyone could do such a thing, especially for their career. What kind of person could do such an evil thing? His opinion of Donna Davenport was about as low as he had ever had of anyone. Just what kind of person would kill for their own gain? And for something as fleeting as beauty, no less? Tony felt shell-shocked. He had actually been involved in an abortion, however inadvertently. He felt horrible. All he could think about were little hands reaching out to him.

He went back to his apartment and promptly punched a hole in the drywall. He let loose a flurry of profanity in his anger, and his pain. Tony was no he-man. Hitting the wall hurt. As his knuckles throbbed and ached he felt stupid. "Violence breeds violence," he thought. "I think I'll stop it right here."

Tony didn't speak to Jewels for 3 days. Jewels called multiple times but Tony never answered. Finally, Tony went back in to the office. "Listen, you jerk," Tony told Jewels. "I'll never run another errand or do anything I even remotely suspect could be illegal or immoral for you again." Jewels was pleased. This meant Tony was back. "O.K.," Jewels agreed, a little too quickly.

Jewels was a weasel. He wouldn't think about his pledge again. The only thing that mattered to him was that things were back to normal, as far as he was concerned.

Tony thought this whole incident was far worse than running drugs could be but he couldn't bring himself to quit. He felt almost responsible for Jewels, like he couldn't leave him. It would be almost like abandoning family. And Jewels needed somebody to keep him from going off the deep end. If only he had known what the three of them were up to perhaps he could have influenced Donna not to abort. Tony felt like he needed to stay involved and quitting was not the way to do it. It was a mixed decision because he was appalled at what they had done.

Tony avoided Dineen unless he was absolutely unavoidable. Unlike Jewels, who was essentially innocuous, albeit self-centered, Tony considered Dineen to be downright evil. Likewise, Tony's image of a certain Indians' left fielder had been badly tarnished.

As for Donna, he didn't really know her beyond seeing her hanging around the concert scene, her parking incident with Dineen, and the abortion. But she wasn't looking too good to him at this point so it was probably a blessing that she hadn't shown her face since the abortion. And life at Family Jewels Productions went back to "normal." Or at least as "normal" as anything in the concert business could be.

Chapter 14 - *Reserved Seats*

Although it might seem that everyone in the concert business was equally corrupt there were still some people who had stronger morals than others, although it would be hard for an outsider to detect the differences. But people inside the industry knew. Tony was considered one of the straight arrows. People could trust him if he said he would do something or handle some matter.

But morality aside, no one could get along with everybody. For example, Tony had a less than perfect relationship with Kenny Loggins. And for the most part it was Tony's fault. Every time Kenny played for Family Jewels Productions Tony seemed to do something that rubbed Kenny the wrong way.

Even before Tony ever became a promoter he managed to put his foot in it with Loggins. In 1972 Tony had run into Loggins in a nightclub in Cleveland, only to spend 30 minutes telling Kenny how much he loved his work in *Buffalo Springfield*. The only problem was that it was his partner Jim Messina who was in *BS*, not Loggins. Tony couldn't figure out why Loggins kept getting more and more perturbed as he spoke with him. Later Tony realized that it was Loggins and not Messina he had been talking to all that time. Tony felt really stupid. Tony could really put his foot in his mouth sometimes.

Luckily, Kenny made no connection that Tony was the same guy when Tony did his first concert with Loggins at Family Jewels Productions. And Tony wasn't about to remind him. Nevertheless, Tony seemed to get into a fight or otherwise make Loggins mad every time they did a show. It might be bad catering, or a reporter making a nuisance of himself (or herself) backstage but somehow what Tony did always aggravated Loggins. Tony couldn't figure out why he kept coming back to play for them.

The coup de grace' came at Hara Arena in Dayton, Sept. 5, 1978. Tony still remembered the date like it was yesterday because of what would happen a year later at *The Who* concert in Cincinnati. Tony had convinced Jewels that crowd behavior had gotten so uncontrollable that someone was going to get hurt. The solution Tony proposed was something that few people thought was possible - go back to reserved seats for rock concerts instead of general admission. Jewels thought Tony was nuts but agreed to try it for the Loggins concert. "How wild can they get over Kenny Loggins?" Jewels asked, thinking it was absurd.

Pretty wild, it turned out. After all, it was Dayton. And it was at "The Pit", as Hara is deprecatingly known in the business. Despite ample warning in the ads, and everyone having a specific seat, the audience contained a huge contingent that simply refused to cooperate. They crushed forward in the aisles and wouldn't let people with tickets into their own seats.

Loggins came onstage to this just as Tony and a whole contingent of security lit into the crowd. Tony was throwing people out right and left trying to clear the aisles and let the people who had paid to sit in front have their seats back. There was a huge melee. At one point, Tony was grappling with two or three thugs when he looked up and Loggins was screaming directly at him to stop it and let them party.

Kenny didn't understand what Tony's crew was trying to do. Loggins was furious, thinking Tony was ruining the excitement of the concert. Finally Tony called off his crew, giving in to Loggins. Backstage he tried to explain it to Kenny but Loggins was too angry to understand at the time. Tony figured this was probably the last straw for Loggins although he had been wrong before.

The following summer Tony got a call from his friend and competitor Abe Pastaks. Abe's company had just gotten permission to stage the first ever rock concert in Riverfront Stadium in Cincinnati. To do this, they would have to cover the Astroturf. Unfortunately, there was only one tarp big enough in the whole country to do it. That tarp was at Arrowhead Stadium in Kansas City and it just happened to be available for the date of the concert. "Why are you telling me all this, Abe?" Tony asked.

"Well, I thought you might like to rent that tarp and make some money," Abe suggested. "O.K., what's the scam?" Tony asked. Abe proceeded to explain that Tony would rent the tarp for $4 grand. Arrowhead would deliver it, Abe's people would deploy it, use it, roll it back up and Arrowhead would reload it and take it back. All Tony had to do was order it and handle the paperwork. $4000 would pay for the tarp, Tony got $1500, and that was it. One call, show up with a bill, get your money. Abe would take care of the rest.

According to Abe this was because Tony's company wasn't awarded the stadium show and it was just a gesture of goodwill. Tony knew this was a lie, but in the entertainment business people think of it as a "story" not a lie. And the better your story the more real it was considered. Besides, Tony figured, better to be lied to and make some money than lied to and have it stolen from you. Tony knew there must be more to it but he was content not to know just yet. His only concern was whether he was being scammed. The last thing he wanted to do was get stuck with a $4000 tarp and no way to get it back to KC.

Nevertheless, Tony decided to oblige. Abe had never cheated him yet. It seemed simple enough. One call, show up and party at the concert, get a check and go home. What Tony didn't know was that Abe was pocketing $2 grand himself, and the company was showing $20,000 in expense, netting a pad of $12,500 as far as the groups were concerned.

Of course, the groups would be padding their own sound and lights bill to do the same thing to the promoter. In the end they probably all ended up even. And that was the way it was done in the concert business. Imagine a circle of people with everyone having their hands in the back pants pockets of the person in front of them, and that just about describes the concert business.

Tony decided to take a new date to the concert and the party at the hotel afterward. She was a hanger-on, in this case a nurse but she could have been from any walk of life, a barmaid, a bank teller, etc. They were all the same, it seemed like to Tony. He had dated hundreds of girls, particularly since he had entered the glamorous world of show biz. Tony showed up, traded checks with Abe and the Arrowhead crew, tried to stay out of the way backstage and enjoyed the concert with his date.

While standing backstage Tony made the mistake of telling one of the usual backstage groupies that she looked pregnant, and she really wasn't. For this Tony earned a smack in the face. Tony was *sure* she was pregnant, and he thought he was being nice (he found out later she actually was). Tony kept his mouth shut the rest of the show. With his luck he'd probably be telling someone that the co-headliner, Steve Miller, wasn't as good without Boz Skaggs in the band, just as Steve walked by. Or mention to someone that the *Eagles* weren't laid back, they were boring, and it would be their road manager. No, Tony decided to keep his mouth shut and observe.

At the party after the show the first thing Tony noticed were the huge bags of cocaine spread out on the tables. It was more than he had ever seen in his life. Jewels was there, too, naturally. The *Eagles* weren't, but Jewels was. Where there was coke, there was Jewels. Tony wandered around talking to folks for a half hour or so and lost track of his date. Finally he decided to go looking for her. He found her with Jewels in the bathroom. Both of them were down in the corner behind the toilet scooping up grains of cocaine off the floor.

Jewels came out of the bath and angrily told Tony to bring a different date the next time. Apparently she was so stoned that every time Jewels offered her the spoon she breathed out instead of in. And that's why they were on the floor scooping it up. Tony was grossed out.

He took his date by the arm and left the party, just in time to avoid a bust. The bad news was his date got sick in the car on the ride home. The good news was she got sick on the outside of Tony's car. Tony found an all night self-serve car wash and ran it through twice. "Why did people do drugs?" he wondered, as the din from the spray and the brushes tried to drown out his thoughts. It didn't seem like any fun to him at all. And Tony mentally crossed one more potential wife off his list.

Tony had managed to make the reserved seating idea stick for all Family Jewels Productions despite the failure of the idea with the Loggins concert. After a year the concert crowds were starting to expect it, at least when Family Jewels did a show. More groups complained but Tony stuck to his guns. He was absolutely convinced that it was keeping people from being hurt. Unfortunately, Abe's company didn't follow suit, citing the overwhelming preference the rock crowd had for general admission seating. That is until December of that year.

The Who had a storied reputation in Cincinnati. They were the last rock group, along with *The James Gang* (which featured a young guitarist and future *Eagle* named Joe Walsh), to ever play Cincinnati's exquisite Music Hall. It was the summer of 1970 and the crowd trashed the place. Jewels was there with *The James Gang*. Tony, who hadn't met Jewels yet, was just a member of the audience and a non-participant in the havoc. It was the loudest concert Tony had ever experienced. *The James Gang* had been so loud it hurt his ears. Then *The Who* came on and turned it up even more! The crowd had practically ripped the hall to shreds. There had been no rock concerts there ever since. The kids weren't alright. They had ruined it.

In December, 1979, *The Who* came back to Cincinnati to perform at the much larger Coliseum on Cincinnati's Riverfront. Tickets were all "festival seating," which meant general admission, you're on your own. The group took a late sound check, delaying the opening of the doors. Normally this was no big deal. But that night it turned deadly as thousands of fans jockeyed for position to make their run for the best seats.

Abe would be blamed because he was the promoter on duty for his company that night. Tony would commiserate with him. Abe had no authority to change the type of seating. He was just a hired hand. Still, he would be the scapegoat. It was always the promoter's fault. The incident would drive him out of the business. Eleven people died, crushed and asphyxiated to death by the crowd pushing against the doors that opened late. No one in the industry could figure out why Southwestern Ohio in the mild-mannered Midwest was one of the most dangerous places in the world to go to a concert. It was like letting animals out of their cages. Every major city in the country soon outlawed general admission seating at all concerts after *The Who* tragedy.

For some reason Tony understood all this and had acted early on. No one was ever killed or even seriously hurt at any Family Jewels Production as long as Tony worked there. It was small consolation to Tony that he had been right. He would gladly have been wrong to bring those 11 kids back.

Jewels was a fool, however. It never occurred to him that Tony's foresight had saved Family Jewels untold trouble, not to mention saved lives. Tony was "*not-cool*." But wisdom was its own reward in this case. Tony thanked the Lord for protecting him from the calamity of *The Who*. Tony was more and more aware of how God had looked out for him in many events of his life, some when Tony used his head but mostly when he had not.

Anthony Joseph Mirakul breathed a sigh of relief. He had dodged another bullet. And he thought about all the petty scams of the industry. They struck him as unseemly and incredibly shallow when kids were out of control and dying. It was the first time the thought of leaving the industry for good crossed his mind. But he wasn't quite ready to take that step yet.

Chapter 15 - *The Stage Pass*

Most people in the entertainment business would like to become famous or do something important to make their mark on the world. Tony was no different, although his desire for this had waned over the years as he grew older and wiser. So it was almost a joke that Tony's claim to legendary status, which has been ignored to date by the *Rock 'n' Roll Hall of Fame*, would turn out to be the invention of the modern day stage pass. To do this he actually needed the help of Family Jewels Productions' Stage Manager, Rob Gullett, and their printer, Tim Totto. It was a group effort.

For years every promoter in the world had been plagued by the inability to control access to backstage, dressing rooms, catering areas, etc. The problem wasn't so much that they couldn't be secured by walls, doors, fences, etc. It was that credentialing who got in and who didn't was so hard to control. The biggest problem involved was the fact that nothing printed on paper would stick to people's clothing. Other ideas they had tried were too cumbersome to administer or too expensive, like hospital bracelets as id's for outdoor shows. The result of all this was that people who should have access were denied it and/or people who shouldn't have access were able to get it.

Tony had complained for years to Tim Totto about the problem of stage passes falling off of clothing, etc., etc. Then one day an excited Tim invited Tony down to the printing plant. There he showed Tony a flexible, almost cloth-like, material that he thought he would be able to print on and had tremendous adhesion to clothing. At the very same time Tony had an idea for something more than just printing the words "Stage Pass" on paper. This turned out to be serendipitous for the whole industry. Tim got the material and Tony came back in with an idea and artwork.

It was 1978 and *Little Feat* had released an album called "Waiting for Columbus." It was a superb live album with a cover that depicted the things that were indigenous to North America that were "waiting for Columbus" when he landed in 1492. Most people know it as the "Tomato in a Hammock album" because a smiling tomato lounging in a hammock dominates the artwork. Jewels had booked the tour through several states, including Columbus Day in Columbus, Ohio at Vets Memorial Auditorium.

Tony decided to go to the library where he found a picture of Columbus landing in the "new world." There just happened to be 6 members of the landing party in the picture, the same number as in the group. So Tony had Tim superimpose the pictures of the group members on the heads in the picture, with lead singer/guitarist Lowell George as Christopher Columbus, of course. Then they titled the Stage Pass - "Little Feat at Vets Memorial, October 15, 1492," and printed it on the new material that stuck to clothing. They were able to do different color material and different color printing so different access areas could be color controlled, making it easy for security to tell who belonged where.

When the group saw it they flipped out. The stage pass was an instant classic. The band ran around yelling "Where's Vano?" trying to find their tour manager because they wanted him to see it. No one had ever seen anything like it before, especially not Vano their manager.

The following week Rob Gullett (or *Popeye,* as Jewels had nicknamed him, because he looked as grizzled as the cartoon character and he actually loved spinach) suggested to Tim that they do a die cut of a Teddy Bear in brown for a Teddy Pendergrass date at the Agora. Tim was able to get it cut to look like a fat panda. Instant classic again. From then on every show became a chance to top the last one for creative stage passes. Jewels came up with the idea of having a generic one for every show that could be sold as a souvenir patch. It would mean additional profit that wouldn't have to be shared with the groups. Jewels saw everything as another possibility for a scam.

It wasn't long before groups were calling Tim Totto before their tours even went out on the road to send him artwork to do passes for every date on the tour. One day Tim dropped in to show Tony an order he had just received. It was for what looked like a stage pass in full color for something called "*MTV.*" Tim said they had just ordered a million copies! Tony scratched his head and wondered with such lousy sound why anyone would want to watch *Music Television.*

Next the *Rolling Stones* called and wanted Totto to print hologram tickets that couldn't be counterfeited for an upcoming tour. Within two years Totto went from fooling around with a few stage passes for Family Jewels to printing nothing but entertainment related products. They even had to sell their small printing plant and build a massive new one to handle all the business, all because of Tim, Tony and "Popeye."

Tony didn't see a dime from being the catalyst for all this. Neither did "Popeye." But Jewels would periodically rag Tim demanding "royalties due my clients Gullett & Mirakul" and "which needed to be paid to me on their behalf." This always drew howls of laughter from Tony and Rob because they knew they would never see a penny of it if Tim was stupid enough to give Jewels anything for their contribution. The hilarity of this running joke was payment enough as far as they were concerned. They were happy for Tim Totto's success. And they loved kidding Jewels about being their agent but never coming up with any cash. Not to be outdone, Jewels would tell Rob, "I'll keep the long green and pay you in spinach, *Popeye*!"

Chapter 16 - *Blind Date*

Tony had just finished the *Running on Empty* tour, or as he had come to call it after being on the road for so long, *Running on Fumes*. Some of the other promoters were calling it the *Summer Blizzard of '78* because cocaine had become the epidemic drug of choice in the entertainment world. It was beginning to be oppressive to Tony. He had been hoping to make a career as a concert promoter but he was beginning to see that if he wasn't prepared to be a drug supplier to the groups and their managers and agents he wasn't going to be able to book any shows if he ever went out on his own. The wheels were slowly turning in his head that there was no future in this business.

Tony ran into Donna Davenport at the deli near the office at lunch time one day shortly after his return. "Long time, no see," he said, distantly. Tony had resented Donna ever since the abortion incident with Doug Dineen and Charlie Fehr. He thought she was the most vapid person on the planet for murdering her unborn child rather than give up her modeling career. "What are you up to?" he said icily. "Just hanging out," she said, happily. Tony looked down and saw a baby carriage with another happy face looking up and gurgling at him. "What's this ?" he asked. "That...is Tyler," she replied. "Whose is it?" said Tony. "Mine,'" said Donna, proudly. "Donna..." said Tony, perplexed, "I thought you had a career. What happened to that?" "I know, I know," she said defensively. "One day someone that I had been seeing in New York just seemed more important to me," she trailed off, as she bent down to stick the pacifier back into Tyler's mouth.

"How about you, Tony?" she asked. "Still single?" "Yeah," he answered. "That's too bad," she said. Now Tony was embarrassed. "I just haven't found the right person yet," he told her. A thought occurred to Donna. "You know, Tony. I know this great girl I could fix you up with." "Oh, that's O.K.," Tony replied. The last thing he wanted was someone like Donna Davenport directing his love life. Still, it was amazing the change in Donna. She practically glowed from within. She had never appeared so happy when she was working the runways in New York.

"Are you living in the Big Apple?" Tony asked. "Heavens, no! New York is great. But I wanted to be close to home so we moved back here. Danny commutes to his office south of Cleveland and only occasionally has to fly to New York," Donna explained. "Man, what a change," Tony thought. "So who's Danny?" he asked. "Danny is Daniel O'Rourke. And I am Mrs. Daniel O'Rourke," she said, holding out her left hand that sported her engagement and wedding rings. "Congratulations!" exclaimed Tony, now realizing what a massive change had happened in Donna's life.

Their sandwiches were ready so they both sat down and continued conversing. It was the longest conversation Tony had ever had with Donna in his life, probably owing to the fact that Donna had scarcely noticed he existed prior to that. Now she seemed overjoyed to be sharing her life with him as if they were long lost buddies. "Where'd you get married?" he asked her. "St. Patrick's Cathedral. Cardinal O'Connor married us," she told him. Tony choked. He tried not to show it but he gagged and had to grab some of his drink. "Sorry, wrong pipe," he said, when he could breathe again. "Now we belong to St. Hilary, out in Fairlawn," she told him. "Do you know it?" "My high school sweetheart was from that parish," Tony replied, stunned.

By the end of the meal Tony had agreed to let Donna fix him up on a blind date. Why not, everything else was so surreal that it seemed perfectly logical to him. Nevertheless, he sat there dazed after Donna left, wondering what he had gotten himself into this time.

Tony had been avoiding women lately. He was so tired of the casual sex and the loneliness that he had all but withdrawn from the dating game. Now he was going out on a blind date with who knows what. He hung his head in his hands. He'd been on blind dates before, and they were usually from hell. How low had he sunk now?

But Tony was someone who never backed out of things. If he said he would do something he did. So a few days later he found himself at the appointed hour and place for his blind date, but with who? The address he had been given turned out to be Donna's parents' house. As he was shown in by Donna he was promptly introduced to Amana, Donna's sister! "Nice to meet you, Amanda," he said as politely as he could, given his shock. "It's Amana!" everyone shouted. "Clerical error," Amana said shyly. "The clerk in Vital Statistics was either hard of hearing or stupid," said Donna. "Or just got a new refrigerator," said Amana, trying to be humorous for the umpteenth time in the awkward situation of having to explain her name. "Great," thought Tony. "My blind date is named after an appliance." Tony almost said, "I hope you're not frigid," but luckily he bit his lip and just grinned stupidly at all around.

And so off they went on their blind date. Broadsided date was more like it. There were only two restaurants in town that anyone went to on a serious date, Tangier and the Diamond

Grille. Tangier was all atmosphere, kind of a Moroccan kitsch, while the Diamond Grille was a funky old bar with the best steaks in town. Long on food with a hole-in-the-wall atmosphere, great hash browns, enormous juicy steaks, the Grille was nothing fancy, just meat and potatoes.

They opted for the Diamond. It turned out to be the perfect choice. Both Tony and Amana were "meat and potatoes" people and not just in food. They seemed to see eye to eye on everything they talked about. Maybe it was that both of them had Italian mothers but they appeared to not only be compatible, they were *sympatico*. Driving around afterwards Tony asked her what she would like to do. "Where do you live," she asked. "I'll show you," he replied.

Amana was appalled. Typical bachelor house. What little there was in the way of furniture had been done in Late Model American Haphazard style. The air was stale, although she could tell he didn't smoke. The kitchen smelled like a Bob Evans' Restaurant - bacon and fried potatoes. "Would you like something?" he asked. "A glass of wine?" she suggested. He opened the refrigerator and it was empty, except for one beer. "How about a beer?" he said. "That's fine." He handed her the beer. "Aren't you having one?" she asked. "I don't drink," he replied, matter-of-factly.

Walking into the living room she looked around and noticed there was no furniture. He strode past her into the bedroom. She followed. He sat down on the bed. She thought it was a ploy until she realized that he was looking at her innocently. He honestly had no furniture. This was the only place he sat, probably because all he did was work and then come home to sleep there. She went and sat next to him. The sheets smelled like stale sex. She took a big swig of beer and then kissed him. "Give him what he wants," she thought. "Get the sex out of the way and find out what he's really like."

"Use protection," she told him. "No!" he answered sternly. "What if I get pregnant?" she shot back. "Then I'll marry you," he said gently. She looked into his eyes, and she saw that he really meant it. He really meant it.

Chapter 17 - *Coming Up for Air*

Starting that night and for every waking minute the next six days and nights, Tony and Amana were buried in passion. They ordered in. They called in sick to work. Tony didn't have any shows so he told Jewels he wouldn't be in for a few days. This worried Jewels. Tony never acted like this. When Donna frantically called Tony's house looking for Amana because she hadn't heard from her sister (not to mention about their date), Tony handed the phone to Amana who told her everything was fine and she'd call Donna next week. Bye. *Next week!* What were they doing, Donna wondered ?

Finally, the following Sunday morning rolled around, and Tony popped out of bed and told Amana, "Come on, we're going to church." "What?" Amana said sleepily. "We're going to Mass." "O.K.," she said dragging herself to the shower.

"Mass?" she thought. "What is this?" as the water warmed and woke her up. She smiled. "He's taking me to Mass. I like this guy."... "No, I think I may love him," she mused. Then she quickly forced it out of her head. "Don't jinx yourself. You'll ruin it for sure."

Sure enough. Off to Mass they went. Amana liked the way Tony put his arm through hers and marched her proudly next to him. She hadn't been in church for a while. She felt estranged yet comfortable all at the same time. It was almost like having a lingering dispute with your parents but coming home anyway. It generated mixed feelings all around. Nevertheless, it was home. And she longed for it. She wanted it to be "all better." Being on Tony's arm was starting to make her feel a little bit of that "all better."

Maybe this was what Donna had been experiencing. For the life of her she couldn't figure that one out. Donna had been the most mercenary of them all, and now she had become virtually transformed. Amana couldn't figure out if it was her marriage, her baby or the church. Common sense told her it was the baby, or Danny, but she had seen other people get married and have babies and although it made them happier, Donna had something extra way beyond that. Amana didn't want to think about it being the church. Still she felt like she was sitting in the palm of a giant warm hand as she sat there with her arm in Tony's. She didn't realize that she was glowing. But Tony saw it. And he loved her for it.

Neither one of them thought about Confession. Of course, they should have gone to Confession before the Eucharist given how long they had been away, and the mortal sins they had committed. Maybe if the priest had been in the box before Mass they would have gone. Maybe not. But they didn't have the choice. Too many priests had stopped hearing Confessions, except by appointment. If there were millions of Catholics in Tony and Amana's position why was Reconciliation so rarely offered?

Well, this morning Tony and Amana's joy overrode their sinfulness, of which they were not fully cognizant. They had been steeped in sin for so long that they couldn't even tell right from wrong anymore. The idea that sleeping together was wrong enough to separate them from God wasn't even close to registering on their desensitized Richter scales of sinfulness. But there would be plenty of time for them to make it up in what they would have to suffer for the Lord. Today they were like children come home to Poppa.

When the time came for Communion, they went up with everyone else, almost in a daze. Their lives were a mess. But they felt drawn to Jesus, and maybe Jesus wanted them back enough to forgive them for this transgression. Just being there was a form of confession to the Lord, however imperfect. He would heal them in due time, and they would be more faithful in following the church's teachings as their sinfulness turned to Godliness and their ignorance to understanding. Today there was much joy in heaven over the return of Tony and Amana. They just didn't know it. They didn't have a clue about anything that was coming. Like their kids.

It was all very sloppy. But it was a start.

After Mass, Donna caught sight of them and rushed up to invite them over for breakfast. "And by the way, where have you been?" she asked her sister. "Never you mind," Amana giggled. Donna smiled, proud of herself for putting the two of them together. They met Danny, a big hulk of an Irishman, with a big grin and a bone-crushing handshake, which he tried to limit but didn't seem to be able to do judging from the way Tony's hand felt after Danny let go. "Sure, come on over for brunch," Danny boomed. Hail fellow well met.

Whether this was what comedian Dennis Miller referred to when talking about marriage as "just a date that worked out," or something far more sublime, Tony did not know. But he was anxious to find out. For the first time the thought occurred to him that one marries into a *family*, not just to another lone person, as if in a vacuum. Danny grabbed his arm and dragged him off while the sisters chattered away. Tony thought, "This isn't so bad. Not bad at all."

Within a week Tony was thinking about just how he was going to reconcile to the Church, now that he had committed himself by going back to Mass with Amana. Lots of questions presented themselves, all of which appeared to have answers that demanded Tony make some changes. He decided to go to Confession that Saturday. He knew there would be Confessions in the afternoon so he called the parish, listened to the recording and headed down to talk.

When he got there the Church was empty. He checked his watch. He was a few minutes early. Sitting down he began to talk to God. Tony really felt in the presence of God in a Catholic Church. Any time he'd ever been in a church that wasn't Catholic it just felt empty to him, like an empty concert hall felt, waiting for the semi's to arrive with the sound and lights. Maybe it was the overwhelming feeling of being "in church" because this particular church was cathedral like in styling, flying buttresses and all. But then he had felt just as awestruck in other Catholic Churches that were not "church-like" at all.

Once outside of San Antonio he had stumbled into a metal Quonset hut church, complete with missalettes all in Spanish, and had been just as awestruck there, especially when he thought of all the people who must come there who spoke Spanish rather than English. Somehow seeing the exact same Catholic things in a foreign language made him feel more connected to being "universal" as a Catholic. Tony didn't know that that's what the word "Catholic" meant - universal - the one, holy, *universal* and apostolic church of Jesus Christ (He also thought "apostolic" was a name used for churches started in storefronts by Pentecostal holy rollers, not a word for "directly descended from the apostles by the laying on of hands." But that's another story).

As Tony sat there in the dim light his eyes fixed on the large candle in the reddish maroon glass next to the tabernacle. *That* was what was different, Tony thought, *the tabernacle*. In fact, Tony suddenly realized that it was God in the tabernacle that made him feel different in a Catholic church. God was really there. That's why the candle was always lit. Bingo ! That's why Tony felt different here than anywhere else. He was in the presence of God. And he could talk to Him because he was right there. In person. Now Appearing, GOD. Tony couldn't help but think in show business terms. "And now, direct from Jerusalem, the Holy City, here's ...GOD!" the announcer in his head boomed.

"Where was the priest?" Tony suddenly thought. He stood up and began meandering his way up behind the altar looking for the door to the rectory attached. He knocked on the door. No answer. He pounded and waited. Finally, he heard footsteps.

When the door opened there stood the priest, Father Studer. "Yes?" he said. "Father, aren't there Confessions?" Tony asked. "Oh, yes," Father replied. "I'll be right there."

Tony sat face to face in the confessional rather than behind the screen. Father Studer offered, "No one seems to come anymore so I just work in my office until someone comes to get me." Tony was a little perturbed but he said nothing. I guess I've got no room to talk about not being around, he thought, as he launched into "Bless me, Father, for I have sinned. It's been...It's been...several years since my last confession." "How many, my son?" "I think 6 or 7," Tony told him. "All right, then. What brings you today?"

Just days after Tony's cathartic return to Confession he had to hit the road. It was his annual tour with legendary comedian Red Skelton. Something he loved and hated at the same time. First off, it was always fun to spend time with Red, and have a part in the show. But it was also nerve-wracking because it was Tony's job to "watch him" as Jewels called it. Red could only physically handle a show every four days, so the rest of the time it was Tony's job to be at Red's beck and call. If Red wanted to go to the mall, it was Tony's job to take him and stay with him at all times, like a body guard. The only time Tony got a break was when Red was asleep, and then Tony needed to get some himself.

Whenever there were people around, Red was always "on." He was always smiling, always ready to sign an autograph. He was a real trooper. And Red knew his audience. People thought of Red as their favorite uncle. They would say, "Red Skel-e-ton, what are you doing here?" and Red would say, "Looking for you!" to their everlasting delight. Then he would tell them he was in town to do a concert to which they would inevitably say, "I didn't know you were doing a show here!" and Red would turn to Tony and say, "Some promoter you are."

Keeping up with Red in public was exhausting work for Tony. The man seemed to get energy from all the people who recognized him. It was like a drug to Red. Tony had to protect him from his fans' adulation while at the same time responding to his every whim. For example, Red loved barbecued ribs. So Tony had to be sure that he knew every rib joint in town, wherever they played.

Luckily, Tony had been introduced by his friend, radio station impresario, Sid LeSurgic, to the splendors of barbecued ribs on one of his trips to Cincinnati. Ribs were simply not a part of his family's diet when he was growing up. But a few trips to Big Ike's Barbecue and Carry-out had made Tony a rib-lover, thanks to LeSurgic. Despite Ike's location in the ghetto, it was not unusual to see white men in suits, fingers dripping sauce, sitting around with the locals, throwing out comments about the fortunes of the Reds or the Bengals. Rib-lovers crossed all ethnic lines.

To be on the road with Red, Tony had to know if ribs were sweet northern or vinegared southern style. He also had to know where the back-down-the-alley joints that only the black folks knew were hidden as well as the uptown eateries catering to whites. Tony had learned enough about ribs that he could have written a book called "Rib Joints East of the Mississippi."

Just for the fun of harassing Red, Tony, who was fairly thin, would eat Red under the table on these rib jaunts they took. Once at the Rendezvous in Memphis, Red didn't care for the ribs, so Tony ate his own slab, then Red's slab, and then half of Red's bandleader's slab - 2 1/2 slabs in one sitting. Red just sat there speechless, his mouth open. Finally he asked Tony in his Freddie the Freeloader voice, "Do you have a hollow leg?" while Red peered under the table as if Tony's leg would burst. Tony laughed and told Red "I'm a growing boy!"

And it wasn't just ribs that Tony would devour. In Baton Rouge, they were out one night with a group of 15 or so people at a crawfish restaurant. After a huge meal the waitress asked if anyone wanted dessert. Just for fun, Tony ordered an extra dozen oysters on the half shell. Red looked at Tony and said, "How do you do that?" Then Jewels, who rarely got to any of Red's tour dates but happened to be along on this one, said, "Hey, that sounds good. I'll have a dozen, too." And Red lost it. "You, too? Now I know where he gets it!" Red exclaimed.

Not to be outdone, when the bill came, Red asked the waitress, "Does it matter who pays the bill?" "No, sir," she said. "Well, then would you take it to that elderly man in the corner over there sitting with his wife?" "Yes, sir," she said, dutifully. She took it over and set it on the man's table. We all watched in glee as the old man picked it up and immediately got flustered (the bill was well over $400). Then he heard our laughter and looked over at our table only to see Red sheepishly waving his fingers at them. Realizing who it was and that they had been had, the man and his wife burst out laughing, came over to our table and had a grand old time having their picture taken with Red. They probably went home and told all their friends and neighbors that Red Skelton had pulled a practical joke on them. It was a memory for a lifetime. And that's the way folks came away from a meeting with Red. He was always everything people hoped he would be.

In private, though, he ached and complained and grumbled to Tony. When it was just the two of them, Red would complain about everything. For example, he would complain about TV. "I've left it in my will to destroy all my TV shows when I die," he would tell Tony. "Those network bloodsuckers aren't ever going to get them." Or he would complain about whatever the latest scandal in the news was and remark about how the world was going "you-know-where in a you-know-what." Tony never heard Red use a four-letter word, onstage or off.

Red would offer how Ronald Reagan was a flaming liberal. "But then I know the guy," Red would say. And then Red would be off on some other story. "You know in *True Grit* where John Wayne has that eye patch on? Well, they're shooting this scene where that young girl has to bring Duke a cup of coffee. And she's real nervous and keeps spilling it, take after take. Finally she gets it to the table without spilling it but she forgets and leaves the spoon in it. So Duke says, 'Upph. Better take this outta there,' removing the spoon. And then he points to his eyepatch and says, 'Wouldn't want this to happen again!'" And Red would laugh. No one enjoyed Red's jokes and stories more than Red did himself. Which made it impossible for anyone else in the room not to laugh, too.

Red would hit Tony with requests out of the blue. For example, he might say, "Let's go out to Graceland tomorrow." Or whatever he was thinking about, depending on the city they were in. In fact, that's exactly what Red and Tony did the first time the two of them were together in Memphis. Tony had a road-weary Pontiac Phoenix that he drove everywhere, and on this trip he took Red out to see Graceland. Red had just bought a new-fangled instant camera with an autofocus electronic eye the day before on one of their jaunts to the mall. Red loved little electronic gadgets, midget TV's, that sort of thing.

Now Red didn't want anyone to know that he liked Elvis, so he had Tony park in the parking lot of the strip shopping center across the street from the entrance to Graceland, and he began to take pictures with his new camera. Except, nothing was coming out. All the pictures were just blurs. Finally Red figured out that the electronic eye was seeing the closed car window, not Graceland across the street.

So Red rolled down the window and began hanging outside trying to take a picture. As he did this he almost fell out of the window so Tony had to grab his legs and hold him inside the car while he hung out the window snapping instant pictures of Elvis' house. Tony just hung on, thinking, "No one would believe this if I told them. Here I am sitting in a strip center in Memphis with Red Skelton hanging out of my car taking pictures of Graceland. And I'm getting paid, too."

Even better than this, Tony always had a part in Red's show. Red, who still did 2 1/2 hours straight for every show, employed some of the worst cornball humor ever... and it always worked. For example, he would yell offstage at Tony as if he was a stagehand, asking for something. Then after Tony threw it to him he would ask Tony, "Hey, what's your name anyway?" Tony would yell back, "Mark!" Red would say, "What?" Tony would yell, "Mark!" a little louder. Red would yell back, "What? I still can't hear you." And Tony would yell "Mark, Mark, Mark!" at the top of his lungs. Then Red would turn to the audience, and say, "Well, Whaddya know. A harelip dog."

This is where Tony learned what "timing" meant. Tony could hear these same old jokes every show for weeks on end every year and still laugh at the punch lines. Red was that good. And the audiences would roar. "Timing" was everything.

Take the time they were doing a show at Louisiana State University. It was in the fieldhouse on a portable stage on the basketball court. This was a big switch for Tony. He was used to playing elegant theatres with Red where there was plenty of room offstage. But at LSU the stagehands had hung a tall, narrow curtain on the side of the stage just wide enough to hide him and all the props for the show.

Besides the "Mark, Mark" lines, Tony had another part in the show where Red would ask for a folding chair. Tony was supposed to be the "stagehand" who brought Red the things he needed during the show. But in the case of the chair request, Tony was to throw it out on stage rather than bring it to Red because this always got a laugh. Well, at LSU,

Tony's depth perception was off because there was no theatre with nice layers of curtains for him to judge the distance to throw the chair.

When the time came for Tony to throw the chair, he threw it too hard. Tony immediately realized his mistake, and so did Red, whose face was suddenly overcome with terror as he saw the chair hurtling at him center stage. Red leaped into the air and the chair flew underneath him, then off the other end of the stage, and bounced out into the audience, to the surprise and glee of everyone in attendance. It was sheer bedlam, they were laughing so hard. The crowd thought something had gone wrong but what they didn't realize is that something actually had gone wrong.

Red turned around and followed the chair, over to the side of the stage, then down some steps and out into the audience, while the spectators continued to roar. He grabbed the chair and started back up the steps, banging it on every one, milking the laugh for all he could get.

When he got back to the mike, he waited for the laughter to die down just enough that everyone could hear him, and then he said, "Strong union, here." And the crowd burst into laughter, and applause.

Tony for his part was cringing offstage, trying to make himself as small as possible. "I'm gonna get fired. I'm gonna get fired," he thought. But no, after the show, Red didn't even mention the incident. It's as if it had never happened. Tony breathed a sigh of relief. "I'm not gonna get fired. Or yelled at," he thought.

A week later they were setting up for the show at a theatre in Memphis. Red was backstage in front of a make-up mirror with all the blazing lights, putting on his show face. Tony was kneeling right next to him in front of the prop trunk, checking everything to make sure it was in working order, hats, balls, glasses, cellophane, Guzzler's Gin bottle, etc., when Red leaned over next to him and whispered in Tony's ear, "Now, you're not gonna throw the chair at me tonight, are you?"

Into this world, Tony brought Amana. He had her fly in to join them on tour a few weeks into it. Amana got a kick out of mall shopping with Red. Red used to carry a wad of cash in his pocket at all times. Tony would eyeball it every time Red would pull it out, trying to figure out how much was there. Tony figured it was equal to at least six months of his salary. And Red enjoyed spending it.

Walking by a dress shop in the mall he turned to Amana and pointing to a particular dress in the window said, "I'll buy that for you if you wear it to dinner." "Sure," said Amana. Then that night at dinner, he turned to Amana and said, "You like that dress?" Amana replied, "Of course I do!" Red then offered, "I'll buy you all the dresses you want if you'll dump this guy over here," pointing at Tony. Tony almost choked on his iced tea while the rest of the table guffawed.

Red liked Amana. He didn't even make any jokes about her name. At least not until Tony told Red he was going to marry her. "Who?" Red asked him. "You know, Amana," Tony took the bait. "You're marrying a refrigerator?" Red replied. Then, pretending to be Gertrude and Heathcliff, his famous seagull characters, he said, "Well, I'm not surprised, the way you eat."

Chapter 19 - *True Cross?*

Soon after Amana had joined up with Tony on the Skelton tour, she tried to talk with Red about his clown paintings. Red's works were fetching $25,000 apiece at the time yet very few people knew what a consummate painter he was. Perhaps it was because his subject matter was always clowns. It may have been the same reason that comedians never win best actor Oscars; it wasn't considered "serious" work. Red would say, "If comedy was easier than drama there'd be more laughter in the world than tragedy. But then what do I know ? I'm just a ham. Well, no, I'm not. Not really. Hams can be cured."

Unfortunately, every time Amana tried to have a serious discussion with Red about painting he would cut up and never be serious about it. Frustrated, Amana told Tony, "I don't think he likes women." Tony told her, "It's not that he doesn't like women. I just don't think he knows how to relate well to them one on one. All the sorrow in his life has been related to women, and believe me, he's had some sorrow. How would you like it if your wife ran off and left you? It might be more common today but in the 50's people didn't normally do that. It broke his heart. If ever there was a classic clown hiding from the world, it's Red. He doesn't really have any close friends at all. In fact, he's downright reclusive." Amana pondered this, and then said, "Well, I sure wish I could get close to him like you are. It would be so neat to talk with him about painting." Tony said, "I'm not close to him. He has to put up with me, that's all."

Maybe. Maybe not. One night a few days later Tony was walking back with Red to their rooms at the Hilton. Amana had already gone back to the room so it was just Tony and Red. When they got to Red's door, Red asked him, "You're Catholic aren't you?" "Yeah, sure," Tony replied, not sure why Red was asking him. "Come on in for a second. I wanta show you something," Red told him. Tony had never been in Red's room when they were on the road. He looked around at all the road clutter - suitcases, books, sketches, partial paintings, dop kit spilling out on the dresser, etc. It was definitely "lived in." Red went digging in all this mess until he found what looked like a small box made of tin or some other metal like that.

Red came back to where Tony was standing and opened the box. The lid was hinged and Red held the box awkwardly in one hand with the lid open trying to steady the shifting weight so it wouldn't tumble over. He was having trouble holding it steady. Red announced, "This is a box of saints' relics I carry with me on the road."

Tony's face screwed up into a "What the...?" look. "I bring them along on the road for good luck, and praying," Red said. In all the years Tony had known Red he never thought of him as being a religious man, even though he knew Red believed in God because of his "Pledge of Allegiance" bit that he used to do on TV and sometimes did in his shows. Now here was Red telling him that he venerated saints' relics. Tony realized that Red probably had the money to acquire saints' relics if he really wanted to, but Tony was still skeptical. He kept waiting for the joke.

Red fumbled around in the box until he brought out a little jagged piece of wood about half the length of Tony's index finger. Handing it to Tony sheepishly, Red said "This is a piece of the true cross that the Pope gave me." Tony took it in his hand and examined it. "Where's the joke?" he kept thinking to himself. As he rolled it around between his fingers he was incredibly skeptical. His first thought was that there was no true cross that anyone had ever found, let alone the Pope giving out pieces of it as souvenirs to American comedians. Tony was sure Red was playing a practical joke on Tony. But Red wasn't laughing.

"What if this really is a piece of the true cross?" Tony wondered. "Nah, it can't be," he thought. "When were you with the Pope?" Tony asked. "A long time ago," Red said. "I had a private audience with Paul. He liked my show." "It must have been more than 'liked'!" Tony suggested. "Well, anyway, after we visited for an hour or so...," Red continued. (*"An hour or so?"* Tony thought, *"The President is lucky to get 15 minutes!"*) "...he said, 'Wait a minute. I want to give you something.' And he went out of the room for a few minutes and when he came back in he handed me this little piece of wood and told me it was a piece of the true cross." Red finished and stood there sheepishly.

Tony didn't know what to believe. He knew one thing. Pope Paul was not known as a practical jokester, so either Red made it up or it was true. And from the look on Red's face Tony knew Red was serious. There wasn't a laugh line visible. Not the least bit of levity in his whole demeanor. If this was a practical joke Red was the best there ever was at keeping a straight face. Very gingerly, Tony handed the piece back to Red. Red took it with utmost reverence and carefully laid it back in the box and closed it up. Tony still wasn't sure if he had just been part of an awesome experience or was just being fooled by Red. But he was beginning to lean toward the awesome experience angle.

Red hid the box and Tony excused himself and headed back to his room. "Amana, do you know anything about such a thing as the 'true cross'?" Tony asked her. "Sure," Amana answered.

"St. Helen was Emperor Constantine's mother and she was supposed to have found the true cross in the Holy Land on a pilgrimage." "How do we know it was the true cross she found?" Tony asked skeptically. "Well, it's a matter of faith. But there've been a lot of miracles attributed to it over the centuries. I guess you either believe it or you don't. Why are you asking me this?" she said. "Because Red just showed me a piece of it that he says the Pope gave him." Tony said, half-dazed. "You're kidding!" Amana exclaimed. "No, I'm not. He's got a whole box of saints' relics in his room." And they both looked at each other in amazement.

Now Tony was a pretty common-sense down-to-earth kind of guy. And Amana was the same kind of person, too. Neither one of them was prone to going off the deep end when it came to fads or cults or the latest kooky ideas ballyhooed out of California or New York. So it was natural for both of them to take anything like this with a grain of salt. But Amana could see that Tony believed that Red really had something. And so she believed because of Tony.

Tony believed because Red had acted totally out of character. Tony was unnerved by the idea of chopping up the cross into fragments. It struck him as almost sacrilegious. But Tony was learning to accept things he didn't necessarily understand when it came to faith. Maybe he would understand better as time went on. He figured that if it was the true cross it only deepened his faith. And if it wasn't, he still believed anyway. Still, if it was the true cross, he understood why people would feel the way they do about this holiest of all relics and why they would want a piece of it. Better to share it he guessed. He felt very odd about the whole incident - unworthy, skeptical and awestruck all at one time - which was the oddest group of emotions he had ever experienced.

Amana, on the other hand, wanted to go see it herself right away. "He's probably already asleep," Tony told her. "Besides, I never bother him until morning once he goes to his room at night." The next morning he told her that he thought they should keep this to themselves, and that they shouldn't mention it because it had been such a rarity for Red to let his guard down. Tony just didn't feel like ruining it by pushing the subject. "He said it was the true cross, so true cross it was," Tony told her.

Amana reluctantly agreed. And never a word was spoken again about the box of relics or the "true cross" between Tony and Red, or by Amana.

Chapter 20 - *The Wedding*

Tony came across all sorts of people in the course of his work. Many of them were famous. Lots of them were unknown. Some of them were infamous. And some were what Tony liked to call "Semi-luminaries." They weren't well known enough to qualify as famous but they still had name recognition on a local or regional basis. One of these "semi-luminaries" was Mick Randall, owner and GM of a Cincinnati rock station, WPAB, or "Pablum," as everyone called it. Another was Sid LeSurgic, the inherited owner of Randall's archrival station WBOG, also known as "the Frog in the Bog" owing to their symbol, a frog, and that the station was located on the Mill Creek in the heart of the industrial valley, where it occasionally flooded out. During the aftermath of the '74 tornadoes, LeSurgic had made himself a local legend by continuing to broadcast from a rowboat tied up on the roof of the station building, in plain sight of I-75, while the Mill Creek raged below.

LeSurgic was a daredevil. The kind of guy who would climb to the top of a railroad bridge and sit on top while a train went under, all for a joint. Or to impress a girl. Randall, on the other hand, was a recluse. Mick's real name was Bernard Kingman. Bernie's grandparents had emigrated from Belarus to New York City to escape the persecution of their wallets. It was Bernie who carried the family "business" gene. Tony used to hatch great promotions on his station by showing up at 3 AM at the studio and sneaking in on him while he was buried in his Arbitrons. Sometimes he would find him asleep with his nose between the pages. LeSurgic, on the other hand, would try anything Tony proposed, as long as Tony insinuated that Sid couldn't do it.

Tony liked them both, although LeSurgic thought he was cooler and smarter than he really was, and Randall needed to get a life. So Tony decided to ask them both to be in his wedding. He had already asked Jewels to be his best man so neither one of them would be jealous on that account. But it was a problem that the two men hated each other.

So he decided not to tell either one. He simply sent them at different times for their tux fittings, and promised them all they had to do was show up for the actual wedding. Neither one suspected the other was involved, especially since the wedding was in Akron. Tony chuckled every time he thought about it. What a wedding picture he and Amana were going to have.

Amana had more relatives than Tony could shake a stick at, he found out when they tried to put together a guest list. By the time they added up all the family who had to be invited, and all the business acquaintances they had to invite, they had almost a thousand. This didn't even count the celebrities Tony was inviting, like Bob Seger and Jackson Browne, knowing none of them would show up. Amana even sent the Pope an invitation, just as a goof.

"Let's move the wedding to the Tuesday night before Thanksgiving at 11 PM in Conneaut so nobody shows up," Tony suggested. Amana punched him in the arm. "Let's just hope not everybody comes then," Tony told her. They decided to invite all of them rather than try to cut back. "We're never doing this again," Amana reminded him. This wedding was shaping up to be about $8 to $10 grand. This was about half Tony's annual salary.

One sticking point was whether to invite Doug Dineen. Amana had met Tony after the *Styx* "small city tour" and was unaware that Doug Dineen, whom she had never met, was actually Simon Wasp. Dineen had not played any concerts or been at any events when Amana was there.

Tony was unaware that Doug Dineen's real name was Simon Wasp because he had only known him as Dineen. Furthermore, Amana had been too embarrassed to tell Tony the whole story of her and Wasp in the stadium, and even if she had she wouldn't have told Tony his name nor have realized he had changed it. She had simply explained her past as having been an "embarrassing and unfortunate incident" with a guy she loved in college. Tony had not pried.

What was even worse was that Amana did not know about the abortion incident with her sister Donna and Dineen. Donna met Dineen through Jewels and so knew nothing of his name change or the incident with Amana in college, either.

Without knowing any of this background, Tony still had to make a decision about Dineen coming to their wedding. Chalk it up to Dineen's incredible obnoxiousness that Tony even had to make a decision about his coming to the wedding. Tony didn't really want him there. It was also a complication that his sister-in-law-to-be had an affair with Dineen and might feel awkward with her husband there. Donna was in the wedding as Maid of Honor, and Tony couldn't see anything good coming from it. He wondered how much her husband, Danny O'Rourke (or "Sarge" as Tony called him) knew about Donna's past. Tony reminded Amana of Donna's relationship with Dineen. "What?" she said. "You mean you didn't know?" Tony asked her. "No," she told him, surprised. "What about the abortion?" Tony asked. "What abortion?" Amana asked, now frightened. "Oh, boy," Tony thought. "What do I tell her?"

Tony hesitated. Amana gave no indication she was about to let it go. "What abortion?" she repeated, emphatically. So Tony told her the story about Tony being gopher for Jewels, and Dineen handling things with Donna, and Charlie Fehr being the father and paying for it, and Donna not wanting to ruin her modeling career. Amana couldn't believe it. "That doesn't sound like my sister," she said. "She might have gotten pregnant but killing for her career can't be true." "Well, people do strange things when they're under stress," Tony said, not doubting the story. Amana continued to insist it was not like her sister. Tony stopped fighting and changed the subject.

"Well, what do we do with him?" he asked. They finally agreed that they wouldn't invite Dineen, but if he showed up they would act like they had and try to downplay the fact that he was there. They would also let Donna know about their "plan" just in case.

Then they went on to the next matter at hand, how to handle the open bar. Since Tony was used to putting on shows he was perfectly calm about all the planning and the details. Amana on the other hand was a basket case. She double and triple checked everything, driving all the suppliers nuts. On the morning of the wedding she even called Tony and asked him if he was still coming. "Of course, I am," he said, "2 o'clock, right?" "One o'clock!" Amana screamed at him. Tony burst out laughing. "Gotcha!" "Oooh, Anthony Joseph Mirakul, you're going to get yours." "I certainly hope so," Tony teased her back.

Everything came off without a hitch. It was the perfect wedding. End of story.

Well, not exactly. Amana started her period at 11 AM, two hours before the wedding Mass. Besides being miserable, her enormous gown required that every time she went to the restroom, the entire female side of the entourage had to go along. "I don't even want to know," Tony told whoever was listening.

Then Tony's uncle, who had offered to film the wedding, was delayed and had sent the camera with another uncle who had never shot film before. He proceeded to shoot a panoramic view of the neighborhood from the church and then set the camera down on the floor while it was still running and used up the entire reel. Tony and Amana's wedding would forever be remembered as that "nice Fall day with the feet." It would provide endless fun at future family gatherings as the family played "Guess Whose Shoes?..."

Not to be outdone, Amana's brother, the amateur photographer, offered to take the pictures as his wedding present. He forgot to put film in the camera and didn't realize it until he got to the reception and decided to change ASA's. "Didn't you think after 50 or 60 shots that there was something wrong with the roll?!?" Amana screamed at him.

On top of all this, Jewels didn't show up. He was nowhere to be found. So no best man. Tony did the next best thing. He asked Rob Gullett, their stage manager, to fill in. "I probably should have asked you first anyway," Tony told him. "What was I thinking to ask Jewels?"

But the best was yet to come. Doug Dineen mercifully skipped the Wedding Mass but in doing so was able to get to the reception and open the bar a half hour before anyone else got there. He was three sheets to the wind by the time the band cranked up their first number. Dineen proceeded to begin heckling the band, which was Tony's cousin's Horn Band. "Tower of Power you're not!" Dineen was howling.

Tony sent some friends to try to get Dineen to eat something hoping it would slow the liquor down. He also told the bartender to stop serving him. But it was too late.

Amana had been circulating through the crowd of guests and caught up with Tony just about this time. "What is Simon Wasp doing here?" she asked Tony with an angry, shocked look, as if Tony had pulled some horrible joke on her. "Who's Simon Wasp?" Tony asked her, dumbfounded. "That guy!" Amana yelled, pointing at Dineen. "That's not Simon Wasp. That's Doug Dineen, and he's making a mess of our reception!" Tony retorted.

Amana looked sickened. It dawned on her that Dineen was a performer and Wasp was, too. She put the two together and realized he must have changed his name for the stage. She was ahead of Tony on this one. Tony was still scratching his head thinking Amana had a case of mistaken identity. Amana whispered in Tony's ear, "He's the guy from college." "What guy from college?" Tony asked her, naively. "The guy I told you about." Now it was Tony's turn to be sickened. He realized that Doug Dineen had taken his wife's virginity, and under bad circumstances to boot. "Nice wedding present," he thought.

While this exchange was going on Dineen moved away from the bar and sat down next to an attractive young lady who just happened to be with Mick Randall. Mick, who was in the wedding party, couldn't be with her so Dineen had moved in taking the seat next to her. Dineen, who seemed to know her, quickly began to hit on her.

On seeing this Mick approached Dineen and quietly asked him to come along with him for a chat. Dineen followed him but darted into the bathroom as they passed it, having had way too much beer at that point. Randall followed him in. What happened next is unclear, particularly in light of the apocryphal way the story has grown over the years. What is known for sure is that there were several loud crashes from within the bathroom, and when the damage was recorded, there were three metal stalls and two toilets completely destroyed. The quiet, seemingly mild-mannered Mr. Randall had learned to fight as a youngster when picked on in his New York neighborhood. And there were no rules on the streets of New York.

It wasn't long before Mick emerged from the bathroom, and when the next brave soul entered he quickly came out running. The room looked like a tornado had ripped it apart and water was gushing everywhere. Dineen was lying bruised and bloody in a puddle moaning "My face. My face." Several guests carried him out to the kitchen and administered first aid. Dineen wasn't so seriously injured that he needed a hospital but his pride was definitely destroyed.

Meanwhile, Mick Randall had calmly checked on his date and then made his way back to the dais with the rest of the wedding party. "Nice shot," Sid LeSurgic told him. The heretofore enemies began talking. LeSurgic suddenly realized that Randall was all right in his book.

The next thing anyone knew they were hatching a plot to team up their respective radio stations as partners. Randall knew a retired Chiquita executive who could fund their expansion. Out of all this, "Big Signal Communications" was born. LeSurgic would sell out for a fortune a few years later. Randall would hold on and eventually become the most successful and feared man in radio with over 2000 stations.

The incident with Dineen would become legendary in the industry. When Randall began to amass his radio empire every time he took over another station the soon-to-be-replaced staff would refer to it as being "taken to the toilet." Pretty soon the entire industry began calling a takeover "being taken to the toilet" or "TT'd." The only thing odd about the whole incident is that no one seems to be able to remember who Randall's date was, not even Mick himself, although there have been several women who claim that it was them.

While everyone else seemed to be congratulatory to Randall for this bit of male bravado, Tony was furious. Amana was crying because of the shambles, and because of the mess Dineen had made of her special day. Tony alternately tried to comfort her while he laid in to Randall for fighting at their wedding. "That's not the way we do things!" Tony told him. "I don't care if he did deserve it. We turn the other cheek." Randall looked at Tony like he was nuts. "No one's going to try to pick up my date, or harass her," Mick told him. "Yeah, but you didn't have to destroy his face or the bathroom!" Tony insisted. "There are gentler ways to handle it." "Not where I come from," Randall retorted. Randall had no idea how lousy Tony felt finding out about Amana and Dineen, and having to maintain his peaceful values in spite of it. It was tempting to just give in and approve of the violence. But that wasn't Tony.

Tony went off to the kitchen and told Dineen it would be best if he went outside. Dineen was quite agreeable at this point. Rob Gullett and Jack Jackson, the owner of the limousine company Family Jewels used for its shows, began walking him to his car. He was mumbling various things in a drunken stupor. "I got her cherry," he slurred to his carriers. "You gather cherries?" Jackson asked, trying to figure out what Dineen was saying. "Stick him in his car. He can gather cherries in his sleep," Gullett said gruffly.

They dumped him in his back seat. He lay there for a few minutes with a big smile on his face and then fell asleep. His carriers breathed a sigh of relief. "He'll be fine after he sleeps it off," Jackson said. And that was the end of that.

The wedding continued but on a much more somber note. There was music and dancing but it wasn't quite as lively as before. Dineen and Randall had managed to cast a pall over the whole affair. And Tony began to have a different opinion of Mick Randall. Ironically, Randall and LeSurgic were starting to find out how much they shared in common, just as Tony began to find out how much he *didn't* share with the two of them.

Amana and Donna were conferring just outside the Ladies Room. Their discussion appeared intense and Tony avoided it. He assumed they were catching up with each other about sharing Dineen. Right then he didn't want to hear any more. He already knew too much. He felt like the whole world was laughing at him even though he knew it wasn't. It was just Dineen. Dineen had a way of soiling everything around him.

After the reception mercifully ended Tony whisked Amana off to honeymoon in Gatlinburg and tried to have a good time. It didn't help any that it was "that time of the month." They couldn't even consummate their marriage. Then they had a fight about Dineen and it wasn't until Amana told him the truth about her tryst in the stadium that they put everything out on the table, Amana's trauma and resentment of men, and Tony's resentment of Donna and Dineen and how he felt small because it was Dineen who had been Amana's first "lover." But out of this truth they realized that despite all this bizarreness they loved each other more than anything else. They made up emotionally but not physically.

They were longing for each other as they came down the mountain not having had any contact with the outside world all weekend. That's when they found the streets abuzz with word that hostages had been taken in Iran. Tony even had a grade school friend who was one of them. And the world was a little more dark and foreboding than it had been just a few days before. It was an auspicious start for any marriage.

After Tony met and married Amana his relationship with Jewels slowly began to grow more strained. Jewels' shenanigans just began to wear too thin on Tony. Things had been deteriorating ever since his "200% scam" on the *Styx* small city tour.

One day Tony and Jewels were going at it even worse than usual. It was actually an argument about being treated with respect but it somehow got blamed on Harry Chapin. "We served his whole group fresh King Crab Legs from the Shuckin' Shack and they didn't touch a bite of it! I thought this guy was big against world hunger? Then on the way to the airport he has me stop at Frisch's, and he buys a whole chocolate cake, which he proceeds to scarf down in my backseat, which is where he's sitting because he's afraid I'll kill him with my driving!" Tony was fuming. "Sounds perfectly reasonable about sitting in the back seat, with your driving," said Jewels. "I'm serious!" Tony cried. "So am I!" Jewels laughed. "We are nothing but caterers!" Tony threw back. "Highly paid caterers," Jewels offered. "Speak for yourself!" Tony answered.

One thing led to another and finally Tony made some comment about not doing something or other because it "wasn't Catholic." Jewels said, "I'm Catholic." And Tony's jaw dropped open. "In all the years I've known you, you never did or said anything in the world that would lead me to believe that you were Catholic," Tony told him. "Yup. Cleveland St. Joe's. I'm a Viking from way back." Jewels pumped out his chest. Tony was dumbfounded. Finally he asked, "Did you play football there without a helmet?"

Jewels proceeded to tell Tony all about growing up Catholic in Cleveland. "When was the last time you went to church?" Tony asked. "Christmas." "What year?" Tony snapped back. "Last year," Tony replied. "No, you didn't. You were in Cancun with Shari." Shari Bergstrom was Jewels' long-time and long-suffering girlfriend. "Shari's Catholic, too," Jewels said, "We went to Mass in Cancun, although I must say it wasn't quite the same feeling of Christmas." Tony was flabbergasted.

Tony thought about it for a few minutes and then he asked Jewels why he hadn't married Shari. "Because I like lots of strange," Jewels replied. "I don't want to be tied down." So Tony hit him. "She does the same you know. Don't you care about her being with other men while you're out catting around?" "Actually," Jewels replied, "She's been seeing the same guy a lot. In fact, she told me she was spending about equal time between us." "You mean she's getting serious about him?" Tony asked. "I'm afraid that might actually be what's happening," Jewels said despondently. "You should marry her," Tony suggested. "Best thing you could ever do."

"To tell you the truth, I've actually been thinking about that myself," Jewels offered. Tony stopped for a second, then jumped up and tackled Jewels. "Hey!" Jewels cried. "Who are you and what did you do with Jewels?" Tony yelled. "Get off!" Jewels yelled at him. "You're an alien and you've sucked out Jewels' brain, haven't you!" Tony cackled while Jewels tried to push him away.

From then on, every chance Tony got, he made the suggestion or comment that Jewels should get married to Shari. If Jewels said something about Tony's wife, Tony would suggest that he could have one, too. If they saw a kid or a teenager, Tony would suggest that Jewels could have kids, if only he was married. "I could have some I don't know about," Jewels would say, bragging. "How sad," Tony would say, digging in the knife. "He doesn't even know where his kids are."

Whether it was the constant digs from Tony or the fact that Shari had managed to make him jealous we may never know. Perhaps it was both. But one Monday when Tony asked Jewels what he did over the weekend, Jewels ran off a litany of things and then said offhandedly, "Oh, yeah. And I asked Shari to marry me. Gave her a rock."

A grin came across Tony's face. "Congratulations !" He put up his fist in front of his face to imitate a microphone and said, "Koossshh! Is this thing on? I'd like to make a toast to Mr. and Mrs. Johhhhhnnnnnn Joooooooooolllzzzz. Annnnnt. Kooossshhh." Tony blew into his imaginary mike. Jewels couldn't resist a big grin. "But wait," Tony said. "I forgot to ask what she said!" "She said 'Yes', you idiot. What'd you think she would say?" Jewels feigned anger. They both laughed and smiled. Tony shook Jewels hand. "Now this is for good," Tony said, not letting go of Jewels hand. "No divorces." Jewels tried to pull away but Tony held him fast. Jewels gave in. "Of course, no divorces. Why even get married if you're gonna get divorced?" Jewels opined.

Why, indeed. Tony had been and still was a sinner. But there was one thing that he was absolutely fanatical about. No divorce. Anthony Joseph Mirakul hated divorce almost as much as God did. But he didn't hate divorced people, just divorce itself.

Tony saw divorce as the complete destruction of civilization. There was nothing more important to mankind moving forward in goodness (and Godliness) than the family. It was the DNA of civilization, and people who destroyed it were mutating the genes of life itself.

Tony placed the devil right at the heart of anything that damaged the family. Even abortion was just a symptom of the disease. Any culture that held marriage as a sacred bond and children as the desirable fruit of love would inevitably pass on values that made abortion abhorrent, and it would dry up and blow away on its own. That's why Tony thought people who spent all their energy trying to end abortion were wasting their time, like putting a Band-Aid on cancer. Tony thought all that energy should be put into defending the sanctity of marriage. Tony thought it was particularly inconsistent when people claimed to be pro-life but used *the pill*, which was actually a form of abortion. They were just as anti-child as the pro-abortion bunch. Neither side saw children as desirable. At least that's what Tony thought.

Divorce was also a major reason Tony had never considered being anything but Catholic. Only the Catholic Church had adamantly and consistently maintained the sanctity of the marriage vow since the time of Christ. For Tony this was a "no-brainer." Christ said divorce was not permitted, and no amount of psycho-babble could reverse it.

Tony didn't go out of his way to make a big issue of it. Most of the time he kept his mouth shut, owing to the fact that he had so many flaws in himself to fix that he didn't want to seem judgmental to others. After all, if he said something, anyone who knew him would surely be able to cite numerous shortcomings on his part. "Who are you to judge?" people had a tendency to say in western culture, usually to avoid acknowledging their own sinfulness. Everybody knew the part of the gospels about not judging people. They just used it to defend evil most of the time instead of the way it was intended, to prevent self-righteousness.

Despite his usual reticence, Tony spoke up to Jewels. "There are no happy divorced people," Tony told him. "But there are happy people who got through a bad time in their marriage and didn't divorce their spouse." Jewels usually thought Tony was a schmo when it came to knowing anything about life. But for some reason this time Tony sounded incredibly wise. And Jewels was touched. "Alright already, Confucius," Jewels said. "Back to work."

Chapter 22 - *Dark Days*

A couple of years after Amana and Tony wed, Tony was still traveling the road promoting various tours. One tour he did every year was *Sha Na Na* through the Southland in late winter, ending up North just about the time Spring broke. It was always a fun tour with the boys, and usually had a few interesting incidents along the way to relieve the tension from the grueling schedule. One year Tony had to duck out of the tour for one night to go to Chicago for a Ferrante & Teicher gig.

This wouldn't have been a big deal except they were in Mobile, and Tony had to pick up a Bosendorfer piano in Memphis and haul it on a trailer to Chicago in one day. It was a thousand miles one way. On Friday night he had to finish the show and settle accounts in Mobile and then hit the road so he could be in Chicago and set up the piano in time for a Sunday Matinee with F & T. Immediately after that show he had to haul the piano back to Memphis, drop it off, and drive back to meet Sha Nan Na in Birmingham in time for Tuesday night's concert. The guys in *Sha Na Na* kept shaking their heads at him. Even by rock 'n' roll standards that was insane. "Why don't you fly and rent a piano?" they would say. "Because it's got to be a Bosendorfer. Nothing else has enough keys!" Tony told them. Sometimes he would say, "It's O.K. I've got my Miraculous Medal." And show them the pendant he carried in his pocket. Tony didn't like to wear jewelry but he carried a few religious medals in his pockets. Sometimes he would give them to hitchhikers he picked up, along with a $5 or $10 bill.

Sure enough, when Tuesday afternoon rolled around, there was Tony back at the hotel in Birmingham. The guys in the band just shook their heads. "Good thing you got that medal," one of the guitarists said sarcastically. Actually, it was.

Tony was an odd combination of naiveté and guilelessness, coupled with worldly common sense. And it was never clear which of these attributes would appear. He could steal blithely in the concert business because that was the way he had been taught that it operates but then be incredibly naive about other things people might do around him. He always assumed the best about others. If someone's manager was rooming with another guy on the road, it never crossed Tony's mind that they might be gay. While the rest of the world assumed that they were, even if they weren't.

One afternoon in West Palm Beach on this latest tour with *Sha Na Na*, Tony walked into the hotel in mid-afternoon only to find John Bauman, otherwise known as "Bowser" in the group, heading through the hallway about to duck into his room. This would not be unusual, except for one thing. He was fully made up and greased down as if he was ready to go onstage, something that was 6 hours away. Tony knew he would never be made up this early. So he stopped him and asked, "Hey, what's with the getup?" John hemmed and hawed for a minute, and Tony couldn't figure out why. Finally, John explained to Tony that he had been out to the local children's hospital visiting the kids in the cancer ward.

It turned out that Bauman had been doing this for years in secret. At various times on the road he would duck out and visit the kids' hospitals and do his routine. "Why didn't you ever tell me?" Tony asked. "Because I've never told a promoter in my life, because they'd turn it into a promotional stunt," John told him. Tony nodded. "I know exactly what you mean," he said. "You have to promise not to tell anyone," Bauman pleaded. "Of course, not," Tony told him, then paused. "Hey, John, that's very Christlike!" Tony offered in praise. "I'm Jewish," John retorted, chuckling. "Well, so was he. So was he..." Tony trailed off, as he began walking away. "Bowser" shook his head and quickly disappeared into his room.

"Best Christian on the tour," Tony said to himself. And he marveled at the pervasive influence of Jesus and his law of love. "Maybe the kingdom really is now. In the Old Testament Jews were only expected to help other Jews. Now they help anyone and everyone, sometimes even their enemies!" Tony's opinion of John Bauman had just gone up about a thousand per cent. And he never told a soul what John was up to. "If only everybody acted like that," Tony mused.

Tony went back to his room. It wasn't long before he heard a knock on the door. "Who wants what now?" he thought, thinking it must be someone with the group or the show bugging him. He opened the door. There stood one of his old girlfriends, Tina. Tina Bracken, a wandering child he had first met in San Francisco but who was actually from Indianapolis. She used to be small but voluptuous when they had been an item but now she looked thin and gaunt.

Tony had just spoken with her a few weeks before when she had called him back home. She was living in West Palm with who knows what guy, and she told him she really should go back to Indianapolis to see her doctor because she was sick. Tony had encouraged her to go to the doctor if she felt she was really that sick. She wouldn't tell him what it was, so he assumed it was cancer. He even offered to give her a ride back to Indianapolis from West Palm if she needed it since he was going to be there in a few weeks, never expecting to see or hear from her. He figured she would have long forgotten about it by the time he got to West Palm. But obviously Tony was wrong on that account.

"I came to take you up on that offer of a ride," she said, walking into the room carrying her suitcase. "Oh, boy," Tony thought. "What have I gotten myself into this time."

Now it wasn't the first time a woman had shown up at Tony's door with a suitcase. It was just the first time since he had gotten married. Rebounding quickly, Tony said, "Sure. But it's going to be a while. We've got a lot of dates before we get back north." "That's alright," Tina agreed. "I don't have any other way to get there." She looked horribly run down to Tony. Something was definitely wrong even as she tried to smile. But she still refused to give Tony any more details. Tony just accepted it and figured he would find out soon enough.

So Tina joined Tony at the show, hanging out while Tony worked. By the time they hit Dothan, Alabama a few days later the guys in the band were asking Tony, "I thought you were married?" "I am," Tony would tell them. "She's just a friend who's hitching a ride back to Indiana." Everybody with the group was sure Tony was shacking up. But nothing could be further from the truth. Tina was sound asleep by the time Tony would get in at night, and she would be up and showered long before Tony woke up the next morning.

Except for one morning. Tony awoke a little earlier than usual to go to the bathroom. When he walked in there was Tina just exiting the shower. This was not anything Tony hadn't seen before when he was single, except that now Tina looked like one of those people in a famine video from Africa. He could see all her ribs with her skin stretched taught over her bones. Tony was sickened, "My God, Tina, you need to eat something," he blurted out. "Eat something?" she replied, "Tony, I'm fat!" she said as she gazed into the mirror.

Tony was stunned. The jigsaw puzzle suddenly clicked in his head. Her father's physical and sexual abuse of her as a child. The abortion she had at age 13. The low end jobs she held. Never eating much when they went out to dinner. Her mother's indifference to Tony sleeping with Tina at their house years ago. It all added up to one thing.

Anorexia.

This was one of those terrible moments when Tony's naiveté was shattered. He hated these events in his life. He could be very child-like in his acceptance of the world and those around him, until, wham, he was forced to see the dark side that destroyed innocence. He suddenly felt like a great weight had been placed on his shoulders, and he didn't have a clue what to do to fix it. He didn't even understand anorexia, let alone know what to do to help someone with it. He'd only heard about it, never seen it or known anyone with it. But he knew this was it for sure. It was glaringly obvious, even to Tony.

"God, what do I do?" he prayed and exclaimed at the same time. He stewed over it. They went on with the tour. That night was Montgomery, Alabama. Another crisis backstage took his mind off his problem for awhile. It seemed that poor Denny Greene, the only black guy in the group, was absolutely terrified and wouldn't come out of the dressing room. "Tony, there's cops everywhere backstage. You know what cops do to black folks in Montgomery. Why are they here?" Denny begged Tony. "I'll find out what's up," Tony reassured him.

So Tony found the hall manager who told him that the cops had just started showing up backstage using their badges to get in. "This is a government facility so they can pretty much come and go as they please," he told Tony. So Tony went backstage and cornered a handful of them and asked what was up. "*Sha Na Na*'s our favorite group," they told him. "We've been looking forward to this for months!" "So there's no trouble?" Tony asked. "Trouble? Heck, no. We're here to have fun!" Tony chuckled. "Freeloaders," he thought. "Oh, well. It's a hard job being a cop. Not many perks if you're honest." Tony decided that tonight they had the best security of any show he'd ever done, and went to find Denny.

"C'mon," he told him, "you're their favorite group." Denny, who was from New York City and had heard nothing but horror stories about touring in the South all his life was incredulous. "I'm not going out there." "Sure, you are," Tony looked at him. "Nothing's going to happen. You'll see." Tony took him by the arm and almost had to drag him out. Luckily, Denny had on his sequined jacket and was ready to go. As soon as he came out of the room a crush of cops swarmed around him. "I'm gonna die" was the look on Denny's face until he realized they were all shaking his hand and slapping him on the back. "We love you, man!" they were all saying.

Talk about the *New South*. A black Yankee was being mobbed by a hundred white sheriffs in Alabama, and they were asking him for his autograph. Tony was laughing so hard it made him forget all about Tina, at least for a while. That night, Denny sang with more energy than Tony had ever seen. Backstage after the show he was all grins. "These guys are great!" he buttonholed Tony. "Did I just say that?" And both of them howled with laughter.

Preoccupied with the tour and with getting Tina back to Indy, Tony never thought about Amana. He often didn't talk with her for days because it was so late when he got in from a show. He did call and tell her that Tina had shown up in West Palm. He also told her he was taking her back to the hospital in Indianapolis after their last date on the tour because she was sick. Amana was perturbed at this. Tony told her he would explain when he got back. And didn't think too much about it.

As the tour wound its way north, Tony got a night off when the group played Knoxville for another promoter. This was an unusual occurrence but the group's management owed someone a favor and Knoxville was payment. Tony had a welcome respite - an extra day in Chattanooga. He picked up some pottery at the Plum Nelly shop for Amana - a vase and a pair of coffee cups, and then, because he was in Tennessee where it was distilled, he picked up a fifth of Jack Daniel's whiskey for one member of the group who was known to have a penchant for the stuff.

When Tony caught up with the group in Johnson City a day later he proudly handed the fifth of blackjack to the group member he had purchased it for, as a gift. All of a sudden he was aware of snickers behind his back from other members of the group in the large dressing room they all shared. Not everyone was snickering. But they were all moving away from Tony and the bandmember with the Jack Daniel's. And several members started to act weirdly toward Tony. Tony couldn't figure it out. This went on all afternoon. Finally, Tony cornered Bowser and asked him what was up. John looked at him and said, "You mean you don't know?" Tony said, "Know what?" John replied, "Oh, my gosh. You really don't, do you?" "Know what?" Tony repeated. "Last night (blank) drank a fifth of Jack Daniel's and beat up two other guys in the band. We thought you were pulling an audacious prank on him, giving him another fifth. As if you were saying, 'do it again.'" Tony felt horrible. "I just got him a fifth because he said he liked it. I didn't know anything about last night. I wasn't there."

Bauman laughed heartily. "I'll take care of it," he said. And he proceeded to let the rest of the band know what had happened. This made all of them laugh, save two bruised and one very hung over player who had decided to pitch the fifth of Jack into the trash. The rest of the night, whenever someone from the band made eye contact with Tony they would chuckle at him, and Tony would blush, feeling stupid. "Last time I buy anybody booze for a gig. Let'em buy their own," he muttered to himself. This wasn't the first time Tony's apparently good motives backfired. And it was not to be the last.

Eventually, Tony managed to get Tina back to Indiana and to her grandmother's house. He took her to Grandma Bracken's house and made her promise to get Tina to the doctor or hospital as soon as possible. Then Tony headed back to Akron for a few weeks downtime from the road.

He was overjoyed to see Amana but she didn't seem to have the same enthusiasm for his being home as he had for seeing her. "Why did you take an old girlfriend on tour with you?" she demanded. "I told you. She was sick and I promised her a ride back from Florida to the hospital. She didn't have any other way and she has no money." "Just what's she got that she had to come all the way back to Indiana ? Don't they have any doctors in Florida anymore?" Amana spit back. She could really cut with her tongue when she wanted to.

"Her doctor is a specialist for anorexia and has something to do with one of the big pharmaceutical firms in Indy. Tina has anorexia and apparently he is the best in the country." Amana was incredulous. "How do you know its anorexia?" she asked. "She's down to 81 pounds. When I dated her she was at least 120," Tony responded. "Which is the point," Amana noted. "You dated her." "Amana, you know that was over before we even met. And I've been friends with her since. I couldn't leave her there once I saw her." Amana was slightly mollified with this. But she still said, "Well, why did it have to be you to help her?" "Because it appears I may be the only friend she has left. And I was certainly the only one headed from Florida to Indiana. Her mom is dead and her grandma is almost invalid. What was I supposed to do?" Tony flustered.

Amana let it go. But there was still a distance Tony felt from her, especially when he tried to cuddle up to her at night. She didn't seem as playful at other times as she used to be, either. It was a bad time between them. "For better or for worse," Tony kept telling himself.

This went on for about six months. Then Tony had to make a short run to visit some ticket outlets in several cities, including Indianapolis. He decided to call Tina's grandma to see how Tina was doing. "Oh, hello, Tony," she answered the phone. "How's Tina?" he immediately asked her. "Oh, Tony. I'm so sorry. I didn't really know how to get in touch with you. Tina's dead," she told him. "Oh, God, Mrs. Bracken!" Tony exclaimed. "How did it happen?"

"She just kept getting worse and worse. They couldn't get her to eat at all. Finally they put her on feeding tubes but one day, she just stopped breathing. It was about two months ago," Mrs. Bracken told him. "They're all gone. My son. Tina's mom. Tina. Lucky for me I'm old. Won't be much longer for me, either." Tony didn't know what to say. He mumbled some platitudes that Grandma thanked him for. About the only thing he said that he would remember was "I'll pray for her." And so he began including Tina in his daily prayers for all his deceased friends and family, and the Poor Souls in Purgatory. Tina wasn't Catholic. In fact, Tony didn't have a clue where Tina stood with respect to belief in Jesus. It was all he could do, to hope and to pray that Tina was somehow in a state of grace when she died. "I hope someone prays for me when I'm gone," Tony thought.

Upon returning to Akron, Tony told Amana what had happened. "Tina died," he started out. "When?" gasped Amana. "Two months ago... I should have done more..." Amana began to cry. Then she began to bawl. She was sobbing uncontrollably, and it scared Tony. "Amana, you didn't even know her," he said, trying to calm her down. She stopped, then burst into even worse tears. "It's not that," she sobbed. "I slept with Doug Dineen while you were on tour with her." Tony had another one of those innocence-shattering moments he hated. Life could really smack you in the head. Or the heart.

He looked at Amana and then reached for her. Despite all the shock and hurt he was feeling he could feel one thing stronger. His love for Amana. And the overriding thing he was feeling was that he had to comfort her. He wrapped his arms around her like a giant cocoon, and he began cooing to her that everything was going to be all right.

"He...had...co...caine...and I was...so...mad...at you," she sobbed. "I'm...so...sorry, Tony... Please...don't...leave me." Now Tony started crying. "I will never leave you. I will never leave you," he started saying over and over again, soothingly. "You're my own flesh and blood. I could never leave you. You're my wife. I love you. I don't care about that. I don't care if it happened a hundred times. We're married. I couldn't anymore leave you than I could leave myself." Tony and Amana held each other for dear life. "I love you," Amana said into his chest. "I love you, too," Tony whispered back into her hair. And they held each other for a long, long time. They were two very badly bruised and hurting lovers. They began to talk about the things that two married people who are very much in love but have sinned against each other talk about. Facing the pain was the only way to heal. Ignoring the situation would have meant the destruction of their marriage.

It made no sense, and it made perfect sense, that Amana would turn to Doug Dineen/Simon Wasp to strike back at Tony for what she thought was going on, and also to try to heal the wound he had inflicted on her in her youth. Unfortunately, Dineen would only reopen that wound and hurt Amana and Tony's marriage even worse than he did before they met.

Amana was distraught because she realized now in hindsight what a dumb idea it had been, even though at the time it seemed like the perfect idea to "fix" things by having an affair with Dineen. Now to find out Tony really wasn't cheating on her made her feel childish and foolish and as low as the gutter. "How could I do something like this to a good man like Tony?" she now asked herself. "What is wrong with me?"

Tony put aside his own pain to comfort her but he would not be able to drive it down deep enough that it would cease to exist. For the next few years it would keep rearing its ugly head until he dealt with it. He had suffered a great loss and could not pretend that nothing had happened. They would both need each other badly to get through this time. But they would emerge from this someday in spite of it all and would be even more in love by the grace of God. It was just going to be a very long and painful journey.

Tony and Amana began by taking some private time for each other, just driving and talking, reinforcing their feelings for each other. They agreed no subject was off-limits. Everything had to be discussible by either person, even if it hurt the other person. If they couldn't get to total honesty with each other they couldn't be married.

They talked about Amana's insecurities after Dineen had hurt her in college. They talked about Tony's insecurities, especially about how Dineen made him feel. Tony was worried that Amana had a weakness for drugs, and a mean streak, too. Tony admitted to Amana that he had a constant struggle with his own desire for money and his use of pornography, the latter of which made Amana feel inadequate as a lover for Tony.

When Tony felt resentful he tried reminding himself of how promiscuous he had been before marriage and how he still liked to look at other women. Every time he felt hurt at what Amana had done he tried to remind himself that even looking lustfully at another woman was adultery. Fear of the Lord seized him. "How am I going to live up to that?" he wondered.

One afternoon they were out for one of their long drives in the country. Tony's mind gelled on the thought that he wanted his "self" back. Amana didn't understand at first, thinking in her insecurity that he might mean he wanted to leave her. "No," Tony explained. "I want my sense of self back. Like when I was young." "You mean your innocence?" Amana asked him. "Kinda... I mean our personal lives are a mess when it comes to sex. Everything's out of order. You know, I not only regret all those women I slept with before I met you, I even regret sleeping with you right away. There wasn't anything to look forward to, to make it special...It's almost like I'd like to start over," Tony told her. "Even beyond this Dineen thing, don't you regret that you slept with me before we were married and so easily?" Tony asked her.

Amana thought for a minute. "I thought it would be the only way to find out if you were interested in me. A man treats you differently after he has sex with you." "I guess!" Tony exclaimed. "But the real question is whether someone loves you enough to make an act of the will to stay with you permanently. That's the only way that the sex has any meaning. It takes an act of the will," he repeated for emphasis.

"Well, I felt like I must have been doing something wrong and so I made up my mind that from then on I was going to get sex out of the way first. The thing is I found you before I went any further," she told him. "That makes me feel great," Tony said amusedly. "I just happened along at the right time." "I guess you did," she said and then hugged him tightly and buried her head in his chest. "We're all scum, you know," Tony said kidding her. "I know!" Amana laughed, letting go of some of the pressure. "I don't know what I would have done if God hadn't sent you to me right then. Instead of you proving my theory correct, now I wish I had only known you and never anyone else, especially not that...," she trailed off, too embarrassed to even say Dineen's name. "Well, I regret everything I did, too," Tony caught the thread. "I want my self back... so I can give it to you."

They talked some more and finally came up with three things to do. First off, they both went to see Fr. Studer and asked him to hear their Confessions, which he did. Unlike Tony's first Confession after he returned to church, this time he touched on everything that he now realized was wrong. He had been blind before when he first came back to church but now he realized he had sins he didn't even acknowledge back then.

Second, Tony and Amana asked Fr. Studer to renew their marriage vows. He was ready to do it right then but they asked him to do it at Mass in a month. He didn't really understand why but he agreed.

Finally, Tony and Amana agreed together not to make love or even touch each other for a whole month before they renewed their vows as a kind of combined preparation/penance. During that time they promised to talk with each other each night as if they were courting to prepare for their marriage. It sounded corny but it worked. By the time they renewed their wedding vows they were dying to get their hands on each other, and they had forced themselves to be better talkers because they couldn't touch each other for a whole month. "That was good," Tony told her, talking about their month of forced abstinence. "Let's never do it again!" And they laughed.

Tony vowed to turn all his attention and energy inward toward his relationship with his wife. First off, Tony quit his job. In fact, he quit the entire industry.

The day Tony did this he walked in to find Jewels schmoozing on the phone with Jerry Springer's campaign manager. It was just about to be announced that Springer, who was then the Mayor of Cincinnati, had dropped out of the Democratic race for the Ohio gubernatorial nomination in favor of Dick Celeste. In return Celeste was to pay off all of Springer's campaign debts. Jewels was on the phone jawboning for inclusion of a $50,000 bill in this settlement as payment for Doug Dineen, who had been scheduled to perform at Springer fund-raisers in Ohio's 5 largest cities. Tony had helped Jewels on one fund-raiser for Springer's mayoral race but had gotten turned off because of Springer's sex scandal.

Springer had taken "spin" into the future of politics years before its time. He had turned his stupidity at paying a Northern Kentucky hooker by check into a virtue by claiming it was an honesty issue. Jerry would never stiff a working woman for her wage. And he wouldn't stiff Ohio, either, he claimed. Jerry had been "pre-scandalized" as he put it, so rather than drop out of politics he had decided to run for even higher office. Jerry dreamed of turning Ohio into the "Saudi Arabia of coal" as Ohio's Governor. But being a smart politician he had sold out to Celeste when he saw the handwriting on the wall.

Now all his fund-raisers had been canceled. Jewels was bargaining to get $10K for each gig. Then he dropped down to $25K total for all five gigs, of which he intended to keep $15,000 and give Dineen only $10,000. Springer's campaign manager was adamantly holding out for nothing, so he could keep as much cash as possible for himself now that it appeared he was out of a job. Jewels finally settled for $500 for "phone and miscellaneous expenses." Jewels was happy with this. He didn't even have $50 in the whole affair. Dineen would never see a penny of it.

When Tony told Jewels he was leaving for good, Jewels didn't believe him at first. He told Tony to take a few weeks vacation thinking he would feel better after that. But when Tony started talking about religious matters and saving his marriage Jewels realized he was serious. He didn't want to lose Tony, and was actually hurt that he was leaving. At least as hurt as his shallow heart got.

Jewels regretted that he had never made Tony a partner, preferring to keep the control and glory to himself, not realizing that Tony didn't want it anyway. Now when he offered to make Tony his partner, Tony turned it down. "Thanks, but no, thanks," Tony told him. "You were the best I ever saw at this business," Jewels told him. And Tony thought he halfway meant it.

Keeping his promise on the homefront, Tony made a conscious effort to turn all his sexual attention inward toward his wife. He and Amana began to make more time for each other, and really talk, not just sit in front of the TV in the same room. It was hard work. But they both wanted their marriage to be loving, not just existing. And they both decided that if they waited for the "right time" to have kids they never would.

So they took a class and made a commitment to begin practicing Natural Family Planning. Tony had always been adamantly against the pill for health reasons but they had done other things to avoid pregnancy. Now they made two decisions. First, they wanted to have children as soon as possible. And two, they were not going to use any contraception even after they had as many kids as they hoped for, just in case God wanted to send more.

"We'll never be rich anyhow," Tony reasoned. "If I didn't make a fortune in the entertainment industry I sure won't make it in any other. So we might as well have lots of kids." It's a good thing he didn't realize how much different it would be raising many kids compared to what he learned about parenting as an "only child." He was almost going to kill himself trying to raise every kid as if they were the only one. Amana would be better at this since she came from a larger family and was not the oldest. In fact, she would find out that she was an incredible mother, and be very saintly by the time the grandkids came along.

But today, it was a struggle just for the two of them to be married unselfishly. There's only one way to stay off drugs, Amana finally figured out. Stay away from them and anyone remotely connected to them. Get all new friends and start a new life. "Maybe there'd be people at church I could meet?" she thought.

Tony burned all his girlie magazines and swore off any visits to dirty book stores when he was out of town. He also burned all 3 sets of sheets they had for their bed one day when he was feeling really angry with Amana in his grief over her infidelity. Then he ran out and bought 3 new sets before Amana got home. "They smelled," he told her. "So I bought new ones." Well, technically, they did smell, especially after being burned.

Tony forgave Amana. There was no question about that. But it would still take him years to grieve over what was lost, and to begin to rebuild their life together. The devil would attack him with insecurity and the various stages of grief during times of the month when he was away for work, or couldn't make love with Amana. It would be "on one week, off one week, on one week, off one week." There was "that time of month" and then there was the middle of the month, which Amana called "Unh-Uhh Time" and Tony called the "Blackout Period" when they didn't make love by choice, to plan their family naturally. "Kind of like re-entering the atmosphere in your space capsule," Tony would say, "It's really not very long but it seems like forever before you splashdown in the ocean."

Tony took a job as a regional fastener rep. He visited lumberyards and contractor supply houses pushing a line of masonry fasteners shot in with a construction type gun. It wasn't glamorous like the entertainment business, but it was steady. Besides, the entertainment business only seemed glamorous. Actually it was really corrupt inside. Tony still had to travel but not as much. And it actually paid better. Well enough, in fact, that Amana could stay home. Which is what she needed to do because Amana soon became pregnant with their first child.

The devil actually became more desperate as this healing and all this blessing occurred. For example, once in Memphis, Tony went to check in to his room at a Holiday Inn on the edge of town and, bleary-eyed after a long day's trip, he unknowingly stopped one door short of his room. When he stuck in his key, however, the door opened right up. The key they had given him was a copy made from a master key. He stumbled into the room only to find ladies' lingerie strewn everywhere, on the beds, hanging on the doors, on the mirror, in the shower, everywhere.

It was like wandering into a *Victoria's Secret* warehouse with no one around to see him. He scratched his head and picked up some lingerie off the bed. "Must be for one of those private show things they do," he pondered to himself. "But why are they in my room?" Then he walked back toward the door and looked at the number on it. Then he looked at his receipt. He was one digit off. "Uh-oh. I gotta get out of here!"

He picked up some lingerie and took off for his room next door. He opened his room and dashed inside. Then he stopped. "What the hell am I doing?" he thought. He took the lingerie and went back to the other room, reopened the door, threw it on the bed, and walked out. "I just hope I don't hear noises next door the whole time I'm here," he said to himself.

Bizarre as this incident may seem it wasn't the last. Several months later he was in Chattanooga at the Read House Hotel. He checked in to his room and there on the bed was someone else's open suitcase and ladies' lingerie strewn about the bed. Tony took one look at it and said, "Oh, C'mon!" He looked at his key and the door number and this time they matched. He slammed the door and went downstairs and demanded another room. He knew the devil was behind it all. Either that or Tennessee had picked a novel way to boost tourism. "*In Tennessee, you get lingerie with your room!* could be their new state slogan," he thought.

Back home Tony and Amana started going to Mass during the week whenever they could, and they began praying together at night, every night. Tony would even call if he was out of town overnight, and they would say their prayers together on the phone. So despite some setbacks, overall the devil was losing, and Tony and Amana were winning, with the grace of God.

Leading a boring anonymous existence didn't seem so unattractive to Tony anymore when he realized he was about to become a father. He was starting to savor little things in life, like sitting on the couch with Amana tossing out baby names. "I'm going to make sure of the spelling no matter what we pick," he told Amana. And she hit him with a pillow. "How about 'Roper' if it's a boy, and 'Whirlpool' if it's a girl?" he asked. And she hit him again.

Through all this the Church was their guide. Tony wasn't really conscious of why. To him it went without saying that the Catholic Church was the world's repository of truth. When Tony finally got to the point where he said, "O.K., God. I've tried it my way and it didn't work. Now we'll try it your way." There was only one way to try, the way that the Church taught.

Tony was like the Centurion. He saw authority in this order - God, Jesus, Holy Spirit, Catholic Church, *Bible & Catechism*, what to do. It was a clear line of authority that he could trust if he wanted to know the truth to live by. It didn't matter if the Church was full of sinful men, he knew God would keep it true. For Tony the Church was his rock. If he didn't know what to do he looked it up in the *Bible* or in the *Catechism*, and then he knew what to do.

It was pretty cool, actually. He didn't always understand or agree but he knew it was right. He had learned the hard way that the Church was always wiser than him. Every time he changed his behavior to follow the Church he would later come to understand why he had been wrong and the Church was right. This reinforced doing what the Church taught even when he disagreed. Following Church teaching had never let him down, whereas his own way always had. Duh! Tony may have been a slow learner but he wasn't stupid. He preferred success to having his own way. It began to seem downright silly to have tried to make it up himself when he had a perfectly good guidebook already in the teachings of the Catholic Church. He understood that the Church was just a conduit for the will of God. So it was really God he was obeying.

Tony didn't know he had passed over to the "other side" of wisdom where obedience to God's authority equaled happiness. He was growing in "fear of the Lord." To him it was as plain as the nose on his face. When Tony saw people self-destructing he would scratch his head and say, "How could they miss the obvious? If you don't want to destroy yourself just do what the Church teaches."

Chapter 24 - *A Charmed Existence*

Anthony J. Mirakul appeared to most people he came in contact with as "salt of the earth," a commoner, peasant, average Joe, etc. And in worldly terms this was most certainly so. He wasn't particularly poor, although he had known some hard times, nor was he by any means rich in terms of money or things. No one would write a biography of him or otherwise chronicle his life or his deeds for posterity. He was of little interest to the world at large except as a number, a consumer, a cog.

When Tony had lived in Hollywood he had hoped to change that but as he grew older and wiser in the ways of the Lord he had gradually come to see his anonymity as a blessing. No one bothered him for the things of this world, except maybe his kids asking for their allowance. In fact, Tony had come to realize that he led a "charmed existence," both in his nothingness to the world, and in his blessings from the Lord.

Tony had always managed to escape any serious disaster. There had been run-ins and near hits but never had anything really horrible happened to him. He had come close with that incident in Conkle's Hollow on a high school field trip when he got trapped on a ledge with no one around and no way down. He had almost slipped to his death. But somehow his guardian angel had extricated him from that one. Tony was sure God and his guardian angel watched over him. Sometimes he thought there must be more than one angel assigned to him.

Tony had a whole litany of stories about how he had "cheated death" by the grace of God. Some were incidents only he knew about. For example, Tony was working on his electric clothes dryer one day when no one else was home. He had the top off, hanging from the ceiling by a string, troubleshooting an electrical problem. He had to keep going back and forth to the breaker box turning the breaker off and on so he could alternately make adjustments and test the wires.

After doing this numerous times he forgot to switch the power off when he began to tinker further with the wires. Blam! His screwdriver crossed two metal tabs and flew out of his hand. He sickened as he realized he had forgotten to turn off the juice. He went to retrieve the screwdriver and found the shaft melted almost in two across the middle. It had only touched the two tabs for a split second. He picked it up and broke it in two with ease. Luckily, he had been holding on to the insulated handle. Otherwise, Tony realized he would be dead.

Tony was now living on the proverbial "borrowed time." He thanked God profusely for saving his life and vowed he would never touch 220 electric again without double-checking the breaker box. He also decided he didn't need to tell Amana about the incident. She would have a fit and worry every time he tried to fix something after that. Some things are better left unsaid.

But there was one incident that he couldn't hide. Tony's territory for his fastener sales job included a number of states, one of which was Indiana. In the late 1980's his company brought out a new product line that had some innovative ideas that made it unique. It was Tony's job to disseminate this information to his many customers. He decided to do this through a seminar format because he could do it more quickly, deliver complete information without having to repeat it multiple times, and also thank his customers for their previous business by treating them to lunch.

Tony scheduled a series of seminars - Memphis, Nashville, Louisville, Columbus, Indianapolis, Cincinnati, etc. Amana was pregnant with their 4th child but still 5 weeks away from term. On the morning Tony was scheduled to fly out of Hopkins for his Indianapolis seminar Amana woke up at 3 AM because her water broke. Tony rushed her to the hospital and then called Marv Gunnar, his largest account in Indianapolis, and asked him if he could call all the other seminar attendees and tell them the event was postponed.

Luckily, Marv was able to catch all but two out of town accounts before they headed for the Ramada at the airport. Then Marv, out of the goodness of his heart, drove across town and met these two, bought them breakfast and sent them on their way home before going back to his own office. In general, there were few complaints. Everyone was very understanding. Tony was well liked by his accounts and most everyone liked hearing about Tony's growing family. They always seemed to be full of life.

The hotel had to send home some of its employees scheduled to work due to the cancellation. This didn't go over as well but that sometimes happened in the hospitality industry. All told, there were 50 or 60 people who were inconvenienced by Amana's premature delivery.

Tony was tied up at the hospital until the mid-afternoon. All went well and their daughter Samantha Louise Mirakul was born. Both mother and daughter were doing fine when Tony went into the lounge and called Marv in Indianapolis to tell him it was a girl and see how canceling the seminar went.

Tony was hoping there were no hard feelings, having inconvenienced so many people.

When he reached Marv on the phone he asked him, gingerly, "Well, anybody mad?" He waited, figuring he would hear some complaints. "Heck, no. You're a hero," Marv told him. "What?" Tony asked, figuring Marv was pulling his leg. "A military jet lost its engines this morning and the pilot tried to ditch into a field. But when he ejected it changed the plane's trajectory and it crashed right into the front of the Ramada where our seminar was supposed to be. They think 9 or 10 people were killed. But if you hadn't canceled the seminar there'd be 50 or 60 of us dead!" Marv exclaimed. Tony couldn't believe it. He got more details and then thanked Marv for getting hold of everyone. "Don't thank me. Thank you!" Marv told him. "Thank God," Tony fired back. "Him for sure!" Marv agreed.

Tony was stunned. He went to tell Amana, and her face turned ashen. "You would have been killed," she said. "Yes, but thank God, I wasn't," Tony calmly told her. Amana kept shaking her head. "All those people killed." "All those people saved," he told her. Tony more than ever realized that we serve at the pleasure of God, as if worrying could add a minute to our lifespan. "I want to be in control," Tony thought. "And I'm not," he answered himself.

Amana brooded over this. Tony had to repeatedly reassure her that things would be alright. All Amana could think of was losing Tony. She was afraid he might never come home from one of his trips, and she would have to raise a family alone. Every time Tony went out of town she felt this way. Now the post-partum baby blues made it even worse. Tony kept telling her he had been "disaster-proofed," so she shouldn't worry. But it wasn't working.

A month later Amana's baby blues had subsided enough for Tony to reschedule his seminars. Amana was still distraught about him leaving but that was his job. Luckily, Amana's mother came over to stay which helped keep Amana from losing it.

When Tony walked into the seminar he had rescheduled in Indianapolis there was sincere and prolonged applause, as well as a few baby gifts. Tony gave out rolls of lifesavers to all present, telling everyone that his new daughter already had been nicknamed "Lifesaver." Tony then led the entire hard-boiled group of grizzly construction supply guys in a prayer of thanksgiving for being spared, and a prayer for those who died and their families.

The group decided to take up a collection for the victims' families, which Tony then took to one of the local banks where a fund had been set up. Some of Tony's customers who thought he was a little too religious for their tastes had decided that maybe that wasn't such a bad thing after all. Several of them actually went back to their respective churches after the crash.

This was one of the more spectacular incidents of Tony's life. But Tony knew there were many more - his plane landing tipped sideways in a rainstorm in Raleigh on a concert tour, deciding to stay in his room at the dorm at Kent State that fateful morning in 1970, finding a culvert to hide in on Tornado Day back in April, 1974, not going to see *The Who* again in Cincinnati, etc. Then there were the omissions he didn't know about. Tony figured there had to have been incidents when he wasn't in a particular place at the wrong time. In fact, whenever Tony encountered some obstacle that threw his schedule off, he had conditioned himself to believe that it must be to avoid some bad situation. This served to increase his level of patience, something he needed to do now that he had kids.

Unlike his younger days when he felt alone most of the time, Tony was getting more and more used to walking with the Lord, and never feeling alone even in the most desolate of places. "Jesus didn't go out into the desert to be alone. He went out there to be with his Father," Tony came to realize.

After Tony quit Family Jewels he forgot about the entertainment business. It no longer mattered in Tony and Amana's day to day life. But not so the wicked. Not so.

Doug Dineen had received an advance of $1,000,000 for his first record with Agravista Records. After management fees he had $850,000 left. Out of this his recording expenses had to be paid. The label assigned him a staff producer who proceeded to take over 4 years recording and re-recording Doug's first album. The end result was a production masterpiece. Unfortunately, it had cost a fortune to record. The record label charged its artists full list price for studio time, production, tape and every other imaginable thing it could. The total cost to make the record finally reached the $500,000 mark.

The average cost to make a record at the time was more like $100-200,000. Dineen had gone way over budget. The remaining $350,000 in advance on royalties he had received had gone up his nose in coke. Dineen was penniless.

He was also too green to understand that the $1,000,000 he had received was all the money he would ever see from his first record. If he ever made another dime it would be in advance payment for his second record, not royalties for his first. That was simply the way the music business worked. Creative accounting made sure that the advance was all anyone received in the way of royalties. When artists signed for large sums of money, or "renegotiated" their contracts, whatever they received was all they were going to get. Dineen was learning this the hard way.

He was forced to hit the road and perform in order to eat. He could have made the record for $200,000, kept over half a million, invested it and lived well off his investments, especially in small-town Ohio. But instead he had squandered it. Such was the fool that Dineen was.

Embittered he worked the various club circuits. He was on the road 45+ weeks a year, barely clearing a grand a week. This would hardly keep him in cocaine. But all this would change, he was sure, when his record came out. Even without any royalties, he could start playing one-set concerts instead of weekly gigs at clubs, and his price would surely go up to a comfortable level where he could make some serious money.

But the wicked and the worldly have a way of tripping each other up. Those who follow their own selfish way end up with no protector except the Evil One, who comes to no one's aid when their world collapses. The devil thinks nothing of crossing the paths of his own disciples so they bring each other to ruin. In fact, he delights in it.

After Randall and LeSurgic had formed Big Signal Communications at the Mirakul's wedding they were met with immediate success. They quickly began to acquire more stations. In their first year they had purchased 50 stations. Then under Ronald Reagan's push to deregulate America Congress took most of the wraps off ownership of multiple radio and TV stations. In their second year they added 200. The third brought in 350 more. By the end of their fourth year they were up to a thousand stations and had gained virtual control of the entire North American radio market, if not directly, then by fear and intimidation.

Nothing happened in radio that didn't have their tacit approval. The record labels suddenly found a gorilla sitting around their house, anywhere he liked. That gorilla was Mick Randall. Mick, more than LeSurgic, understood power and how to use it. Mick was quietly greasing the way for LeSurgic to leave the corporation, unbeknownst to Sid, who was thinking about it independently anyway.

Randall had not forgotten what Dineen did at Tony and Amana's wedding. And in his first real test of power, Randall had let it be known to all the radio promo guys for the major record labels that nothing by Doug Dineen would ever be played on a Big Signal station. Clay Davids at Agravista Records called to say, "How dare you..." to Randall, chewing him out royally. But when not a single Agravista song was played on any Big Signal station anywhere in the country for the next week, Davids was back on the phone claiming it was all a big misunderstanding and would Mick please forgive him. Randall made him crawl. And he made sure everyone in the business knew it. From that moment on no one in the entire music industry would ever challenge Mick Randall again.

Clay Davids delivered the bad news to Dineen. His record would never see the light of day. They were locking it into the vault for posterity. What's more, Dineen still was under contract to Agravista so he wouldn't be recording for anyone else any time soon. Davids was forced to promise Randall that Dineen wouldn't be released to go elsewhere. Randall wasn't going to futz around with anybody else in the industry who wanted to back Dineen, either. Randall had paid Dineen back and taught the industry a lesson all in one fell swoop.

Dineen was crushed. He didn't really understand why all this was happening since Davids wasn't about to explain how Mick Randall had rubbed his nose in it. Davids made up some story about lack of support from the radio industry for airplay on his product but Dineen knew there was something else going on. Eventually he heard the real story from Jewels. Dineen was the laughingstock of the industry. He had crossed the most powerful man in the business. People would use him as an example. "You don't want to end up like Dineen, do you?" they would ask.

Nothing guaranteed Dineen's everlasting enmity more than attacking his ego. But just who should Dineen be angry at? Clay Davids? No, Clay had invested a bundle in Dineen. He wanted his money back but had to take a huge loss on him. Besides, Clay pumped sunshine up Dineen's skirt, telling him he was "still the greatest."

What about Mick Randall? He was the one who had blackballed Doug. But if he went to war with Randall there was no hope. Randall was the key to radio airplay and success. He couldn't focus his anger and hate on Randall. He needed him.

What about Jewels? No, Jewels was still a friendly supporter and periodic coke supplier. Many a time Dineen had crashed on Jewels' couch and it was still open to him. Besides, Jewels still wanted Dineen to be successful, too.

No, the person most responsible for Dineen's plight was obviously Tony Mirakul. Mirakul was that moralizing son-of-a-bitch who had caused all of Dineen's problems. It was Mirakul's wedding that had started it. Everything was fine until then. This whole mess was Tony's fault. It never crossed Dineen's mind that he might be responsible for his own plight. Nothing had ever been his fault before. No, it was always someone else's fault, not his.

Dineen was glad of what he had done to Tony's wife in college. He was even happier that he had hurt him by his affair with her after they were married. It gave him great delight.

From that moment on Dineen began to dream and plot how he would exact his revenge on Tony for destroying his life. Dineen had found the fuel that would slowly consume him, his hatred for Tony.

Dineen stayed on the road. Every club, every hotel, every slight, imagined or real, threw more gasoline on the fire that kept Dineen going. He became obsessed. He would still be famous someday in spite of Mirakul and his buddy, Randall. He just knew it. He was one of the hardest working acts in show business, and totally ignored by all those whose favor he courted.

For ten years he labored, spiraling ever downward. He was finding it harder and harder to pick up women. He was losing his looks and his charm. Eventually he couldn't afford to keep a band together anymore. The clubs wouldn't pay him enough. He wasn't drawing flies. He tried going solo but this failed after about a year, too.

He finally quit playing altogether. But he didn't know how to live anywhere but on the road so he began to wander from town to town, still focused on his hate and his dream. Over time ridding himself of Tony had become equivalent to overnight success in the music business. As long as he was touring he had hope of making it in the music business. Now he had switched his focus to ridding himself of Tony. The minute Tony was out of the way he knew he would become a star overnight.

He began to track what Tony was up to. But he was patient, savoring every moment he dreamed of revenge. He still had plenty of fuel left to burn. And he was in no hurry. The longer he took the more savory would be the final prize.

He began to practice some of his plans on strangers. When the women stopped responding to his advances he became a rapist. After all, they all belonged to him anyway. They just didn't know it. He enjoyed the feeling of power this gave him.

As he meandered around the eastern half of the U.S. several men figured out he was up to no good. He had to kill two of them. He practiced on them, imagining them to be Tony. It just whetted his appetite for more. He was the hunter. Soon he would be ready to seriously hunt Tony.

Chapter 26 - *Sweet Surrender*

The spiritual transformation that had been happening in Tony was only apparent over time. From his concert promoter days to now he had become a far more spiritual, holier person. Of course, to him it was still a constant struggle with sin. The only thing different was that the sins he struggled with had changed over time. Whereas he was a liar and a thief as a concert promoter, now he was trying to control his anger with his children and his tongue in general. He was trying to be chaste in his marriage. The skirmishes he had fought and won with the grace of God he no longer thought about. How he had quit the entertainment business and gradually changed his behavior to be more ethical never crossed his mind. Anthony Joseph Mirakul was on a journey and he was moving forward.

Because he had sought it, and loved it, the Lord had been blessing him with increased wisdom. Like most men his wisdom was the result of his experience but unlike many men Tony actually learned from his mistakes.

One of these things involved Amana. They had weathered many hard times together and survived. They now had five children as the fruit of their love. Yet there was still something missing.

One day it struck Tony after reading part of the book of *Sirach* in his *Bible* that there was still a distance between Amana and him that should not be there. He decided to discuss this with her and kept looking for an opening to bring it up. This had been going on for two weeks and he still had not found an opening. They were both too busy.

Finally, Tony told Amana to come with him, walked out the door, got in the car and just started driving. Amana wondered what was wrong. She felt a little apprehensive.

Tony began to talk about how Amana was the love of his life, which Amana liked hearing, but she wondered, "Why is Tony taking me on a drive to tell me this?" Tony continued, talking about how a man and a woman were supposed to become "one" when they were married. Children were a natural result of that but it was more than that. Finally, Tony told her that he wanted to be one with Amana but felt like she was holding something back. Tony thought they should think of each other as "owning" each other. This was not the best choice of words, and Amana told him she didn't want to be "owned." Tony replied that he meant that "she belonged to him and he belonged to her." By that he meant that they were giving up their personal selves for the love of each other.

Amana didn't like this. She wanted to maintain her own self as separate from Tony. Tony told her that he felt like she was "holding back herself" from him, and he wanted all of her. Amana began to cry.

"You're dissatisfied with me," she said. "No, I'm not. If I was dissatisfied with you, why would I want more of you?" Tony replied. "I love you." Amana continued to cry. Tony became exasperated. "Why is that so hard for you to understand, that I want you to give me all of yourself, and I feel like you're holding something back from me?" Amana cried even more. Finally she said, "I don't know how," and burst into more tears. Tony reached over and hugged her as best he could without wrecking the car. He felt like a heel. He never thought about

the fact that Amana might not know how to be more loving.
He then began to talk soothingly to her. "I didn't know that,"
he said. "I'm sorry."

Amana didn't know how to love. It was as simple as that. She
had no example to go by. Her parents had been lousy teachers
about love, never showing any affection toward each other that
the children could see. Lucy Bartini thought that love and
affection meant only sex and had limited that to the bedroom
with her husband, John. John was certainly no better, being an
old-school male of European descent. John prided himself on
his lack of emotion. Now his children were emotionally
incapable of giving themselves in real intimate love because
they had no teachers.

Amana's sister Donna was experiencing the same dryness in
her life with "Sergeant" O'Rourke, who was just as frustrated.
Both couples were experiencing this as the children took more
time and energy and the active sex lives that had masked the
problem dwindled to almost nothing.

Tony was low-key but blunt with Amana. "If you don't want
to end up a stranger to me someday when the kids are grown,
you've got to make an effort," Tony told her. "I will make an
effort, too," he promised her.

One more step on the road of God's will for Tony and Amana.
After all, if God was love, then he wanted intimacy for his
loved ones more than anything else so that their love would
blossom. It was odd how so many times Tony had chosen to
follow the will of God without necessarily being conscious of
his decision to do so. God's will was like a natural compass
deep in the heart. If it was properly maintained it would
always right the ship. Tony and Amana's ships were moving
closer together and faster toward their mutual destination.

There was nothing amusing or particularly spectacular about this phase of Tony and Amana's life together. Growing in true love together was a little like watching grass grow. Better to fertilize it and check it in the morning. Or every few days. Better to build in a routine that reinforced good habits.

Tony began to give Amana flowers at unexpected times for no reason at all. He would make up funny cards to go with them, like "Just because it's Alamo Day" or "We're having chicken tonight." Amana would leave greeting cards in his briefcase that would fall out when he opened it in clients' offices. This was all well and good but what they really concentrated on was learning to touch each other. They had both gotten lazy when it came to kissing, so now they lingered in this area far longer than they had ever done before. And Tony learned to give Amana back rubs, which she loved, having ruined her back carrying five children. Tony could have started a second career as a masseuse he became so good at it. But he preferred keeping it all for Amana.

The bottom line was that things got better because they made a serious effort at it. This entailed making time more than anything else. Once they set aside the time for each other, almost anything would have worked, save watching TV. The latter was actually a destroyer since vegging out in front of the TV was basically a form of ignoring each other.

Over time grass grew, paint peeled and Tony and Amana's relationship entered a new phase. The kids would go "Yecch!" whenever Tony and Amana put on a PDA, public display of affection, but they were also learning about love. With a little luck the cycle of distance would be broken for Tony and Amana's children, and they would be more loving people when they were adults.

Donna and Amana had been exercising their sibling rivalry by competing over the number of children they each had. Amana was winning 5 to 4. But Donna had noticed a change in Tony and Amana's relationship that went beyond numbers of children. She saw it and wanted it for herself. So, putting down the rivalry for a moment, Donna asked Amana what was different between her and Tony.

Amana tried explaining it to Donna by starting with an explanation of what they were lacking from their parents, the ability to be intimate and loving. At first Donna denied that she was unloving, thinking that all that sex she had experienced must have been love. But eventually the lights began to go on and she began to understand what Amana was talking about.

Donna took this to heart, and even managed to trump her sister. She and Danny registered for a Marriage Encounter weekend, and came back raving about it to Tony and Amana. Of course, then Amana had to go on one, dragging Tony along. Tony had learned to let his wife have her way for certain things, like color schemes and furniture, even if he thought they would be hideous. Having no serious objection to a Marriage Encounter weekend, he went along figuring it might not be much help but it certainly couldn't hurt any. Tony was not big on group activities, preferring to work things out on his own.

Surprisingly, both Tony and Amana loved it. They couldn't stop talking with each other. Instead of having nothing to talk about like a usual weekend, they couldn't shut up. When they got home and the kids asked how it went, Amana tried explaining it to them while Tony muttered under his breath so only Amana would hear, "The sex alone was worth it." Amana turned and slugged him in the arm. It was just like old times when they were first married and still playful with each other.

Chapter 27 - *Black Gospel Choir*

Tony's life had settled down from his concert promotion days. Fasteners could be boring but they put food on the table every week. And that's what a family needed. Tony's priorities had gradually shifted from his selfish single days to his full-up family days. Every once in a while he would stop just long enough to remember how lonely he used to be before he met Amana, and before they had a family. He would try to remember this at about the same time as he began to wonder why he had this big family and all the stress of this responsibility. He would remember how empty his house used to be when he was alone, and how much he hated the quiet. How any extraneous sound could make him hit the ceiling like a cartoon cat. And how people had actually tried to break in to his place regularly in the crummy neighborhood he used to live in, including the guy who took a pickax to his window to get in. Tony had scared him off, and then put in bullet-proof glass.

Now he lived not far away in a bigger house. It was a safer neighborhood but without a moment's quiet. No house creaking would ever scare him in these surroundings. He was a happy man, with that inner happiness that could not be taken away by the problems of the world.

Not that Tony didn't have any worldly problems. He most certainly did. It was almost a certainty that if things were going well at home, there would be trouble somewhere else in Tony's life, work, in-laws or some other family member, parish, etc. It was just the way it was. Tony would remind himself that it was better to have a stable home, with problems elsewhere, than to have the messed up homelife so many other families had. Tony was an optimist. He had learned somewhere along the way that it was better to appreciate the good that you had than be preoccupied with the bad things happening at the moment. He hadn't always been this way, nor did he always act that way now. Sometimes he would forget and get stressed out and explode, or lose sleep. But for the most part he would right himself, regather his senses and get back on an even keel. Life was good. The show must go on.

Tony was deeply in tune with the Eucharist. A day without Holy Communion just didn't feel right to him. Believing in the Real Presence of Jesus in the Sacrament bred in him a sense that his day was a success no matter what happened, as long as he was able to go to Communion that day. Amana had started to go to Mass almost everyday, too, although they had to go at different times because of their schedules. It would have been nice to go together but it was the best they could do under the circumstances. Daily Mass and Communion had the effect of strengthening their marriage because they were growing in the same direction spiritually. Nothing helped a marriage more than spiritual growth together.

Both Tony and Amana were active in various ministries and activities in their parish, good old St. Hedwig's, where Tony grew up. Tony did have one run in with Fr. Studer, however. After several years of trying to interest the pastor, staff and congregation in evangelizing to the neighborhood without success, Tony had taken matters into his own hands and started going door to door giving out pamphlets and inviting people to the parish. There had been complaints to the parish and the bishop from both members and non-members of St. Hedwig's who lived in the neighborhood and didn't want to be bothered.

Fr. Studer didn't care too much if Tony wanted to trudge around in the neighborhood wasting his time but when the bishop called him on the carpet because of the complaints, he had to do something. Like most people Father only wanted to remain in the good graces of his boss. So he tried to explain to Tony that the parish wasn't prepared to provide the services that an influx of the poorer people now moving into the neighborhood would need, nor did he want the church to be perceived as a nuisance. Tony told Fr. Studer this was a copout because "making disciples of all nations" was the job of the church. Fr. Studer said it had to be done in other ways in order not to offend anyone. Tony told Father he didn't know of a way that wouldn't offend someone. They had reached an impasse.

Tony was extremely uncomfortable being at loggerheads with a priest. For his part, Father decided he couldn't trust Tony any more. He thought of him as a "loose cannon" he could not control.

Father decided to sidetrack Tony while he made it look like an accommodation. He asked him to sing the opening song and participate in an upcoming planning meeting on Evangelization for the various area parishes. Naively taking this at face value, Tony accepted, and learned how to play "City of God" on guitar just for the occasion.

One of the priests who pastored a black parish in town, St. Martin DePorres, heard Tony at that meeting, and asked him to come and hear his church choir. Tony obliged a few weeks later. He was impressed. It was a black gospel choir based out of the Catholic parish but it was inter-denominational, including members of Protestant churches from the ghetto, who didn't seem to mind being regular members of a Catholic church's choir. Tony was introduced by the priest, who told the choir how he had met Tony. They asked Tony to sing, which he did. It was a fine time all around. Tony left and thought nothing more of it.

A few days later he got a call from the choir director from St. Martin asking him if he would like to join their traveling gospel choir. Tony laughed, "You're not serious," he said. "What's wrong with this picture? I'm a middle-aged white guy who gets red in the face." "We don't care," she told him. "We voted to ask you to join. We need another tenor." Tony was flattered. He thought about it, then concluded, "What a hoot. It's not every day a white guy gets asked to do this!" "All right," he told her. "I'm game."

So Tony was suddenly thrust into a world he knew little about - black culture in America. Tony told Amana and his kids, who thought it was cool. But when he told his mother-in-law he had joined a black gospel choir, she said "Why'd you have to go and do that?" obviously irritated. "Because they asked me to, and I figured it was what I was supposed to do," he said. "Besides, it's not so weird. They're Catholic just like us." "I don't care if they're Catholic," she shot back. "They can stay in their own church on their own side of town."

For the life of him Tony could not figure out why Italians and Irish and other descendants of Catholic immigrants from Europe were so prejudiced against black people, especially when they were their own faith. It was as if being Catholic meant nothing to them. What was even stranger was when they had black friends. "He's not like those other people," they would say. Mrs. Davenport, formerly Bartini, was no exception. She had one black friend she had met playing

Bingo, and they rarely went Bingoing without each other. Elizabeth Doolittle was her name, and she was one of Mrs. Davenport's best friends. Tony just scratched his head.

Shortly after joining the choir, Tony asked his choir director why they had decided to ask him to join their otherwise all-black choir, and she told him, "We decided you weren't like those other people." "What do you mean, those other people?" Tony asked, dumbfounded. "You know," she said. "No, I don't know," Tony answered, realizing the truth but wanting to have some fun with her. "You know, you people," she squirmed. "What *you people*?" Tony milked it. "You know, white people." Tony looked at her stonefaced and said, "But I'm just passing," meaning "passing for white." His choir director burst into laughter. She then proceeded to tell the story to every other choir member as they arrived for practice, producing the same guffaws. Tony was in. He was part of the family.

From then on, whenever someone would make a comment to one of the other choir members about Tony being white, they would always tell them that he was "only passing," to their utter disbelief. It was a great running gag. The family joke. It was also very disarming.

The only problem Tony had performing with the group was bumping into people. Tony was notorious for bumping into people. The choir director placed Tony right in the center of the group where his tenor could carry the melody. "We look like a giant oreo sandwich," Tony thought. "That must be what people think when they see us." When the group began to sing it would sway back and forth. Tony would inevitably start out in the wrong direction from the group. This went on for 6 months or more before Tony finally figured it out. "White people lead with their left foot and black people with their right foot!" he announced one day at practice. "I've been watching and that's how they start out. That's why I'm always bumping into the person next to me." Sure enough, he was right. The rest of the choir expressed disbelief. "No, seriously," Tony said. He knew he was right. He had been observing. "You're just a klutz," one of the choir members yelled at him, to everyone's laughter.

Tony decided to have some fun. "You know how water spins the opposite direction in the southern hemisphere from the northern?" he asked. "Well, your ancestors are from Africa, south of the Equator and mine are from Europe, north of the Equator, so that's why we start with different feet." They all thought this was plausible, and besides the white guy said it, so it must be true. Tony was laughing inside but kept a straight face. From then on if Tony started up in the wrong direction he would mutter "ancestors" and everyone would nod their head in understanding. Hence started the "right foot/left foot" stereotype about blacks and whites. "Well, they all start with their right foot, you know," white people would say, as if that explained something deeply cosmic about the races.

The group toured for the next few years, playing lots of other churches of all denominations, plus other events like arcade openings, prisons and Black History Fairs. Tony would occasionally book them into non-traditional venues, like street festivals and county fairs, where they were well received. He did make one boo-boo, however. He booked them into a Sorghum Festival that turned out to be all Appalachian whites.

It was really tense from the time they arrived until the time they began to sing. Then the crowd loved them. It wasn't long after their performance that a bunch of the choir members were leading several hundred white folks in the "Electric Slide," which is not much different from country line dancing, so they morphed into that next. The crowd ended up loving them so much that they got invited back to the festival every year thereafter. "I guess they're all passing," Tony told his choir director.

News of the group spread over the years. They never charged for a performance, although they did accept donations for expenses. They just showed up and sang, for the sheer love of it.

One day in the spring of 1993 they got a call from the organizers of World Youth Day in Denver, Colorado, asking if they would like to come and sing for the Pope's visit. The group thought it was a fantastic honor. So preparations were made. The white, suburban parish that Donna and Danny O'Rourke belonged to, St. Hilary's, collected and donated enough money for the whole group to go. Tony, owing to his background in concert promotions, took charge of the logistics, van rentals, lodging, food, equipment, etc.

They rented two 15-passenger vans which are notoriously unsafe. One of them was brand new, while the other one was on its last leg. Tony was dubious as to whether the old one would make it from Akron to Denver and back. But it was the only other van he could find to rent that was large enough so they were stuck.

After months of planning, they were off. Things were relatively uneventful until they hit St. Louis. Bypassing the town to the North, following the belt highway around town, the two vans stopped for gas. 30 people spilled out of the vans for a pit stop, with Tony and Amana being the only white faces. As Tony stood there pumping gas he noticed a number of glaring white faces staring at him from other pumps in the station.

Tony thought to himself, "They hate me because I'm black. Wait a minute. I'm not black. But they hate me because I'm with all blacks. So I must be black, too." A shudder went up his spine. For the first time in his life he knew what it felt like to be black in America. And it scared him. Suddenly he thought about how vulnerable they were to attack. Any fool could drive by and shoot them, for all he knew. After all, THEY WERE JUST A CARLOAD OF NIGGERS to the rest of the world. They were expendable trash. Images of burned out Freedom Rider buses in Mississippi suddenly flooded his memory. "They treated them like they were less than human," he thought. "We're strangers on the road and they look at us like we're sub-human, too." Tony felt frightened, and crushed. He found himself doing what black people do. He looked at all the faces glaring at him, and he smiled a "please don't hurt me" smile, and quickly finished filling the tank. Over protests he herded everybody on to the vans as fast as he could and they took off.

Later that night they stopped in Columbia, Missouri, at the hotel Tony had booked. Tony was busy unloading the vans so he told several of the others to go get the room keys. When he was done unloading the vans he went looking for everyone else. He found a group of them waiting in the outer hallway of the motel. "Why didn't you get the keys?" he asked. Sheepishly one of the choir told him, "We were waiting on you." Tony couldn't figure this out. So he got the keys from the surly motel clerk, and asked his choir director what the deal was. She told him, "We don't like to have to deal with motels. Too many of us have been turned away when they found out we were black. They say they can't find our reservation." "You're kidding!" Tony exclaimed. "You mean that still goes on in the 90's?" "Yes," she said. "It's not as bad as it used to be, but it still happens."

Tony thought about how he felt at the gas station earlier that day. "So this it what it feels like to be black," he repeated to himself. "I am so glad I am white. I don't think I could take the indignity. I just know I'd be a militant, and that's no way to be."

Then he thought about all the prejudiced things he had overheard coming from the mouths of black folks. Tony had been around so long that folks forgot he was white and said stereotypical things about whites all the time. In fact, there was no virtue among blacks when it came to racism. Some of the most virulent racist remarks he had ever heard came from the mouths of black people. Tony was offended but it just didn't seem as bad because whites were not disrespected in the society overall.

"What a mess," Tony said to himself. "I don't like it one bit but I also don't know the answer. It seems like we should all be a little more respecting of each other." Tony thought about how he felt like family with the other choir members, and often forgot they were black. He liked to think of them as his brothers and sisters in Jesus, and they really felt like siblings because he knew God loved them as much as God loved him. Tony thought it was awesome that he had been given the chance to experience this. "Maybe everyone should have to travel in an interracial group of some kind," he thought. But then he remembered how often people, black or white, thought he was nuts when he told them he was in a black gospel choir. "Maybe in a hundred years we'll all be chocolatey," he mused. "A nice tan would look good on me."

Aside from one incident of overheating somewhere in the sunflower fields of Kansas, the old van made it to Denver unscathed. It was actually fortuitous that the van broke down where it did because Amana discovered a winery at the exit where the van ended up. A winery in Kansas? It must have been the only one in the state. Amana loved fine wines. While the men got the van fixed, the ladies went taste testing. They pronounced the wine "passable" given the circumstances. All fixed, the van headed on for Colorado with a few extra bottles on board. The new van just purred on alongside them.

Once in Denver they began a whole series of concerts on various stages throughout the World Youth Day park. The first show drew a few thousand people. By the second show the word was getting around. 10,000 showed up. The third show saw 25,000. The crowds were forming snakelines and weaving all over the park to their music.

Amana came backstage and told Tony, "I overheard two priests talking. One said, 'They sure sound like Baptists to me.' The other one said, 'I don't care. Let's dance!'" Tony laughed.

But the funniest thing of all to Tony was how the group reacted. On the way out to Denver a number of them had been grousing, saying things like, "They only want us because we're black." Now that they were there, all such talk had stopped. People of every color were everywhere in every kind of dress imaginable! And a black gospel choir fit right in. Tony found it all quite amusing.

Some of Tony's compatriots were heard to say, "These are Catholics?" They had never seen such a rainbow of people. "The Catholic Church is awesome!" Tony thought. It made him feel connected not only to the people he saw there but to all Catholics through history. "This is what Jesus intended when He started the Church. Everyone who wants to go to heaven should see this," he thought. "These are your roommates."

Chapter 28 - *Been to the Mountaintop*

The next day the choir had two concerts planned. The first was a sunrise service in front of the gold-domed State Capitol, and the second was a concert at Mile High Stadium for the Pope.

The choirmembers dragged themselves out of bed at 4 AM, dressed, ate and loaded onto the vans to rush downtown just in time for the service. "Why couldn't we have a sunset service?" someone asked.

Bleary-eyed the group took the stage in the darkness. Within a few minutes a gorgeous sunrise began stage left. As the light began to wash the crowd the group saw more people than they had ever performed for in their lives, even if you added up every concert they had ever given before they came to Denver. There were over 50,000 souls that had arisen before sunrise just to see them. Several of them froze at the sight of so many. Tony, who had seen larger crowds, and had to pacify angrier ones, too, was unfazed. Grabbing the mike, he introduced the group. "My fellow brothers and sisters in Christ, allow me to present to you, the group you've heard so much about, from St. Martin DePorres Parish in Akron, Ohio, the all-most all-black, *Poormouth Gospel Choir*!!"

The light hit the golden dome of the Capital and they launched into "The Rivers of Babylon." Stiff at first, they began to wake up and loosen up. They hit their stride on "Victory is Mine" and then swung into "He's Able" followed by "The Holy Ghost." The crowd was on its feet. Twenty-five minutes later they finished up with "Thank You, Jesus!" and passed into legendary status. The place was in shambles. The crowd was exhausted, and the day had just begun.

After the big start the group had a layover until 4 PM when they were to be at Mile High. Half decided to stay in town and check out the rest of the event, while the other half decided to head for the mountains, this being their only chance of the trip. So Tony took the old van loaded with half the group and headed north and west toward Rocky Mountain National Park.

"What a beautiful August day!" Amana exclaimed. It was sunny and 90 degrees, in the city. The van wound its way into the Rockies. They ate in Estes Park and headed on. They decided they would go up to the park's Visitor Center at the top of the mountain near the continental divide. It looked so easy on the map. Tony should have known better. The thought that this was a high point didn't seem to occur to anyone.

There were two roads on the map that seemed to go up to the summit where the Visitor Center was. Of the two the shorter looking one had alternate sections of white and black shading to indicate the road on the map. Tony decided that this was the one to take, thinking it would be shorter.

Following it up the mountain they were already a mile or two up the road when they realized that a) it was all dirt, b) it had hairpin turns, and c) it was one way only. They could not turn around. As they started their actual ascent, Tony realized he had made a terrible error in judgment.

The entire road was made up of hairpin turns crawling up the mountainside. What was worse was that the van was too long, being a 15-passenger size. On every turn Tony had to back up toward the edge of the precipice to swing the van around and make the turn. This meant constant stress on the transmission. And they were in the old van, with 140,000 + miles on it. One slip, and they would tumble over the edge to certain death.

Tony tensed up and started sweating, and praying. What had started out as a fun trip with singing and carrying on had suddenly turned terrifying. The group grew silent as fear gripped them. Amana had the presence of mind to start the rosary out loud. Gradually everyone joined in. 2/3rds of the group were Protestant so it was remarkable how quickly they picked up on the words of the *Hail Mary* and the *Glory Be*. Of course the *Hail Mary* was in Luke but they still weren't used to saying it. Tony continued to drive slowly, with Kenny, their bass player, hanging out the passenger side window giving directions to him. The rest of them prayed like they had never prayed before.

Up they twisted. Tony was bargaining with God. "Oh, God, if you'll just get us out of this one, I'll never ... again." They found one flat rest area, and they all got out to walk off some of the tension before resuming their ride. They were all wishing they could just stay there. But they had to press on. What's more, they had to get up the mountain, then back down again and back to Denver in time for their concert in front of the Pope. Time was awastin'!

They kept pushing. It got steeper, and colder and more barren as they went. Thank God it was sunny day. Rain would have made it impossible to maneuver the van around the turns. They looked down and saw a swatch of land that was washed out. One of the crew remembered reading about a sudden flood that had washed down the mountain and killed two campers that spring. Everybody got more uptight. The rosary went on. The second set of mysteries was half over. Then it was the third set. Still they climbed up the mountain. It was only a few miles on the map, as the crow flies, but unfortunately, they weren't crows.

They finished the third set of mysteries. The road began to smooth out and take longer, easier turns. They could see the Visitor Center up above. Everyone began to get excited. It looked like they were going to make it. Yes, it looked like they would make it.

A few more minutes and they were there. Tony felt like getting out and kissing the ground, but it was freezing! They had left 90 degree weather in shorts and it was now 30 degrees. There were snow flurries drifting by. Quickly they ran inside, hitting the bathrooms. "Ten minutes and we leave you behind," Tony yelled. Tony felt stupid. And thankful. His knees were a little shaky yet.

Now for the ride down the mountain...

The old van's transmission had made it up the mountain. Now it was time to see if the old van's brakes would make it down. As they left the Visitor Center they rounded the corner, and looked down. It was beautiful. And also terrifying. Tony began to realize how much demand he was about to put on the brakes. Quickly he downshifted to first gear. "We're going to almost creep our way down," he thought.

This road was better. It was paved. It also moved a lot faster. Unfortunately, it had no guardrails. Every turn gave the van's passengers a view ten thousand feet below. One wrong steer and they would all hurtle to their death. Tony was thinking, "This doesn't look as frightening when you're flying over it in a jet."

Down they went, Tony trying to keep it under control. Even in first gear it was going pretty fast. The brakes began to burn. Another rosary started up. They were fighting the clock to get back, and at the same time trying to slow down to make it down the mountain. The first few miles were the worst because they were above the tree line. There was nothing but rocks and crevices below. About halfway down the scenery changed. Now there were trees with the green leaves of summer. "It will be over soon," Tony thought. Not so. They went on for miles and miles amidst the greenery. "You folks try and enjoy the scenery," Tony said feebly.

Finally they were out of the park. But now they decided to head east for the freeway to try and get back to Denver in time for their papal show. This meant miles of winding roads through towering canyons of sheer rock walls, following a rushing stream that alternated from one side to the other like a double helix of road and river. It was beautiful, and Tony didn't see a thing. He was too busy race-car driving the van down the canyon like it was an obstacle course, trying to beat the clock. Amana was trying to enjoy it but it was mostly a blur. Oh, well, the Pope was waiting.

"You don't have to race," Amana said, interrupting Tony's concentration. "He didn't make our wedding, you know. Why should we worry about being late." Amana's attempt at humor brought only a slightly less hectic pace out of Tony's leadfoot on the gas. "Find the best way to Mile High on that map, would ya?" Tony asked her. She looked at it and told him. Tony filed the order of the interchanges and streets in his head.

Luckily, rush hour traffic was headed out as the van made its way into town. They pulled into the reserved area for performers and exited the vehicle 5 minutes before their scheduled appearance. The rest of the group was frantic, wondering where they were. "How were we supposed to go on

without you guys?" they asked. They were worried but then
when the van load showed up their worry turned to anger.
"We'll tell you after the show what happened," Tony told
them, feeling foolish. It had all been his fault.

He raced onstage. His choir director told him to introduce
them. Tony was still feeling foolish. Then he realized the Pope
was sitting just a few feet away. He began to thank God for
bailing him out again. "Mother Mary, pray for me," he
whispered as he went to take the mike.

"Ladies and gentleman, I hope we're not too late. You see,
we've been to the mountaintop, and what we found there was
deliverance by our God who answered our prayers!" Since the
group was black many in the crowd thought he was talking
about some metaphorical mountain, ala Dr. Martin Luther
King. But Tony meant the real thing, the rosary and the
mountain. "Let us thank God the Father, God the Son and God
the Holy Spirit for this fantastic day to be alive! And now I
would like to introduce to you, from St. Martin DePorres, in
Akron, Ohio, the..."

85,000 people roared their approval. "Reminds me of the
Breakneck Music Festival in Kent," Tony thought. "Hope they
don't burn down the pressbox." The participants in the
afternoon's escapade sang their lungs out. There was nothing
to lose. They had been delivered, and tomorrow it was back to
Akron. They ripped it up. The legend of the *Poormouth
Gospel Choir* was secure. Thank you, Jesus.

Chapter 29 - *The Fastener King*

If we measure time by the significant events that we experience, then only a few months had gone by for Tony and Amana, even though they had been married now for over 15 years. The most eventful thing, of course, was the birth of their 5 children, Luke, Amy, Philip, Samantha, and Michelle, all within 8 years. Their youngest was now five years old. Amana was 25 pounds heavier but then so was Tony.

Life in the city proper could be rough. The neighborhood continued to deteriorate. Crime was creeping up. Houses were changing from owner-occupied to renter at an alarming rate with all the downcomings of disinterest attached. Too many of the street urchins were permanently fatherless, and left to wander while their mom worked. The city leaders were concentrating on keeping programs that made people dependent on the government rather than freeing them. They didn't seem interested in keeping middle class families in town, either. The only time they paid any attention to them seemed to be when they wanted a tax increase. Then it was back to the same old "same old" after that.

Despite this the Mirakuls stayed. They would have liked to live in Fairlawn near Donna and Danny O'Rourke and the rest of their extended family but instead they stayed in Akron because that was all they could afford on one income. They had an old 4 bedroom house with only one bath that seven people used in shifts. Despite this relative deprivation they considered themselves blessed to have a roof over their heads. They realized there were far worse off people than themselves, whether it be really poor people financially or really poor people spiritually. On the surface they appeared to be like so many other lower middle class families in the country struggling to live paycheck to paycheck (which they did). But in reality they were going about the day to day revolutionary process of raising up disciples to the Lord.

Just because everybody else did it didn't mean that the Mirakuls did it. The older kids were already getting used to seeming odd even in their inner city Catholic school and their Catholic parish. The Mirakuls didn't have much money but, because they tithed, they always seemed to have some dollars to give when it came to any church, charity or civic need.

Amana stayed home and really nurtured her children. The kids felt safe there. Plus there were always tons of other kids around since Amana was home and many parents were not. Sometimes Amana resented being "Mom" to so many other kids whose parents were working when the Mirakuls gave up so much to live on one income but Tony told her it was a blessing to be able to stay home. Some couldn't. Others had made the wrong choice and were missing it. Either way, Amana should feel lucky. "Then you clean up," Amana said and walked out of the kitchen, leaving Tony standing alone.

Tony chuckled. He was used to helping out when he was home. He put on an apron and put all the food and condiments away. Then he loaded the dishwasher and turned it on. Finally, he started scrubbing the non-stick pots and skillets making sure he used a teflon pad rather than steel wool. He wiped off the table with a soapy rag and then removed the apron and walked out himself. There was nothing exciting about day to day life at the Mirakul household, yet somehow it just felt right.

What Tony and Amana once had in variety and excitement they now had in stability and routine. Oceans of it. The excitement of the last 15+ years would scarcely have filled one half-hour sitcom. Yet they had accomplished much. The children were well-grounded and learning their faith. Tony and Amana were both growing in faith themselves. Each one of them was just a little bit more Christlike with each passing month, with each passing year. Like plants growing, it had to be observed over time to realize the difference.

Amana was put on the planet to be a mom. No one was more sure of this than Tony. He had lucked out by the grace of God. After all the women he had been through it was miraculous to him that he had found such a good spouse, friend and partner. Amana could testify to the same. Given her traumatic past she had fallen into the sugar bowl herself. It was only the grace of God that they had ended up so well matched. They even knew how to fight without hitting below the belt or talking about irrelevant things just to win. Randomness said it shouldn't be so. But there they were, blossoming. It was serendipitous.

They knew that if they were successful with their five children that meant that those children would be likely to have successful homes themselves. This would multiply the effect. Good homes bred more good homes just as so many bad homes had bred so many more. Tony and Amana were dug in for the long haul. They had seen the rest of the world and it could go its own merry way.

Amana was a whirlwind of activities at church. She started a Sunday school. She was a pack leader for the Girl Scouts. She was a retreat leader for a women's retreat group. She volunteered at school as a kitchen worker in the cafeteria and in the summer as a tutor. She was a founding leader in the "Young Mother's Social Club" that gathered once a month to have fun and forget they had kids.

Tony had stumbled into a small ministry of his own that Amana ended up helping with half the time because Tony traveled so much. Tony wanted to build a basketball hoop for his kids to play on much like his father had built for him. But they didn't have a garage to build it inside of. All they had was an alley. So Tony put up a hoop in the alley.

To his surprise the hoop was overrun with kids immediately. It turned out that there was no safe place for the kids to play. The city parks were run down and inhabited by dangerous miscreants. Nor did the city have the resources to keep the undesirables out. Unfortunately, none of these inner city children had any social skills or manners. They were like wild animals. The minute Tony would leave his house some showoff would break the hoop down trying to jam it. Tony replaced the hoop twice, trying to keep the place up for his own kids and any other decent ones to play on. But he had numerous altercations with kids who refused to behave.

One night after another fight with these hooligans Tony walked down into his basement and saw an old forgotten plaster of Paris statue of the Blessed Virgin Mary that had been left behind by the previous owner when they had bought the house. In total frustration he picked up the statue, carried it out behind the hoop in the alley, slammed it down and said, "You watch over them. I can't do it anymore."

The next day he put up a hand lettered sign that said, "Mary's Hoop" and posted a set of rules. Then he managed to talk Fr. Studer into coming over and having a ceremony to bless the hoop with all the kids in attendance. They even had Father stand on a ladder and dunk the first ball after the blessing.

Exactly what combination of factors came together is always subject to interpretation but one thing is sure, the kids at the hoop began to settle down. They no longer broke the hoop.

They slowly stopped behaving like animals. Tony had fewer and fewer altercations although poor Amana got stuck trying to discipline everyone when Tony was out of town. Of course, the perpetrators would disappear after hassling her because Tony would go on the warpath with anyone who messed with her. Tony learned to pick out the biggest, meanest bully of a kid that came to the hoop and then hound him until he obeyed every rule. Then all the other kids followed. Sometimes wisdom had to be street tough.

Even though things settled down at the hoop some of the neighbors complained to the Akron Beacon Journal, which dispatched a reporter to do a story. He ended up writing a glowing report about the atmosphere at "Mary's Hoop" being "fit for the angels." This brought even more kids who had no place to play. When black kids started to show up regularly, too, some neighbors would call Tony and tell him they didn't belong there because they didn't live in the neighborhood. But Tony would tell them that all God's children were welcome at "Mary's Hoop."

As the years went on Tony added on to the hoop. One of his neighbors let him pave part of his lot off the alley to make the court bigger. Other neighbors let him put up lights and fencing. Tony held a 3 on 3 tournament and most of the kids won the first thing they had ever won in their life, a trophy and ice cream. Tony even talked some of the Kent State players into coming to do a clinic for the kids.

The original statue of Mary accidentally broke when a basketball hit it so Tony put up a vinyl statue of Mary holding the baby Jesus so the kids would all get the connection. Then he put up permanent signs with rules and an explanation of who "Mary" was. "Mary's Hoop" was neutral ground. Everyone was safe there. Tony made it clear no gang colors or violence of any kind would be tolerated, and he enforced it adamantly.

In a few short years "Mary's Hoop" had become the center of the neighborhood. Nothing brought this home more than when tragedy struck. One of the kids who had played there regularly was killed in a car wreck. Kids began showing up at the hoop the night after it happened. A few brought candles. Then kids began leaving and coming back with candles. Tony wasn't home so they asked Amana if they could sit at the hoop and just talk together past closing time that night. She agreed. 15 or 20 kids assembled around the statue of Mary with her child Jesus and the kids placed candles all around the statue and sat around quietly talking until well past midnight. Tony shut the lights down for the night and then left them alone to mourn in their own way. Tony and Amana were pleased that they had given the kids a place of their own even if it was only by accident. "Of course, we can't move now," Amana told people. "Who would keep up the hoop?"

Over the years Tony had become a successful regional rep for a company called Big Shot Fasteners. Big Shot manufactured pneumatic gun-type power tools to install nails and other fasteners in construction. This had both commercial and residential applications. Tony had recognized the advantages these power tools had for the Do-It-Yourself market and had begun marketing Big Shot products to the so called "Big Boxes" like HQ, Home Depot, Furrows, Lowe's, etc., long before any of his contemporaries had.

He had also refused to market the company's "coil" type pneumatic nailers because they shot on touch and were far more likely to injure people accidentally. He had always pushed the more expensive, slower but safer "sequential trip" style nailer guns. Tony had long been a proponent of the position that even if it meant longer install times and fewer sales, it was still more profitable to sell only the sequential trips. What they lost in sales would be more than made up for by the lack of litigation payouts for injuries.

Big Shot had been slow to come around to Tony's thinking but he had hammered it home for so long at annual sales meetings that the field force had followed suit unofficially and eventually the company stopped offering the coil type altogether.

The result was that when litigation skyrocketed very little of it involved Big Shot and the company surpassed many other manufacturers hit by the suits. Big Shot became a coveted stock purchase in the markets. Much of this could be attributed to Tony's moral leadership, although no one in upper management would ever have admitted this publicly. Tony might ask for a bonus or a raise, they figured.

They did, however, ask him to speak to the combined field force and dealer network at Big Shot's annual Convention this particular year. So Tony and Amana packed the kids up and headed to Disney World in Orlando. Just when they needed a vacation it seemed that the Lord provided them with one. And it was all expenses paid, too.

So off the family went in their minivan packed to the gills, from Akron to Chattanooga in one day, then from Chattanooga to Orlando the next. Amana could have been head of logistics for a small army given what it took to move 5 youngsters on the road. She seemed to know what to have on hand at any given moment for every possible need, from gum and candy to Tylenol and anti-histamines. Everyone called her "the pharmacist."

"Go ask the pharmacist," Tony would say. "Does the pharmacist have any gum?" the older kids would ask. The little ones would say, "Farm-a-sissy" and put their hands out as if Amana could read their minds. Most of the time she could. Tony would watch her and smile. "What are you smiling at?" Amana would demand when she caught him looking at her. "You!" he would snap back. Sometimes he would grab at her and she would push his hands away. "Now stop that, Anthony Mirakul," she would yell at him. "Those are for later." "Promises, promises," Tony would say. "Keep your mind on the wheel and out of the gutter," Amana would mock scold him. The kids would have no idea what they were talking about, or if they did, they didn't want to know.

This year's working session at the convention was to be highlighted by a speech Tony had been asked to give on the topic "The Secret to My Success." Tony thought it was a typically arrogant, pompous business idea. "*My* success," Tony thought. "How ridiculous. As if I was responsible for *my success* and not God." Nevertheless he had been strong-armed into giving a talk because someone had figured out that over the last 10 years Tony had sold more pneumatic nailers and more fasteners in his territory than any other territory of the company. He wasn't always first but his area had been the most consistent.

Tony had decided that his speech would be short and sweet, in keeping with his topic's alliterative use of the letter "s." So while Amana took the kids on the monorail to enjoy the amusement park, Tony went to talk to the conventioneers. Carson Penney, Big Shot V.P. of Operations, introduced him proudly. "My fellow Big Shot associates, without any fanfare today's speaker has led the company in sales of both pneumatics and fasteners overall for the last ten years. He must be doing something right. Let's hear it for our Regional Rep of the year, no make that the decade, Tony Mirakul!" Tony took the podium amid a burst of applause.

He opened with the obligatory joke. This one was about Danny Glover who used a Big Shot Pneumatic Nailer in a scene from *Lethal Weapon 2* (or was it *3*?). It made a play on the word "trip" which was the nickname for sequential trip pneumatic nailers vs. the more dangerous "coil" type. The punch line was, "It must be a trip. I only shot myself twice!" These insiders laughed hysterically while the wait staff yawned.

Then Tony explained that he was reluctant to speak because he didn't feel that he was responsible for his success. He explained that he paid attention to his market and his customers needs, especially what the field told him.

But more than anything else he credited his success to the blessings of God. He told the group that virtually every morning he got up and went to Mass. Then during the Petitions in the middle of the service he would always ask God to "bless the work of my hands by sending me some people who needed to nail things down." And that was it. "The Secret of My Success," as Tony put it. He then suggested that those who were so inclined should do the same thing, and if they weren't Catholic, they should do the same in their Morning Prayers. "Oh, and don't cheat your wife, your customers or your company," he said. Then he sat down.

"That's it? That's all he's going to say?" the Big Shots wondered to themselves. Tony's speech lasted less than 5 minutes, joke and all. Well, it certainly was about the topic, Tony's "secret." But now what?

Tony had copied the movie *Cool Hand Luke*. In the movie Luke convinces the whole chain gang to rush to complete their day's work spreading gravel on the road so they will have nothing else to do all day. In the same way the Big Shots had the entire rest of the day off to do with as they pleased. The golfers were out the door before anyone in management could think of a reason to keep them there. The rest of them quickly followed.

Whether any of them were buying what Tony had said, he didn't know. But he certainly knew why he had been successful. And his prayers for the courage and the wisdom to know when and what to say were being answered. Whether Tony's fellow Big Shots adopted or rejected his philosophy and approach, they would never forget that speech. It was short, sweet and to the point.

"I'm going to take my little ones and stand in line for 45 minutes to ride Dumbo," Tony told Carson. Then he walked out himself. Tony might lead a routine existence but he still knew when it was time to have fun.

As the years rolled on the Mirakul household continued to grow and mature. The kids were making it clear that they had 5 different and distinct personalities, all of them some unique combination of their mother and father. The influence of their parents was obvious. They were being "raised up" in the Church.

Tony was commenting to Amana on how great it was that the kids were permitted to proclaim the readings from the scriptures at Mass at such an early age. "They don't think anything at all of getting up in front of 500 people and reading out loud," he told her, amazed. "Sure, they don't know to be scared," she said.

"I was afraid to go anywhere near the altar when I was a kid. It took all the courage I could muster to be an altar boy. Once we were practicing and I was nervous and I burped and the priest chewed me out royally. But actually I wasn't so afraid after that because I managed to survive burping," Tony was babbling. Amana was amused. "It's different now. The kids think it's just normal." They both nodded that this was good.

"Hey," Tony started up. "How'd you like to go out Saturday night?" It was getting close to Amana's birthday. "What? On a date?" Amana asked, playfully. "What to?" she asked. "A concert," Tony answered. "A concert? What's that?" Amana asked, sarcastically. Tony and Amana had not been to a concert in more than 15 years. Once the kids came along a hot Saturday night date had become driving around with the kids asleep in their car seats, listening to "A Prairie Home Companion." Tony smiled wryly at Amana's sarcasm. "Oh, you mean a concert like last year!" Amana said, and started laughing. "Alright!" Tony said, curtly, pretending to be miffed.

The year before Tony had decided to be extra romantic for Amana's birthday. He wrote a song for her called "The Prettiest Sound I Ever Did Hear." It was about her name being the prettiest sound he had ever heard, until he heard her voice. It was very romantic. The only problem was he never got to play it.

On the night before her birthday he decided to surprise her by going outside their 2nd floor window to serenade her with the song he had composed. He helped her put all five children to bed. Then he encouraged her to put her pajamas on, and he would meet her for some "mommy and daddy time" when they could "visit." Then while she went to their room, Tony slipped out to the side yard below their window with his guitar.

Now Tony was down to just one guitar, a $50 Aria with a bowed top. He had sold his really nice guitar, a Martin D-35, to come up with the downpayment to buy their house years ago. His Aria wasn't much but it would do the job tonight.

Tony began strumming his guitar and calling for Amana to come to the window of their bedroom. When she finally figured out where the sound was coming from she did just that. She flung up the old double hung and put the stick under it to prop it open. "Tony Mirakul, what are you doing?!" she demanded. "I'm serenading you," he responded, and began playing his tune. He played about 12 bars of intro and in four more bars was about to begin singing when an ambulance roared by, siren blaring, drowning him out. Tony and Amana's bedroom was in the front of their house no more than 25 feet from the street and they lived on a fire route.

Tony continued strumming waiting for the sound to die off. He was just ready to start again when he heard shouting and arguing next door. Houses in their neighborhood were built about ten feet apart so you could often hear what your neighbors were doing, especially if it was fighting. Their new neighbors were young and fought a lot. It was also becoming apparent they were dealing drugs from all the cars pulling up and people running in and out quickly.

Tony heard what he thought was a gunshot, then a woman's voice screaming "You're trying to kill me!" He yelled up at Amana, "Call 911. They're at it again." He waited, still strumming his guitar, while Amana called in a report. Then she returned to the window. Before Tony could start, however, one of the kids came in and tugged on her pajamas asking for a drink of water. Amana told Tony to wait a minute and went to the bathroom.

After watering their errant child Amana returned and said, "O.K.," and Tony began to strum in earnest. He had just finished the first line of the song when the phone rang. Amana looked perturbed and yelled, "I better answer it in case they're calling back about next door." Tony kept strumming while Amana got the phone. In the meantime a car came down their street playing obscene rap music with the bass turned up so loud that it rattled their windows. Amana returned and said, "Telemarketer."

Tony swung into the first verse again and got through the whole 4 lines. He was just about to hit the chorus when two squad cars pulled up, sirens blaring. They were obviously there for the domestic disturbance call next door. Tony was standing in the dark by a bush with his guitar strapped on. Unfortunately from a distance it looked like he had a weapon, like a shotgun or a rifle. One cop came toward him from the squad car in front of his house, and he figured the other cop was already descending on the porch next door, so he swung his arm toward his neighbors and yelled, "You want next door."

He no sooner got these words out than the second cop whom he had not seen tackled him from the side, toppling him into the bushes and down on the ground right on top of his guitar. The old Aria exploded in smithereens under the weight of Tony and the cop. "Hey!" was all Tony could yell as he went down. Amana was screaming up above "Leave my husband alone!" The cops were ignoring her because they heard this all the time in domestic disturbance cases. The same woman who called in the complaint would then defend the man who was abusing her.

The two cops handcuffed Tony and dragged him out of the bush toward the squad car. Then they realized that he had a busted guitar on a strap around his neck. "You have the wrong address," Tony was protesting. "I was serenading my wife for her birthday. You want the drug dealer next door!" He was biting his lip so he didn't say what he was really thinking of these two Keystone Kops. They would surely take him to jail then.

The cops leaned Tony against one of the squad cars. Beginning to realize they might have made a mistake they checked the address of the call against Tony's address. Amana, meanwhile, had run down to the door and was yelling to let Tony go but wouldn't go outside because she was in her pajamas.

The cops finally figured out they had the wrong address but now they were worried that Tony would make trouble, so they were trying to justify what they had done. Tony had calmed down enough to just want to be let go, so he suggested that they all forget the whole thing, that as far as he was concerned nothing had ever happened. He even told them it would be a good excuse for him to buy himself a new guitar since the old one was practically worthless anyway. And he told them he would be much obliged if they would do something about his neighbor where the gunshots had actually come from. The two cops seemed very pleased with this compromise. It meant no paperwork. So they uncuffed Tony and with apologies escorted him to his porch. Then they headed next door.

Tony presented himself at the door, covered in dirt and with a smashed guitar strapped around his waist. Amana looked at him with relief that he was alright and then began laughing. Tony was trying to maintain some "cool" about the whole fiasco so he dredged up a line from Woodstock and said, "It's a free concert now!" as he opened the door and headed for the basement to hose himself off. Amana let him in, saying, "Oh, poor baby," and laughing.

That was the end of Tony's birthday "concert" for Amana. He never did play the whole song for her, insisting that it was far more memorable as the song she had never heard than anything he could have actually written.

So when Tony proposed a concert for her birthday this year Amana could not pass up the opportunity to kid Tony about "last year's concert." She just did it with a soft heart. No other man had ever tried to serenade her. Only Tony. She loved this man who was not afraid to make a fool of himself for love of her.

After Tony quit Family Jewels Productions he had wanted nothing to do with the concert business anymore. Then as time went on concert prices kept rising and Tony and Amana's money went to tuition instead. They rarely went to hear music anymore unless it was free. Tony couldn't bring himself to pay for a show, having been in the business where he could always obtain tickets as a "professional courtesy." It must have been his "cheap" bone.

On top of all this, Mick Randall had been building his empire of stations for almost 20 years, and radio content had become so bland that there wasn't much to get excited about hearing. Every single bit of airplay on the radio had been bought and paid for by the large conglomerate record labels so indigenous music was all but dead. Regardless of the genre, corporate music prevailed.

Mick had once told Tony that he could make money in some markets running a test tone. Mick was proving this theory correct. With a virtual radio monopoly he was showing that people would listen to whatever they were fed.

Tony couldn't blame him for playing it safe. The investments were huge! Wall Street demanded good returns. Radio was a business, not an art form. The idea that the public owned the airwaves was just silly. Tony knew all this. Still, he wished Mick would open up a little bit. It was just plain boring. But Mick and Tony didn't talk much anymore. Their lives had taken such dramatically different courses.

In fact, Tony had lost touch with all his old friends. Jewels was reduced to booking has-been groups for charity events because he got old and the new groups didn't think he was "cool," not to mention that he wasn't "corporate" enough for the suits that now ran the concert business.

Rob Gullett, on a goof one day, had dressed up in a red cape and tights, dubbed himself the "Spanish Fly," and started marketing multi-lingual software on billboards, the Internet and Mexican sitcoms to multi-national firms doing business in Latin America. This allowed him to bring back certain desirable commodities for his own personal use and hide money offshore to boot. Not to mention dress funny. He only spoke to Tony once in a blue moon or by Christmas card anymore.

The only thing remarkable to Tony was that both Jewels and Gullett had gotten married and stayed married. "Popeye" Gullet's wife even looked a little like "Olive Oyl." Tony liked to think it was partly do to his influence that they both had stayed married but he didn't know for sure.

Sid LeSurgic, on the other hand, had sold all his Big Signal stock within a few years after it was formed and then moved to a Caribbean isle to try and live the idyllic life of leisure Jimmy Buffett liked to sing about. LeSurgic used to hang out with Buffett on his annual weeklong concert foray into Cincinnati every summer. Buffett made enough money in that one week that he didn't need to work the rest of the year. Cincinnati was the Parrothead capital of the Midwest, if not the world, and no one, least of all Buffett, could figure out why, not that Buffett cared.

LeSurgic had stars in his eyes from dreaming of life in the tropics just like Buffett described it. But now that he had moved there he was finding it just as impossible to live like a song as Buffett had. That's why Buffett wrote about it. If Buffett had really been able to live it no one would have ever heard from him again.

Buffett had made a public issue out of rejecting the Catholic Church, thereby eliminating the possibility of paradox in his life. The one thing he had rejected was the one thing that could save him - the Church. LeSurgic was in a similar boat, trolling after Buffett. The experience of these "good time boys" had not produced any wisdom. They both thought life was strictly the result of "luck." Nevertheless, God kept pulling them back, even though they didn't want to go.

LeSurgic couldn't figure out why his life was such a nagging dissatisfaction. He was only trying to live the "life of Riley." He had plenty of money but no inner peace. He had married, divorced, remarried, divorced and then remarried the same woman, looking but not finding anything better than the bride of his youth. He knew she was best for him yet he still wasn't satisfied. He was floundering like the fish he hauled in off his boat. He had long ago forgotten about Tony and Amana, least of all as a good example of marriage and happiness.

No one seemed to know where Doug Dineen was. The collapse of his musical career after Mick Randall blackballed him had seen him reduced to playing in bars and dives during the decade or so after Tony and Amana's wedding. After that he just seemed to disappear. And no one, least of all Tony, was looking for him. Amana rarely, if ever, thought about him and neither did Donna. Little did Tony know that not a day went by without Dineen thinking of them.

The only "old friend" Tony had kept was his beautiful Amana. Beautiful to him because he saw more than just looks when he saw her. Despite the years and the ravages of bearing 5 children on her body she was ever more beautiful to Tony with each passing day. There was nothing sweeter to a man's heart than a faithful, loving wife. She was his heart's desire even after all these years.

Sometimes Amana would act insecure, particularly about her looks. Tony would tell her she grew more beautiful with every day. She would think he was just saying that to appease her but he really meant it. Tony could see her soul, not just her body. Tony knew her heart not just her looks. And her looks weren't bad, either. She had just spent too many years in Donna's shadow. Tony reassured her whenever she needed it. And she liked hearing it.

Tony and Amana couldn't afford to go out very often but Tony had ignored his "cheap bone" and decided to treat Amana to some great music for her birthday. He had procured tickets for what he hoped would be a fantastic show. He just had to go quite a distance to find it.

"So who're we going to see?" Amana asked. "It's a surprise," Tony told her. Amana bugged him. "C'mon, who is it?" "No," Tony said. "It's a surprise for your birthday. Just be ready to go in the afternoon. We're going down to Columbus."

Amana was excited. She and Tony rarely got a night on the town together. Tony was excited because he knew who they were going to see. It was his favorite guitarist of all time, even more than Jimi Hendrix, Phil Keaggy. He was hoping Amana would love Keaggy as much as he did.

When Saturday rolled around Tony and Amana rushed through their Saturday morning chores and kid things, anxiously waiting for Amana's mom, who was taking over for the day. They were ready to go an hour before she showed up.

"There's plenty of food in the fridge. The beeper number is on the speed dialer. Don't wait up, we'll be back late. Thanks, Mom, Bye!" Amana said, as they hurried out the door. "O.K. Tell me now," she said, as Tony pulled away from the curb. "Tell you what?" Tony answered, pretending not to know what she was asking about. "Where are we going?"

"O.K." Tony told her. "We're going to see someone that I think you will love. When I was growing up he used to play around everywhere in Northern Ohio in a band from Youngstown called the *Glass Harp*. His name is Phil Keaggy." Amana squealed. "Where's he playing?" she said excitedly. "You know him?" Tony asked, surprised. "You bet I know him. The greatest concert I ever saw growing up was the *Glass Harp* in Eden Park in Cincinnati. There must have been 25,000 people there and they were incredible!" "Well, I'll be...," Tony trailed off. "All this time I thought they were my secret." "Are you kidding?" Amana told him. "I still have two of their albums packed away." "I never knew that," Tony said. Now he *was* surprised.

Tony went on to explain that they were headed for what he thought was a small club called "The Lord's Place" or "The Kingdom" or something like that just outside of Columbus where Keaggy was playing. It was supposed to be some kind of Christian concert venue. He had sent away for the tickets by mail. They were both excited. A night out, and a Phil Keaggy concert!

"You know, I made them a pizza once," Tony told Amana as they were driving. "I was working at this nightclub bar-type joint that had a pizza parlor in the rear. At first I worked there as a bouncer checking ID's until some drunk punched me in the throat. I sounded like Rod Stewart for about two weeks. That's when they had me make pizzas, while I was recuperating. Then I just stayed there for awhile 'til I quit."

"Anyway, about that time the *Glass Harp* played a show there, which I got to see, and then I went to work in the back. About an hour later Keaggy and Pecchio came in and wanted a pizza. I think they had to move all their own equipment back then. But they couldn't seem to agree what to put on it. They must have argued for about 10 minutes while I stood there waiting before they finally agreed on something. So I made the pizza and then gave it to them no charge. I told them, 'See, you could have each had one.'" "My husband, pizza man to the stars!" Amana exclaimed and laughed.

They arrived in Columbus with enough time to have a birthday dinner in German Village at Engine House #5, and then headed for the concert. They both thought the evening was going to be great! When they got there they found their seats were way in the back in the last two rows of the hall but they didn't mind because it was small enough that they could see and hear everything just fine.

"All I see is an amp," Tony said, wondering. "Where's the rest of the equipment?" When Keaggy took the stage he was by himself. "I thought he'd have a band," Tony whispered to Amana. The place was jammed and Keaggy took off. Combined with a few black boxes Keaggy proceeded to put out as much sound as an entire band, almost an orchestra. It was amazing. He would play a guitar section, loop it, then start playing another part with himself. Before long he had multiple tracks going all at once. It was like watching a kid doodle in his basement, except it sounded great. The entire crowd was spellbound.

He went on like this for over an hour, playing various pieces neither of them had ever heard before. Then he quietly excused himself and took an intermission. The crowd started buzzing, getting refreshments, lining up at the bathrooms, etc. Tony and Amana just looked at each other. "This is awesome," Tony said. "I know," Amana said, almost dazed.

A few minutes into intermission a man came on stage and began speaking into the microphone. This being a "Christian" club he proceeded to begin delivering a sermon to the crowd. Tony thought this was an interesting idea, sermonizing at the intermission, and he listened to see how this would go over with the crowd.

The man wasn't more than a minute into his talk when he began to attack the Catholic Church as the "Whore of Babylon." Tony couldn't believe it. He figured this was an overwhelmingly Protestant crowd but he never expected to be hearing this kind of diatribe at a supposedly "Christian" concert. He also noticed that some of the people around him were murmuring things as they began to pay more attention to what the guy was saying. Some of them were squirming in their seats. Others were making it vocal that they didn't much care for what was coming from this guy.

The man went on attacking the Church and had now turned his attention to Mother Teresa. "Mother Teresa thinks she can earn her way into heaven with her good works. But I tell you she's going to Hell!" he proclaimed. "That's it," thought Tony. He stood up. Amana immediately said, "Tony, don't!" Tony, who was already moving toward the stage, turned to her and said, "Sometimes we have to speak."

Quickly Tony headed up the center aisle toward the stage and at the top of his voice yelled, "Excuse me. How do you know what Mother Teresa thinks?" The crowd fell silent, people shushing each other. It gradually worked its way back even to the concession stands where people turned to see what was happening.

"I know because that's what Catholics believe. That they can earn their way into heaven with good works," the man said. "That's a lie!" Tony shot back. "Catholics believe we are saved by the grace of God, and that we 'put on Christ' and do good works to show that we accept the gift of faith. Jesus said our actions would be judged, and the book of James says 'faith without works is dead," Tony exclaimed. The man didn't know it but Tony was scared, breathing fast, heart pumping, adrenaline rushing. Tony wondered what he had gotten himself into this time. He was actually afraid the crowd would kill him. "Holy Spirit help me," he prayed to himself.

"You don't know the *Bible*," he yelled at Tony. "The *Bible* says that you have to come out of Babylon, which is Rome. The Pope is the Antichrist. It's all in the book. That means you have to leave the Catholic church to be saved."

"That's another lie!" Tony cried. He wasn't as afraid when he was speaking. "There wouldn't even be a *Bible* if it weren't for the Church. Who do you think put it together and decided which books were in and which were out, or numbered the verses?" "We all know the *Bible* was given to us by God. It's divine revelation," the man said. "It's because the Church was given the authority by Jesus Christ that they could decide which books were in and which weren't. It didn't just fall out of the sky!" Tony yelled. "It's tradition..." the man said feebly. "I thought you guys didn't believe in *tradition*," Tony nailed him.

"You worship graven images... and Mary," the man changed the subject. "We do not. That's another lie of the devil!" Tony yelled again. "We only worship the Lord our God, Father, Son and Holy Spirit," Tony practically spit it out like nails to make his point. There were a few noises of approval from the crowd, and a buzz started in the background.

"You still think you can earn your way into heaven," he returned to his original idea. "Now let me get this straight," Tony came back. "Because Mother Teresa is trying to lead a holy life, that means that she thinks she is earning her way into heaven and so she's going to hell? And the Pope is really the antichrist who is just posing as a holy man so he can deceive everyone into being holy, too, so we'll all go to hell, right? It sounds like we should all do evil rather than good so we can go to heaven."

The man was perplexed. All he could think of was to say, "It doesn't matter what we do as long as we have faith," the man explained. At this some of the crowd jeered. There were a few shouts of "It does matter."

Tony grabbed control of the situation again, "You, sir, do not have any idea of what it means to be a true believer in Jesus Christ. I don't hear any love coming out of your mouth, only hate. And woe to you for trying to mislead these little ones. You are trying to divide the flock because you are under the control of Satan! I'm going to have to ask you to leave the building." Tony was up on the high wire now, working without a net.

At this, the man grew livid and jumped from the stage at Tony, growling like a wild animal. Tony braced himself for the attack but before the man could get to him, three men closer to the stage jumped out and intercepted him. When the crowd saw this there was bedlam. Several more men and a couple of women joined the first three men in restraining the man who wanted to attack Tony.

Then they began to drag him back toward the stage, then off to the side and out an emergency door on the side of the building. When the crowd realized what was happening they began to yell their approval. When the group of interceptors got to the door they pushed it open, setting off the alarm, and threw the man out into the parking lot. Then some of the group pulled the doors back shut, slamming them and shutting off the alarm. The crowd went wild, cheering. One of the group that threw the man out yelled, "And stay out." The crowd cheered and laughed at this.

Tony meanwhile had taken the opportunity to disappear back into the crowd. No one grabbed him or paid any attention as he went. By the time the other shenanigans were over Tony was back safely in his seat next to Amana. Only a few people near them realized it had been Tony who had gone up to the front.

"It wasn't the greatest defense ever," Tony told Amana, "but it will have to do." Tony was shaking from all the adrenaline he had been pumping. All he could think of was, "Most Protestants don't hate Catholics." The crowd had obviously felt much the same way about the speaker as Tony did. Tony felt good, surrounded by these brothers and sisters who had defended him. He felt hopeful.

He told Amana, "I couldn't let it go. There would have been people in the crowd who thought it was true because it wasn't challenged." "I know," she said. "I just wish it didn't have to be you," Amana told him. "Somebody's got to do it," Tony answered.

A few minutes later Keaggy came back to the stage, apparently oblivious to all that had transpired. He continued where he had left off. But Tony was too wired to enjoy it now. He tried to get into it but the concert was ruined for him. He stayed to the end only because it was Amana's birthday.

On the way back to Akron he told Amana he was too wound up to enjoy the second half of the show. In fact, Tony's system didn't finally calm down again until they had been home and in bed for about a half hour. Tony said, "O.K. now I'm ready for a concert." Amana snored lightly next to him. "Happy birthday, dear," Tony said to her sleeping ear. "I wonder if Keaggy ever serenades *his* wife?" Tony asked himself. "I bet nobody crushes *his* guitar," he mumbled as he fell off to sleep.

Chapter 31 - *The Plastic Rosary on the Mirror*

Y2K had come and gone with barely a blip of trouble. It had been over a year and a half since Tony's accident that killed the young man. Tony still prayed for the boy every night before he went to sleep. And he tended to slow up, look to the side and cringe when he went through intersections that reminded him of the one where the accident occurred. Sometimes he wasn't conscious that he was bracing himself to get hit.

The new millennium seemed pretty much like the old one as far as Tony's job was concerned. Big Shot had been bought and sold twice by larger parent corporations, big fish swallowing smaller fish, but nothing operationally had changed.

Tony had been making a bi-monthly trek to Tennessee to see his customers for over 15 years now. He would fly from Cleveland into Memphis early Monday morning, rent a car one way, spend the day in Memphis, then work his way to Nashville on Tuesday & Wednesday, then over to Knoxville on Thursday and Johnson City for half a day on Friday before dumping the car back in Knoxville and catching a flight back to Cleveland.

If it weren't for the parochial school tuition he would have handed the accounts off to someone else. But as it was they needed the money, so he made the trek because you have to see the people to do business.

He missed being home with Amana and the kids but *Volunteers* are agreeable folks, so he didn't mind the time he spent with his accounts. Most of the time he was invited to visit their homes, having been their rep for so long that most of them thought of him as more of a friend than a business acquaintance. His customers led quite normal lives, except for the ones in Nashville where everyone had stars in their eyes.

Once, Tony had made the mistake of staying in Nashville during Fan Fair week. This was the one week a year when all the stars came to Nashville and all the fans came there to meet them. There were endless autograph sessions and concerts galore. You couldn't go anywhere without running into somebody famous or stumbling on to some shindig. Tony didn't miss this business at all. But he did feel a few pangs of that old *concertlust* as he watched all the adulating fans and the famous people congregating.

To complicate things Tony was staying at Shoney's on Music Row, not because he had business there but because he just liked the hotel. He ran into Reba in the lobby before he even checked in. Her bus pulled in right behind his car. "Don't I know you?" she said. "Tony Mirakul... from Family Jewels Productions," Tony reminded her. "*Not-cool!*" she exclaimed. "I haven't seen you in years!" she hugged him, something she never did when he was actually working for Jewels. "You look great!" Tony told her. And he meant it. "What are you doing?" she asked him.

"I sell fasteners," he said, sheepishly. "What do you fasten?" she queried. "They shoot them into the walls in construction work," Tony explained. "You got family?" she changed the subject, not being the least bit interested in construction fasteners. "Yeah. Five kids, boy-girl, boy-girl, girl, all within 8 years," Tony enumerated. "Well, it's good to see you." "You, too." They parted.

Reba was already practicing for her grueling week with the fans, making them feel special when there was no way she, or anyone else, could possibly remember all the details of their lives, even if anyone wanted to. Picture, picture, kiss, kiss. It might seem phony to some but at least country stars understood what their fans meant to them and their careers, even if they could care less about them. They still showed up because it mattered. There were even country stars who actually did love their fans, although it was getting fewer every year.

Tony realized that the concert part of his life was really over. No more hanging out on the bus with the *Oak Ridge Boys* singing just for the fun of it. Tony remembered how his tenor voice had fit right in. He loved this not because they were famous but because they sounded better than any back porch bunch of singers you could imagine, and Tony was just one of the guys. He also missed Barbara Mandrell, the prettiest, most talented, and shortest woman he had ever met. Tony could remember her sitting on a table backstage picking banjo, her legs dangling off the floor, and she was so good that Tony momentarily forgot both how short she was and how beautiful. He could still see her smiling at him. "Good woman," he thought to himself, nostalgically.

On this trip Tony checked into his room, once again at Shoney's, and drifted in thought back to his "scufflin' days." Memories began to wash over him in waves as he daydreamed on his bed.

Once he had gone just a few blocks away to the old Ryman Auditorium, long before it had been restored. He had managed to sneak in to what was then a shuttered building that no one wanted. The *Opry* had moved to the fancy new Opryland on the outskirts of town and abandoned the old Ryman. Tony went in and sat down in one of the pews a few back from the stage. The whole place was decrepit. Splintery. Tony looked around and thought about the Beverly Hills Supper Club that had burned down in Northern Kentucky, across from Cincinnati. The only time he had ever been there was to see Charo just a few days before the inferno, one more example of his "charmed existence."

He had sat in the back of the Beverly Hills during rehearsal and was struck by what a fire trap the club room was. Everywhere there were red velour seats, and two corners of the Cabaret Room looked like they should have exits but didn't. That's where they found most of the bodies, he had read. He imagined the horror of being trapped with no exit. It made him shudder. He had only gone there to see Charo to please his date so she would sleep with him. After the club burned down he began to have second thoughts about casual sex. That lightning bolt was too close. A year or so later he met Amana, perhaps because he was finally ready.

His thoughts came back to the Ryman. He looked around for the exits. "This place is a fire trap, too. I hope I'm not a jinx," he thought. Then his thoughts wandered back to the stage, as he imagined all the greats standing there in front of him, Patsy, Hank, Jimmy Rodgers, Bob Wills. He wasn't really a connoisseur of country music. He didn't know all the trivia or all the stars. After all, he was a northern city boy. Still he appreciated what it must have meant to look forward to those weekend shows when the *Grand Ole Opry* was all about music from poor white folks' souls and not just another Hollywood business with a twang.

Tony thought about the time some useless New York music business transplant to Nashville had castigated him for calling it "country and western" music. "It's *country*," the guy told him, arrogantly. "And we sell it to country folk who have to live in the city." "Country and western" music's success had been its downfall.

Tony remembered leaving the Ryman feeling a little spooked, as if he had escaped the Twilight Zone but the greats were still trapped inside and could never leave. As he pulled the door shut, a chill ran up his spine. He jumped and wiggled as he shook it off. Traffic whizzed by in the sun and not a soul on the street paid any attention to him or the Auditorium as he hurried away.

Returning from this daydream, Tony called Amana and told her he was safely in his motel room; they said prayers, and Tony hung up. He didn't dare turn on the TV for fear there would be dirty movies on, and he would be tempted too much. He turned in early. He was beat.

Just outside of town a dirty derelict from the road was breaking into a suburban home, ransacking the bedrooms for cash and rummaging through the kitchen for food. Luckily, no one came home, for this wretch had been on a rampage across several states. He was not above murder if there was something or someone in his way. But mostly he was into rape.

He laughed when he found the booze on the top shelf in one of the cabinets. People were all idiots. Their cash was always in a top drawer with their underwear or in the *Bible*, and the booze was on the top shelf of a kitchen cabinet if they were secret alcoholics. He sat at the table, stuck his feet up on top of it and leaned back, toasting the owners of the house he was violating. "Whoever's bottle this is won't be able to claim it's been stolen," he mused to himself. "Ahhh. The perfect crime," he thought.

He lit out the back door when he had grabbed everything he wanted. He figured the owners were gone for the night so he could pawn a few things in town in the morning without fear. He found a stand of trees near a large interchange off I-65 and sacked out for the night. He loved falling asleep to the rumble and the noise of the interstate. Tomorrow he just might get lucky.

Tony made the rounds of his accounts as usual the next morning. One of them, Rit Blackmun, had some southern home cooking for lunch with him at Monell's Mansion. "Do you know why the University of Tennessee is in Knoxville and the State Prison is in Nashville?" Rit asked Tony. "No, why?" Tony answered. "Nashville got first choice!" Rit guffawed. Tony laughed, too, mildly amused. It was obviously a much funnier joke to the locals than to a Buckeye. He would store that one away. But he wouldn't use it in Knoxville.

Why was so much of regional rep work actually about being able to tell the latest jokes? Was Tony just a wandering minstrel without his lute? Tony had made a career out of being a good listener, and retelling jokes from one town to the next, never making up one of his own. In fact, he had no idea where all the jokes came from. Who was out there actually churning out new ones ? There seemed to be an ample supply of indigenous jokes, especially off-color ones, although the really great rep jokes were never gross. They were always witty, even if they employed something off-color. Bawdy was alright. Crude was not.

Tony's joke-telling delivery was dry and subtle. He was known for slipping in a joke so slyly that his guests often thought he was in the midst of general conversation when they would suddenly realize he had snuck in a story with a comical ending. As a result, he rarely bored or put his customers to sleep. They had to stay on their toes or they might miss a great joke.

Today was no exception. Rit loved to fish so Tony was telling him about a new hybrid gamefish the Ohio Fish and Wildlife hatchery had developed. "First they crossed a walleye with a muskie. And they got a pretty good tasting fish but they wanted one with a little more fight. So they took that fish and crossed it with a coho salmon. Now they were pretty sure they had the perfect gamefish. So they decided to give it a name that was a combination of all three fish. So they took *co* from coho, *wal* from walleye and *ski* from muskie and called it a *Kowalski*. But when they threw it into Lake Erie, it drowned," and Tony paused. Rit looked perplexed, then got it and groaned. Tony said, "What's the matter?" and gave Rit a deadpan look. Rit burst out laughing and then so did Tony. Knowing the best Polish jokes was one of the advantages of growing up in a Polish parish. Of course, there had been a world-wide shortage of Polish jokes ever since a Pole had become Pope and Poland had overthrown communism.

Besides jokes Tony was always pulling some story about somebody famous out of his hat. Nor did it ever seem like he repeated one, except when one of his guests would clamor for a particular story about someone famous that they had been told before but wanted Tony to share with someone new at the table. Some would have called Tony a namedropper but he didn't really tell a story unless it was funny or had some relevance to the conversation. It was just what he knew and had experienced. They could have been stories about strangers as far as he was concerned.

Tony and Rit parted after lunch. It was time to hit the road for the city by the Smokies. Tony always liked Knoxville, although he wished it was a little closer to the National Park.

He caught the belt highway around the center of Nashville and headed for I-40. Merging on to I-40 he noticed a ramshackle man on the berm hitching a ride. He stopped and picked him up. It was second nature to Tony. He couldn't leave anyone on the road in need.

The man had an old bag with a few things which he threw into the back seat. He was greasy and disheveled in appearance. Tony could barely make out his face for all the scraggly hair and the dirty clothes. Turning his attention to the road Tony and the stranger struck up a conversation.

"Where ya headed?" Tony asked. "Where ya goin'?" the man answered. "Knoxville," Tony replied. "Funny thing. That's where I was headed," he said. Tony noted the slight sarcasm in his voice. It made him a little uneasy. They drove a while in silence. Then Tony tried again.

"Where ya been?" Tony inquired. "Oh, around," the man said, elusively. Something about the man's voice was familiar but Tony couldn't quite place it. "I been around." "Anyplace interesting?" "Well, can I trust you?" he asked. Tony answered, "I don't see why not." "I'm on the run from the CIA," the stranger confided. Tony had heard wacky stories before so this, in and of itself, didn't disturb him too much. "Oh, boy. Another one," he thought but said nothing.

The man continued, "The CIA is running my life. They operated on me and stuck a computer chip in my neck which they control me from. Except I escaped, and I'm out of range for their transmitter as long as I keep moving." Tony was unnerved now. He hadn't heard this story before. The voice was also eerily familiar. The man showed him what looked like a little scar on his neck. "Sometimes I just want to rip it out myself. But I have to find a doctor I can trust to remove it," the man said.

Tony looked at the man and was scared. He tried not to show it but he began to think about escape plans. Tony noticed the man wasn't wearing his seatbelt while Tony was. "If he makes any dangerous move at me I'll slam the car sideways into a guardrail, and he'll hit the window or the dash," Tony planned.

As Tony drove he kept his peripheral vision on the man and on the side of the road so he would be aware of any sudden move, as well as the upcoming terrain should he have to ditch the car.

Then the man laughed. "Meer-a-*not*-cool, you gullible old fool. I don't have any receiver in my brain!" Tony recognized the voice now. "Dineen. What the...? What are you doing hitchhiking in Tennessee?" "Looking for you," he replied. Tony laughed but Dineen didn't. "Reminds me of what Skelton used to say," Tony laughed again. Dineen didn't.

"I figured it was just a matter of time before you picked me up. I know you always pick up hitchhikers. Your wife told me about it when she called me and had me come over to stay with her while you were gone," he told Tony, snidely.

Tony bristled. The memory of his wife's infidelity with Dineen was being thrown into his face. "Keep control," he thought. "Things are different now."

But Dineen was just getting started. He proceeded to revile Tony with detail after detail about first his affair with Amana before she met Tony, then a lengthy description of the 3 days he spent with her while Tony was on the road with *Sha Na Na* and Tina Bracken. Tony bit his lip. This was really starting to hurt. "Keep cool, *not-cool*," he reminded himself. "She called him. He didn't instigate it."

"I laughed like a jackal when I found out you were taking that girl to the hospital. You can't even cheat your wife right, you loser, '*not*-cool,'" he laughed. "I've done many things I've been ashamed of," Tony offered. "Things I wish I could undo. But I'm not about to brag about them to make you think I'm 'cool'," Tony lashed back.

"Ha, you goody two shoes. Always acting like Jiminy Cricket with Jewels." Dineen began mimicking Tony in a high, squeaky voice, "'That's not right, Jewels.' 'That's not fair, Jewels.' 'You wouldn't want that done to you, would you Jewels?' Ha! Mr. Conscience," Dineen mocked him. "I am very much aware of my own sinfulness," Tony retorted. "I wasn't trying to be 'holier than thou.'"

Dineen continued to berate Tony. Tony started to drift away, not listening. "This guys gone off the deep end," he thought. Tony drifted back in to the conversation.

Dineen continued, "I heard about you ragging on Jewels about Donna's abortion. You're both fools. I knocked Donna up, and I got her to have the abortion. I only told Jewels it was to save her career so he wouldn't know it was me pushing her into it. He would have been against it, and then I'd have had to listen to him repeat what you would say, Mr. Conscience... She would have gladly had my baby, the little fool. But I told her it was Charlie Fehr's because I was sterile, and it would ruin his marriage and his career and she had to abort it because she didn't love him, she loved me. The stupe bought it." Dineen had Tony's attention back now.

"You mean, Donna didn't want an abortion and you browbeat her into it?" Tony asked, stunned. "Yeah. The last thing I wanted was some kid running around and her always bugging me to act like a father," Dineen replied. "So I pinned it on Fehr."

"So it wasn't really Charlie's kid?" Tony asked. "Hell, no! I just didn't want to pay for it. I knew he'd slept with Donna once so I just told Jewels to get the money from him. It was brilliant. I got everything I wanted, and it didn't cost me a dime," Dineen said proudly. "You know what's even funnier? I found out a few years ago that Charlie was the one who was actually sterile! The big ballplayer was shooting blanks!!"

Dineen laughed demonically. Tony's mouth dropped open. He thought he had seen and heard just about everything despicable someone could do in his days in the concert business but this hit a new low. He was speechless.

Dineen saw his face and laughed even harder. "Well, look at this. Goody two shoes is speechless," he teased. Tony was thinking about Donna and how he had resented her. Dineen was having a field day laughing at him, thinking it was because he had pulled off such a great scam. "Not even Jewels would have thought of this one," Dineen sputtered.

Tony slowly turned and looked at Dineen. It was all he could do not to throttle him. Dineen was enjoying making Tony see red. "Why are you doing this?" Tony finally asked. "Why?" Dineen looked at him in disbelief. "You mean you don't know why I've been waiting for you to pick me up the last three times your office said you had gone to Tennessee? Or do you mean why am I going to kill you?" Dineen asked. "What did I ever do to you that you would want to kill me?" Tony said in disbelief.

"You ruined my life, you idiot!" Dineen told him. "You just had to invite Mick Randall to your wedding, and then he blackballed me so I couldn't get on the radio. Clay Davids said I was a star but, noooooo, Mick Randall owns all the radio stations so I can't get any airplay. Agravista dropped me like a hot potato. My record still sits in the vaults, never to be heard. DO YOU KNOW WHAT IT MEANS TO BE BANNED ON RADIO WHEN IT'S YOUR WHOLE LIFE?!?" Dineen screamed. "And it's all your fault because you just had to invite him to your wedding!!"

Tony countered, "I don't believe it! You crashed our wedding. I let you stay. Then you trashed our wedding, and it's my fault you hit on Randall's girlfriend?!? Do you see anything clearly?" he shouted. "She wasn't Randall's girl, she was one of mine, just like Donna and your wife are," Dineen insisted. "You're nuts. You don't own them," Tony spat back. "I'll always own them," Dineen told him, menacingly. Then, pouring it on, he said, "You know, I can't wait 'til those daughters of yours are grown." The insinuation was clear. Tony looked like he was going to pop. Then an unearthly voice of controlled rage worked its way out of Tony's throat. Very quietly it said, "That's enough." It was so quiet, in fact, that Dineen barely heard it above the road noise. But he heard it. It was like the tiny, whispering sound of God passing by Elijah in the desert rocks.

Dineen stopped for a minute then slowly pulled out a knife he had in his coat. Bringing it around in slow motion, he said, "Now don't get any ideas there, Jiminy."

They sat there breathing shallowly, both of them poised to strike, while the car sped on through the mountains.

And they sat.

Dineen was trying to savor the moment he had been waiting to enjoy for over 15 years. But it wasn't happening for him. He had imagined killing Tony in so many different ways and so many times that now that the real thing had come it was a letdown. Now he had to choose only one way. He wished he could kill him 10 or 12 different ways. Oh, he would still kill him but it wouldn't be as pleasurable as all those years of mentally doing it. He wanted to savor it just a little longer.

And so he sat, waiting.

Tony was watching for the slightest movement by Dineen, adrenaline rushing through his body. His eyes were fixed on Dineen while he steered the car out of the corner of his eye.

His blood was pounding in his ears with every rapid heart beat. His mouth was bone dry. He wasn't about to make the first move. He would defend himself but he wasn't going to be the aggressor.

And so they both sat, each one waiting for the other to move first.

Sweat began to pour off Dineen's forehead in anticipation. Tony's did the same in fear. The windshield began to steam up. Still they continued to sit there, crouched like cats.

Finally, Dineen could wait no longer. It was time. He leapt at Tony, skyhooking the knife like Kareem Abdul Jabbar. But Tony was quicker. He spun the car to the left as hard as he could, throwing Dineen first against the dash, then around against his door. The car slid sideways and struck the guard rail. The impact threw Dineen back at Tony but wildly so he couldn't control the knife. The blade came loose and embedded itself at an angle in the ceiling upholstery. The car rolled over one and a half turns and wedged itself between the guardrail and some rocks on the mountainside, driver side in the air, passenger side down, right over *Window Drop*, a hole in the limestone outcropping that I-40 hugged on the eastern rim near Monterey. It was several hundred feet straight down, and a miracle that the car had come to rest without plummeting over the side or falling through the hole.

Both of them were shaken up, Dineen worse than Tony since Tony had on his seat belt. The two airbags had exploded, shooting that peculiar combination of glitter and powder everywhere. Tony had known enough to close his eyes. Dineen hadn't so he was blinking his eyes uncontrollably, obviously in pain. The two airbags drooped sideways, hanging down like kids' punching bags. The car was crumpled all around. Dineen's door was slightly ajar from the impact. Tony's door was less damaged but he wasn't sure if it would open.

Coming out of their daze they both realized they were still in a fight. Dineen started climbing up to grab Tony, who was still strapped in his seatbelt. The two grappled and Dineen snapped Tony's seat belt loose. Tony headbutted Dineen, which caught him totally by surprise. Dineen was pleased. The last thing he wanted was for Tony to roll over and play dead. Like a deep sea fisherman, he wanted more fight out of his prey.

"Finally, you're using your head," he taunted Tony. "Someone must have dropped you on yours to make you this way," Tony countered, breathing hard. "Am I wrong to defend myself?" he wondered. "Should I just give up and die?" Tony chose life. He had no desire to kill Dineen but he wasn't going to let Dineen kill him if he could help it.

They rolled around with their feet balanced on the side door that was ajar. It was a precarious base. Suddenly, as they spun, the door gave way, and they started to slide out. Tony grasped at the rosary hanging from the rear view mirror, where he always kept it. Miraculously, it had spun around in the crash but not come loose. It was still hanging downward from the side of the mirror as Tony slid by and grabbed at it. He caught the loop and swung toward the windshield.

Dineen slid down Tony's clothes and grabbed at his legs, then his feet. He was holding on to Tony's shoes as he hung out the door. Now he realized that there was nothing below him but the valley floor below. Dineen screamed in panic and started clawing at Tony. Tony was praying that the rosary didn't snap and that the mirror stayed attached to the windshield. As for Dineen hanging there, Tony didn't know what to do. He couldn't do anything to help him, even if he wanted to, which he wasn't sure he wanted to do since Dineen would surely kill him if he had the chance. But he also didn't feel like kicking Dineen off his shoes because he knew it meant certain death for him. So Tony just hung there holding on for dear life.

"Doug, you need Jesus!" Tony cried. "Doug, pray to Jesus."
"Doug, ...*Our Father*..." Tony prayed the *Lord's Prayer* out
loud. After this he started a *Hail Mary*. There was silence from
Dineen other than grunts of trying to hold on. Dineen was
mentally scrambling, trying to figure out a plan to save himself
and still kill Tony. "Maybe I can jump and grab the door and
pull him down past me at the same time," he was thinking.

When Tony got to "Pray for us sinners now, and at the hour of
our death. Amen." Dineen yelled, "Would you shut up?" That
was his final answer to God's continued pleas for Doug to
return to him. The Lord had used the man who had the most
reason to hate Dineen to convey his message of love to him.
Tony was trying his best to "love" his enemy.

Just then the knife which had been stuck in the ceiling almost
sideways came loose. Since the car was on its side, it was now
headed downward, with gravity pulling it. The knife slid out
of its place and flipped over. Tony couldn't see it exactly but
it hit Dineen right on the forearm slicing him, then it fell away
into oblivion. Dineen screamed and recoiled at the pain before
he realized what he was doing. First his cut arm, then his
other arm, broke free of Tony's feet, and he was gone with
a blood-curdling scream.

Tony was shuddering, still praying his *Hail Mary*'s over and
over again. He swung his feet up, one against the dash and one
against the seat, pulling himself up by the rosary. He grabbed
at his shoulder harness with his left hand and yanked on the
rosary as he swung his right hand to the belt also. When he
pulled in a different direction the green string of the rosary
snapped at the loop, the mirror broke loose, and both the
circle of beads and the mirror tumbled out the door and down
the mountainside. Tony was left with a broken string and the
bottom few beads and crucifix in his right hand as he clung to
his shoulder belt with both hands.

He got a foothold on the center armrest and scrambled up the seat. He realized that his driver side window was shattered but he didn't know it was his own head that had smashed it during the crash. He pushed his head through the crinkled glass which crumbled around him. It fell inside the car and then back out the passenger side door down the mountain. Tony hoisted himself through the broken window. He climbed up on the side of the car which was now on top. He took a quick look around to make sure which direction the road was and jumped.

The car stayed right where it was. It did not fall. It did not explode. It just sat there. Tony stared at it. Then he began to shake and collapsed on the ground. He began to cry.

And cry.

And cry.

Never had he experienced so many emotions at once. Fear, relief, despondence, thankfulness, fatigue, horror, anger, pain and guilt. He was in shock. His head throbbed. He was wet but he wasn't sure from what. There might have been blood, too. If there was, he wasn't sure whose it was, his or Dineen's. There was nothing heroic or Hollywood about the way he felt or looked. He was an utter mess.

He sat there for what seemed like an inordinately long time just sobbing, holding the crucifix and what was left of his plastic rosary. In fact, it was less than a minute before another motorist saw him, and the driver stopped to help. "Duyuhafasellfone?" Tony tried to say. "Calmywifepleez!" Then Tony passed out.

When Tony woke up he was in Baptist Hospital in Nashville. He had no recollection of the helicopter flight. Dazed and confused, he saw strangers in his room. There was a nurse and two sheriffs. Tony didn't know it yet but one was Sheriff Avery Holler and the other was one of his deputies, Cleon Ledbetter, both from Cookeville in Putnam County. They were investigating the crash.

As they questioned Tony they began to piece together what had happened from Tony's disconnected comments. As Tony described the sequence of events, how he had swerved the car and the fight with Dineen, Holler and Ledbetter began to realize that there was another occupant of the car. "You say there were two of you fighting?" Sheriff Avery questioned Tony. "Yeah," Tony answered. "Didn't you find Dineen's body?" Tony asked.

Sheriff Holler looked at Deputy Ledbetter. The deputy got up and said, "I'm on it." And so began the search for Dineen's body at the bottom of *Window Drop*, the ridge where Tony had crashed the car. The sheriff said, "I'll come back," and left.

The next day Tony was feeling better. He was definitely more coherent. Amana had arrived and Tony had told her what had happened. He reminded her that he was "disaster-proofed," trying to put some humor into the situation. Amana was aggravated and relieved at the same time. She also felt a little guilty, as if it was her fault that Dineen had been stalking Tony. She was quietly saying a rosary of thanksgiving while Tony napped when the Sheriff returned.

The sheriff's attitude was different today, although Tony had no recollection of him from the day before that would cause him to think so. Today the sheriff was there to question Tony about the death of Dineen as a possible homicide.

The sheriff asked Tony if he had any objection to answering any questions. Tony was perfectly willing to cooperate. Sheriff Holler then took Tony's statement about the entire incident, including a history of the relationship between Tony and Dineen. Tony said nothing about Dineen and Amana, nor did he go into details about what Dineen had said about Amana or his daughters, wishing to spare Amana any trauma over the incident. The sheriff seemed satisfied, and told Tony it sounded like self-defense and not to worry about it. Tony wasn't. He told the sheriff briefly about the auto accident where they had taken his license while they investigated and then cleared him. The sheriff left and Tony figured that would be the end of it. "Just don't leave the state without talking with me first," Holler told him. "Yes, sir," Tony answered.

Later that day they released Tony, and he and Amana checked in to Shoney's on Music Row. Meanwhile word of Dineen's death reached Dineen's family and then Jewels. Jewels called Dineen's manager-attorneys in New York. "Dineen's dead. What's the status of that album of his?" Jewels was sharp. He gave the bloodhounds the scrap of clothing and they ran with it. In no time the M-A's had Clay Davids on the phone. "We can press CD's overnight in Hong Kong," they told him. Clay loved it - the sympathy angle - the potential "Legendary" hype - and best of all, no Dineen to make trouble or shoot himself in the foot.

First, Clay alerted the entire Agravista field force. The next thing he did was call Mick Randall at Big Signal. When Randall learned that Dineen was dead he was quick to figure out that this would mean big bucks for his stations. He quickly withdrew his long-time ban on Dineen and instead told Clay that he could count on non-stop airplay from every station in the chain with even a remotely close format to Dineen's music. Plus he would have Dineen's life and death become a topic for all his news-talk stations. The public wouldn't know what hit them. Clay knew that every competitor of Big Signal would quickly fall in line not wishing to miss the Dineen bandwagon. Doug Dineen was about to become the legend he had always wanted to be but had been denied, courtesy of the very man who had blackballed him years ago. Randall loved it because it was so poetic for him to now make Dineen a star after preventing him from becoming one all those years. After all, what good was all that power if he couldn't enjoy it?

So the "fix" was in. Doug Dineen was going to be as famous as Dylan or Presley. The machine moved into high gear. Suddenly the airwaves were awash in Doug Dineen songs. The CD's were ubiquitous. The requests for his ballad songs began to pour in. The young girls loved his voice. He was a modern day heartthrob like Sinatra or Elvis had been. *Rumbling Rock* magazine ran a picture of him on the cover with the headline, "He's Hot! He's Sexy! And He's Dead!" Doug Dineen became a household word. Doug's mother sued his ex-wife over the rights and royalties to Dineen's music and persona. Clay Davids was already wondering if there was enough material and outtakes for a second Dineen album. Everybody was making money except Dineen.

Just as all the hype began to hit the airwaves Tony was trying to get permission to leave Tennessee and go back to Ohio. Amana had left after a few days to get back to the children, and Tony was anxious to leave. He called Sheriff Holler for the third time in as many days to see if he could leave Nashville yet. The Sheriff told him, "Son, I need you to come on down here before you head for home and testify before this here grand jury." Tony was annoyed. But he thought it was better to cooperate than refuse, since he didn't want anyone to think he had anything to hide.

So Tony went over to Cookeville and testified before the Putnam County Grand Jury, telling them the whole story all over again. Everything seemed to go fine. The prosecutor, Lanny Hicks, didn't press Tony in any way. Tony just told his story and was dismissed. They even gave Tony his driver's license back. Tony was sure that would be the end of it.

Back home in Akron, Tony was amazed at all the airplay Dineen's record was receiving. "Oh, no! Now we've got to listen to this from now on?" Tony asked Amana, rhetorically. The last thing he wanted was to be reminded of Dineen every time he turned on the radio. "I used to give up listening to the radio as a penance for *Lent*," he told Amana. "Now I think that will be the only time I'll listen."

Dineen became the top-selling artist of the year. He was nominated for Grammies for Album of the Year, Song of the Year and New Artist of the Year, plus various Grammies in both Pop and Rock categories. Unfortunately, Tony had to watch all this from a hotel room in Nashville. That was because by the time the Grammies rolled around the Putnam County Grand Jury had indicted Anthony Joseph Mirakul on murder charges for the death of Doug Dineen. Tony was caught in the wheels of something he did not yet understand.

Unbeknownst to Tony, County Prosecutor Lantham J. "Lanny" Hicks was the brother-in-law of Sheriff Avery Holler. Nor did Tony know that Lanny Hicks was running in the Democratic primary for the U.S. Senate. On top of that Hicks didn't have as much cash as his opponent, a former radio station manager and well-known disc-jockey from Knoxville. Prosecutor Hicks desperately needed some name recognition, and Tony was going to be his siren, at least if he had his way.

Sheriff Holler had done some investigating and found out that Tony's wife and her sister had both been one time girlfriends of the deceased. When he turned this information over to his brother-in-law, Hicks had quickly realized that he now had a motive that would allow him to portray Tony to the grand jury as a jealous husband seeking revenge. Things were slow in Putnam County and he needed a case, any case, that would produce some media hype. It was particularly helpful, as Hicks saw it, that Tony was an outsider, and a Yankee to boot, since anyone else local he might prosecute was liable to be a relative, or at least a potential voter. Tony just happened to be in the wrong place at the wrong time.

Hicks managed to convince Holler that the "knife and prayer beads" he and deputy Ledbetter had found at the bottom of *Window Drop* needed to disappear with no record of them ever being found. This gave Prosecutor Hicks a hole in Tony's story to get his indictment. He then had the venue switched to Nashville in order to "guarantee Tony a fair trial," not to mention much more publicity.

Now Tony sat at Shoney's Motel on Music Row, anxious, lonely and longing for home. His world seemed to be coming apart at the seams. Carson Penney, his boss, had gone ballistic when Tony totaled another car. Then after almost twenty years of loyal service he had been fired from his job at Big Shot Fasteners when he was indicted. The company assumed he was guilty. Now Tony was stuck with a court-appointed attorney named Newman Blaylock because he had no money. Newman was not the type to inspire confidence. Tony wondered what Newman had done to Hicks to cause him to be stuck with Tony as a client.

At least Tony wasn't sitting in the jail. He could still move around freely. That is, he could have moved freely, if it weren't for the massive press presence. But Tony was under indictment for the murder of one of America's most beloved new musical artists. He was protected by armed security at the hotel, provided by Putnam County, of all sources, primarily because Hicks wanted to keep Tony alive long enough for him to hang him. If Tony were to be killed before the trial Hicks would get very little publicity. And since Nashville didn't want him in their jail they released Tony on his own recognizance, and

Tony had to pay for his own motel room and meals while he defended himself. His brother-in-law, Danny O'Rourke, was footing his living expenses.

Newman didn't want to put Tony on the stand but Tony pointed out that it was his word against the prosecutors, since no one was at the scene except Tony. How could they stop Hicks from character assassinating Tony in front of the jury if Tony didn't take the stand?

Hicks had hand-picked Newman Blaylock because he was timid and plodding. Hicks knew this would give him free rein in the courtroom to monopolize the media's attention. Hicks had even put up a weak objection to the trial being televised causing the TV stations to fight for it. When Hick's objection was overruled it all but guaranteed gavel-to-gavel coverage for the trial. Lantham J. Hicks was about to take the stage. Tony was Tennessee's newest monkey.

The trial began on a Monday with opening statements to the jury. Hicks got really wound up and made it seem like Tony was Adolph Hitler, who had come to Tennessee to destroy the talented Doug Dineen. He twisted every single thing about Tony's story that he could, playing up the "old girlfriend" idea as a motive for revenge on Tony's part.

Tony couldn't believe that the person Hicks was portraying was supposed to be him. It was almost like an out-of-the-body experience. He was being railroaded by a corrupt prosecutor. Tony wanted to interrupt him almost every 30 seconds but Newman kept telling him to stay calm. When it came time for his attorney to speak, Tony was livid. "You don't look very sympathetic to the jury," Newman Blaylock told him. "Calm down." Tony tried his best but he was furious with the prosecutor's distorted presentation of the truth.

Blaylock made a brief statement, which simply amounted to, "People of the Jury, my client is completely innocent and was only defending himself, which we shall prove." Tony put his head in his hands, and thought to himself, "O.K. God, how are you going to bail me out of this one?"

The prosecution laid out its case, which basically amounted to Hicks saying that Tony was guilty because Dineen was dead, and Tony must have pushed him off the cliff because he hated him. There was no hard evidence to prove the allegation, although the prosecutor planned to make it appear that way by concentrating on creating a scandal around Tony. To this end he called on Donna O'Rourke because he couldn't force Amana to testify about her relationship with Dineen because she was Tony's spouse. So he took the next best thing, Tony's sister-in-law.

He grilled Donna about her love affair with Dineen while she was a model. Dineen's ex-wife could be seen fuming in the back of the courtroom but the prosecutor didn't mention that Dineen was married at the time and Donna wasn't, not wishing to put Dineen in a bad light. Then the prosecutor asked Donna about her sister Amana's affairs with Dineen. He had managed to get a picture of her very public affair at OSU off the Internet since everything remotely related to America's newest star, Dineen, had somehow found its way onto the *'net*. Then he asked about their second affair, after she was married to Tony, trying to paint Tony as a jealous husband who killed Dineen in a rage.

Tony was doubly angry at this because Hicks was not only trying to character assassinate him but he was hurting his wife as well. Amana had her head buried in her hands until she realized the cameras were on her. Then she turned and beat a hasty exit from the courtroom, covering her eyes. Tony wanted to run after her and hold her but he couldn't leave the proceedings. He was trapped in a nightmare.

To make it even worse, Hicks set upon Donna next, asking her about her abortion with Dineen's child. Donna's mouth dropped open. So did her husband's. "I never had an abortion with Dineen's child," Donna said assuredly. "But you did have an abortion?" the prosecutor pressed on. Donna paused and bit her lip. This was horrible. She was being publicly executed. "Come, come, now, Mrs. O'Rourke. It's perfectly legal. Remember, you're under oath," Hicks pursued her.

Finally, Donna answered, "...Yes," she said quietly. "Did you know that it was Dineen's child?" Hicks continued. "It wasn't," Donna quickly responded. "Were you not having an affair with Dineen at the time?" "Yes, but it was someone else's child," she answered. "Whose?" "Do I have to say?" she asked the judge. Newman raised no objection. Tony was ready to kick him. The judge told her to answer. Donna paused. "Charlie Fehr, the ballplayer," she said. "Isn't Charlie Fehr married?" the prosecutor pounced on her response. "Yes," Donna said. "Does he have any children?" he asked. Donna thought for a moment. "No, I don't think that he does." "Then it never occurred to you that possibly the child you aborted wasn't Mr. Fehr's at all but was actually Doug Dineen's?"

Donna sat stunned for a moment. You could see the wheels turning now and Donna was getting upset with the possibility that Dineen might have tricked her into aborting his own child. This horrified and angered her. But that wasn't what the jury was getting. The prosecutor continued, "Who gave you the money for the abortion?" "Doug did," Donna answered, angrily. "Doug Dineen?" "Yes. He said he would pay for it out of his own money, as a friend, to protect me," Donna explained, sarcastically spitting out the phrases. The prosecutor ignored her petulance. "So he paid for it out of the goodness of his heart?" "That's the way it seemed at the time," Donna answered, lips pursed. She now doubted anything she used to think was true about Dineen actually was.

Tony sat there knowing what the real story was but unable to explain it because he wasn't testifying. Dineen's mother must have told the prosecutor about Donna's abortion and about Amana' affairs with her son. It would be just like her to do anything she could to pin a murder on Tony for killing her boy.

Hicks now began another line of questioning of Donna. "Mrs. O'Rourke, your mother's maiden name was what ?" "Bartini," Donna replied, not understanding why he would ask this. "Any relation to Cosmo Bartini and the Bartini crime family of Detroit?" he continued. "No!" Donna answered, emphatically. "You mean that with as unusual a name as 'Bartini' you're not related? Remember now, you're under oath," Hicks asked her. Donna thought for a minute. "If we are it goes back 150 years to the mountains of Sicily," she finally answered. "Then you are related?" Hicks returned to the same question. Donna had recovered now from the abortion attack and was starting to get angry. "Mr. Hicks, are you responsible for the actions of every low-life named 'Hicks,' or just your own?" she asked him. The courtroom crowd, including a few jurors, snickered. Hicks was slightly taken aback. He had expected to breeze through this trial looking like a champion of the public interest. But Donna had decided to put a face on the term "hostile witness" after Hicks had attacked her.

Hicks took a few steps back and leaning against his prosecutor's table, a safe distance from Donna, he asked her, "But you were aware that Cosmo Bartini, the reputed crime boss, was the financial backer of the company Mr. Mirakul worked for in Akron, Ohio, at the time Mr. Mirakul first met Mr. Dineen?" Donna was ready to fight now. "Mr. Hicks, I know that the only Italians you've ever been exposed to must have been what you saw on your satellite TV in your trailer back up in the holler, but not every person with an Italian surname is a mobster." More snickers in the crowd. "Whoa," Tony thought. "Related or not, never cross a Bartini!" Donna was pissed. Still Hicks wouldn't give it up. "But you were aware that Mr. Bartini was the backer of that company, were you not?" "Actually, sir. I have no knowledge of that being true," Donna concluded. Finally, Hicks decided it would be smarter to let it go. He would use other means to introduce the "guilt by association" angle. "Thank you, Mrs. O'Rourke. Your witness," he said, turning toward Tony's attorney.

Tony wanted his attorney to cross-ex to show how Dineen had manipulated everyone but Newman simply said, "No questions." Donna was excused. Tony watched her walk out. She was so angry she was shaking. Danny put his massive arms around her and hugged her. Then he heard Donna burst into tears. "Thank God for Danny," Tony thought. "It will be O.K., somehow." Tony said a silent prayer for healing for his sister-in-law and brother-in-law.

He had gone past anger now. Trying to paint Tony as a mobster? He knew he was caught in the wheels of the corrupt machine that Lantham J. Hicks was driving. Tony got steely. "I'm taking the stand and if you won't do it, you're fired," he told Blaylock. Court was adjourned for day one.

Tony went back to his motel with Amana. He insisted that all four of them eat together, Tony, Amana, Danny and Donna. Over dinner he explained the whole truth about Donna and Dineen and Jewels and Charlie Fehr, and how Dineen told him in the car with delight how he had manipulated them all. He explained that Dineen was surely the real father since Charlie Fehr had later been found to be sterile. Somehow Dineen had figured out that he was probably the father back then and had played Donna for his own ends. He also explained how Dineen had talked crudely about Amana and Donna both, and how he had claimed the two of them were "his." He even explained how Dineen had threatened his daughters.

Danny, who didn't speak much through all this piped up and offered that if he had been in the car he would have done the same thing Tony did. Tony told him, "I didn't kill him!" "Well, he deserved what happened," Danny told him, angrily. He looked at his still furious wife and put his arm around her. Tony looked at his despondent Amana and did the same.

Both women felt publicly humiliated. It was hard not to blame Tony, except that they knew Dineen, and both of them had fallen for the guy's charm. They knew now that even if Dineen hadn't hitched a ride with Tony he would have found some other way to attack him. Both of them regretted ever having laid eyes on Dineen.

Then Tony told them all, "Not only was he after me to kill me, but he made it clear he had been on the road and had killed other people who had picked him up." They all looked at Tony. Amana asked, "You mean he told you he was a serial killer?" "In so many words, yes. And a rapist, too!" Tony answered. "Then you had to stop him," Danny said. "I didn't kill him," Tony reiterated. "He attacked me. I defended myself. He fell." They all looked at him. Tony began to doubt himself. Waves of sinfulness roared up from his memory. He knew *he could have been Dineen* were it not for the grace of God. Had he actually killed Dineen in a rage and then come up with this story, like the prosecutor said?

Then he remembered the broken rosary that had saved his life. He had clung to the crucifix hanging at the end of the string even as he exited the car. He still had the piece that was left and carried it with him along with his black *Knights of Columbus* rosary from Italy that he always had in his pocket. No, he had done exactly what he had maintained all along. He defended himself but did not kill Dineen. The doubt on his face cleared and he sternly looked at his wife and in-laws. "I know what I did, and I didn't kill him. I never wanted him to die." He pulled the broken rosary out of his pocket and held it up for them to see. Tony's faith had saved him.

Amana was thinking, "Sometimes I wish he would be more like a man and defend us." Then she felt ashamed of her thoughts, realizing that Tony would surely give his life to defend her and the kids if necessary. She just found it hard to understand how Tony could take so much from Dineen without killing him. "This 'love your enemies stuff' is tough," she thought. She put her arm in Tony's and said, "We believe you, honey." Donna followed suit once she saw what Amana was doing. Danny saw both girls locking arms with Tony, jumped in and said, "Me, too, honey!" in a falsetto voice, which started the girls giggling in spite of themselves. Danny put his massive arms around all three of them like a big shield. Somehow smiles began to return to their faces. "Let's all pray for healing, and deliverance," Tony said. And they prayed with brave smiles on their faces for each other.

Tony didn't sleep well that night. He tossed and turned. Anxiety kept waking him up. He would say a few prayers and then doze off again only to be reawakened by the adrenaline his body was pumping. He had dream after dream. He was unable to do something that he needed to do to save Amana in some of them. In others he couldn't seem to escape himself. He woke up exhausted.

When he arrived at court the next morning there was a surprise waiting - an extra face at the defense table. He introduced himself as "Arthur Goodman... from Goodman, Goodman, Goodman and Hungadunga in Cincinnati." He told Tony an anonymous benefactor had asked him to come down and act as backup counsel, if he didn't mind the extra help.

So this was the answer to Tony's prayers! He couldn't have been more pleased. Tony knew things were going to be alright now because his sense of humor was returning. He asked Arthur, "Which Goodman are you, anyway?" "The middle one," Arthur told him. "Good answer. I want to take the stand," Tony told him. "We'll see," Goodman answered noncommittally. "We have some other things to do first."

When the session started the prosecution wrapped up its case. There really wasn't much else to do since Hicks couldn't get Amana or Tony on the stand. Nor was Hicks comfortable putting Dineen's mother on the stand, and certainly not his ex-wife. In fact, there wasn't anyone who would take the stand and offer a good character reference for Dineen. Hicks was amazed. There was always somebody who would stand up for even the lowliest trash. But not Dineen. Hicks realized his case was best left as it was. He would rely on the public image of Dineen as a great musical artist to make Mirakul look like a jealous murderer.

When the torch passed to the defense, Goodman immediately called Herzel Dobbin to the stand. Tony didn't know who Herzel Dobbin was but Newman Blaylock immediately exclaimed, "That's *Country Croc*!" as if that should mean something to Tony. Newman looked impressed.

It turned out Herzel "Laney" Dobbin was *Country Croc*, the morning drive time disc jockey on the "Country Monster" radio station back in Cookeville. Something about him made Tony think "Big Signal." He was just the type of personality Big Signal Communications would hire. "Did Big Signal own stations in Cookeville?" he wondered. "They must. They own them everywhere else," he answered himself.

Arthur Goodman proceeded to ask Herzel Dobbin about a knife that he apparently found at the sight of the crash. It turned out that Dobbin was part of a climbers club, and they had just happened to climb the ridge where the accident occurred that past Saturday. Herzel then explained how he had come across a knife on a limestone outcropping 2/3rds of the way up the side of *Window Drop*. At first he hadn't thought anything about it but one of the other climbers who had been following the story remembered that the accused, Tony Mirakul, had claimed that Dineen had a knife that had stuck in the ceiling of the car when Dineen supposedly attacked him, only to fall out and cut Dineen while he was hanging on to Mirakul. Dineen then fell to his death from the cut of his own knife.

His climbing club had taken the knife in and delivered it to Deputy Ledbetter on Monday, the first day of the trial, and the Deputy had given him a receipt for it, which Herzel showed to the court. Tony noticed that Sheriff Holler was squirming in his seat. Cleon Ledbetter sat behind him as low as he could squeeze himself down.

Goodman then went over to Hicks and said a few words. Then he and Hicks strode to the bench and asked for a short recess. Tony didn't know what was up. Newman sat there puzzled as well.

Hicks and Goodman disappeared out the back of the courtroom. Fifteen minutes later they returned. Goodman sat down while Hicks approached the bench. "Your honor, in light of this new evidence the state would like to request a dismissal of all charges against the defendant and also request that the record of his arrest be expunged." The judge looked at Hicks and was perturbed. "Case dismissed," he said. "I'll take the request to expunge under advisement." Then under his breath he said, "small town hicks!"

Meanwhile, the courtroom erupted, some of it with cheers, but mostly with disbelief. Amana squealed with delight and ran to hug Tony. Tony squeezed her as hard as he could then he whispered in her ear, "Let's go live happily ever after."

Reporters scrambled to get out the door and file their reports. Others descended on Tony. Some went for Hicks. Both of them tried to avoid the press and get out as quickly as they could. It was just for different reasons.

Tony wanted to take his family and get out of Tennessee as fast as he could. But first, he had to thank Goodman. "Couldn't you get me the commencement speech at Tennessee Tech while you were at it?" he kidded Goodman. Arthur smiled. "Call me about a settlement," he told Tony and walked out. "Settlement? What did he mean by that?" Tony wondered.

Hicks wanted to avoid any reporters who would ask too many questions about the knife. After what Goodman had told him out in the hall, he not only was ready to dismiss the charges and expunge the record, he was going to lay low and avoid politics. It was the end of his primary run. And he would do a better job of checking out his opponent next time, too. If there ever was a next time.

Goodman had allowed him to stay on the ballot to save face but Hicks had agreed not to actively campaign from that moment on. This was all because Goodman told him that the next person he would call to the stand was going to be Cleon Ledbetter, and he was going to force Ledbetter under oath to answer the question about the original knife they had found and why they had destroyed evidence. Goodman knew Ledbetter would wither under his examination and would own up to the destruction.

Goodman also told Hicks that there was a 4th witness to their collusion. Goodman knew that the knife Herzel Dobbin supposedly found wasn't Dineen's. And if he didn't dismiss the charges and expunge the record he was going to see that not only Hicks but Holler and Ledbetter all went to jail. Goodman then suggested that Hicks might want to consider a run for some other office some other time. But, of course, he wouldn't be able to do that from a jail cell.

Hicks had caved immediately preferring to salvage what he could. He didn't care about Dineen or Mirakul anyway. He could see he would be lucky to get out of this without being destroyed. There were people with more money than he who were willing to do whatever they had to do to stop him.

Luckily for Hicks, the FBI held a press conference later that afternoon and announced that they had matched DNA from Doug Dineen to at least 2 murders and 3 rapes across the South, and they were studying 7 other cases. All the attention shifted overnight away from the trial of Mirakul and on to Dineen. Tony was quickly forgotten. And Hicks was, too.

Tony had begun to put all the pieces together. He had a good idea who the anonymous benefactor was who had bailed him out. He was pretty sure it was Mick Randall at Big Signal. There were just too many Big Signal people hanging around for it to be coincidence, even with the media attention. If there was any doubt in his mind it was erased when he found out that the ex-station manager running against Hicks in the Senate Democratic primary was a former Big Signal employee.

Chapter 34 - *Would You Like To Settle?*

Tony avoided the reporters like the plague. He simply would not give interviews. Nothing he had ever said to anyone in the press had ever been quoted correctly. And he wasn't about to be any more fodder than he already had been.

Talk radio was even worse than the legitimate press. It was a complete aberration against the 8th commandment, detraction, calumny, false witness. He wouldn't talk to anyone.

Luckily, the public's attention span was short. They were now pre-occupied with the dirt on Dineen, the serial hitchhiker. If anything, the pendulum was swinging the other way. Some people wanted to lionize Tony for doing away with him. But Tony would have none of it. He didn't kill Dineen nor did he wish him dead.

The press still was such an annoyance that Tony took Amana and the kids and disappeared for a week. "If this were a commercial we should be going to Disney World," he told Amana, as they crossed the border near Niagara Falls. "But Toronto will do." The kids didn't seem to mind the vacation, especially since they got out of school, although they did complain about having to catch up on all their homework when they returned home.

Tony and Amana gave them each a wad of Canadian dollars to spend as they saw fit. They called it "play money" because it came in all different colors, and didn't seem like they were spending real money. This was the best part of all on vacation- "Mad Money." Tony was convinced that the different colors were part of an elaborate scheme to make tourists spend more than they should while on vacation there.

Tony and Amana tried to interest the kids in the various cultural attractions in Toronto, but all they really wanted to do was shop. The kids thought that Eaton Center looked like the *Titanic*, which was enough ambiance for them to spend their whole vacation there. They were selling glycerin soap by the pound at Eaton's, cutting it off in large chunks from massive blocks that looked like wheels of cheese and then weighing it on a scale. This fascinated the girls. They had never seen a department store sell product in bulk before. The boys were busy making fun of the girls for being so interested in soap. Tony put his arm around Amana and admired their flock. It felt good to be unknown and unrecognized again.

Eventually the parents got the kids interested in a few attractions but mostly it was the various ethnic "towns" that the kids came to love - Chinatown, the Filipino section, the Hungarian "Honkeytown." They browsed the shops and ate the food. Finally, they had spent all their money, and they headed back to the States. For the next few weeks everyone in the house went around saying, "eh?" after every sentence. Best of all, no reporters came around or called.

The first few days back Tony didn't know what to do with himself. He needed to find work and luckily someone in his parish referred him to someone else they knew who knew a guy who needed someone to rep plumbing supplies. Tony went to see the guy and he needed someone to "start yesterday." The next day Tony was a plumbing rep. The Lord will provide.

He also put in a call to Arthur Goodman in reference to his cryptic comment about "settling." It turned out that Big Signal was willing to settle with him to avoid any potential litigation for slander. Mr. Goodman told Tony he was authorized to offer him $250,000. Tony was pleased but suggested to the attorney that they set up 5 college funds, one for each of his children, and purchase prepaid tuition units equivalent to a 4 year private college education for each and either call them "scholarships" or pay any necessary taxes on them. Goodman said he would check and get back to him.

A few days later he called Tony back and said that his counteroffer was accepted. They would work out the logistics and the tax ramifications and take care of it. Then Tony surprised Goodman. "After all this is done I want you to call me back," Tony told him. "I have a proposition for you."

After all the settlement paperwork had been completed and returned, Goodman called Tony back. Tony proceeded to ask him if he would represent Tony in another matter now that there was no conflict between Tony and "Big Signal." Goodman said he would listen.

Tony explained how he had been summarily fired from Big Shot Fasteners when he had been indicted. Tony wanted Goodman to settle with Big Shot for wrongfully terminating him. Tony wanted enough money to pay Goodman and buy a small business for himself so he would be his own employer from then on. "I'll think twice before I fire myself," he told Goodman. Goodman agreed to represent him. "You sure you don't want me to sue everybody else who slandered or libeled you?" he asked Tony. "No," Tony told him. "I'm not going to be vindictive. Just getting money from them won't be a serious enough penalty to cause them to change."

So Goodman started the ball rolling against Big Shot. They were afraid they were going to be sued for mega-millions after what they had done to Tony. Not only had they hurt Tony but they had hurt themselves even worse. Their other employees had figured out just how little the company actually thought of them because Tony had been a star performer. People were heard to say more than once, "Just think how they'd treat me, if they treated him that way!"

In this environment the company was more than anxious to settle, especially if it meant less than multi-millions in payout. Goodman quickly arranged a deal that did what Tony had asked and took the paperwork back to Tony. Tony was pleased. This whole sad chapter was just about to end.

It was pretty obvious to all concerned that Big Signal Communications, which meant Tony's old friend, Mick Randall, had played a significant role behind the scenes in the dismissal of the case against Tony. Tony knew that there were ulterior motives for Randall's actions but he was thankful nonetheless. He decided that he would invite Mick to lunch just to say "thank you."

After a few calls to Mick's office, Tony finally got a call back from Randall while he was on a plane headed from Cincinnati to Dallas. Tony asked him to lunch and Randall accepted. They set it for the following Wednesday at Dee Felice's, a Cajun restaurant just across the river from Cincinnati. Tony knew Mick loved Cajun food.

Tony had an extra treat for Mick, too. He brought along Amana. There were hugs all around when they met. Mick seemed rushed initially but soon dialed it down a notch or two as he began to relax with his friends.

They began with some catching up. Amana told him about all the kids' exploits. Mick was still divorced (after a six month marriage) and had remained single for the last 15 years. Tony was now a plumbing supplies rep, but he described for Mick how he planned to open a specialty hardware store in Akron when the settlement from his former employer, Big Shot, came through. "We're going to be the Aufdemkampe's of Akron," he told Mick, referring to the legendary Cincinnati store on Central Parkway. "Where every rep knows how to solve every problem and the parts are always in stock," Tony said in his best TV commercial voice.

Talk then turned to current events. Mick had over 200 stations with all-talk-show formats. Naturally, he liked to hear about anything controversial, and for him that meant last year's priest scandal and now the schism unfolding in America's Catholic Church. He asked Tony, "What's your take on the priest scandal?" "I just know that every priest comes from a family of lay people so if there's corruption or a lack of faith among the clergy it reflects an even bigger problem in the laity," Tony told him. "If we don't encourage our kids to become priests or religious we have no right to complain about the clergy we get." Mick was surprised at this. "I hadn't heard that angle before," he told Tony.

He hesitated, processing Tony's answer. Then he said, "But what about the schism? Which side's gonna win?" Tony told him, "Follow the head." Mick puzzled for a minute, then said, "Ah, you mean the Pope." "Yeah. Wherever he goes, there goes the Church." "Must be pretty risky, depending on one man," Mick said. "Not really," Amana chimed in. "It's not just the Pope we're following, it's the Holy Spirit who keeps the Church safe, and that means we're just following God. That's a much better bet." "I don't understand that," Mick answered. "He's just a guy!"

Tony tried explaining. "God sent Jesus. Jesus set up the church and told Peter he had the 'keys to the kingdom', which means Peter, and each of Peter's successors, would be God's straw boss here on earth. Then to make sure the Pope wouldn't screw up, Jesus promised to send the Holy Spirit to lead the Church and he guaranteed Hell would never win. It's been that

way ever since, even when Peter's successor was a skunk."
Tony's fractured history of the Church actually seemed to
make sense to Mick.

"I guess then, all you have to do is believe there's a God,
and then the rest of it makes perfect sense," Randall suggested.
"Well, people get off the train at every stop along the way,"
Tony told him. "But if you stay on the train all the way,
eventually you get to where you know you have to follow
the head."

"But what about this new 'American Catholic Church' that is
claiming to be the real Church?" Mick asked them. "The head
wasn't chosen by the rest of the Cardinals, who are apostolic,
so it's a false church," Tony explained. "They're claiming they
carry the torch but it's just another schism." "What about all
the fights over control of the property? This bishop claims that
and that bishop claims this. Some of them are split within their
own diocese!" Mick went on.

"It's a terrible time in the Church for sure," Tony said. "But it
happens periodically. People go off the deep end on the right
or the left and they leave. Then the Church renews itself and
hits the happy medium. Then after a while things swing too far
the other way and the same thing happens again. It's always a
question of obedience. Somebody gets a wild burr up their butt
and they go off and start their own church because they don't
understand it's about obedience to God's will, not theirs. They
give you lots of excuses but it's still always the same reason
they leave."

"Sounds like you could make a lot of money in the futures
market if there was one for religions," Mick said, trying to
be humorous. "Always bet on a sure thing," Tony threw
back, pointedly.

"Food's here," Amana said, wanting to keep the conversation from going too far out. Her husband had the tendency to overwhelm people when it came to talking religion. Tony continued anyway, "You know, Mick, the really amazing thing is what's been happening quietly. The really spirited fundamentalists are coming into the Church in droves, especially the ministers. It seems the more they study the *Bible* the more they want unity with other Christians, and after a while they realize they can only find it in the Catholic Church. It's the only place where it all fits. It's just a process of elimination."

Mick squeezed a word in edgewise, "I didn't know that was going on. We should get some of those guys on the radio." "You should," Tony agreed. "I'll tell you one you ought to get. Tom Turkey. Tom used to have a whole organization that printed anti-Catholic pamphlets. Then one day he just up and converted. It seemed the more he studied the Church to rip it up the more sense it made to him. He also said he was having a recurring dream where a voice kept asking him why he was persecuting "him." He said he became convinced that the voice was either Jesus or the Holy Spirit."

"Great!" Mick answered. "Bob Pollard." "Who?" Tony asked. "Bob Pollard. He's a guy from Dayton with a group called *Guided by Voices*," Mick explained. "I suspect they're not the same voices," Tony surmised. "Well, whatever. Radio audiences will love it." Mick was thinking more about controversy and ratings than about whether the voice Tom Turkey heard was true or not.

Tony tried to get him to understand the gravity of it. "Do you know that when Tom announced it to his staff they almost beat him to death? It took real courage to turn around. Most people would ignore the signals and keep doing what they were doing rather than risk it all. This guy has guts!" Tony said. "Perfect,"

Randall answered. "Then he won't mind it if he gets peppered with angry phone calls." Mick was obviously in a different world than Tony and Amana's.

"Tell him why we came," Amana cut in. Tony took the hint this time. "Oh, yeah! What we really came for is we wanted to buy you out." Tony waited. Randall was the second largest shareholder in Big Signal, with almost 2000 stations. Mick's net worth was conservatively estimated at more than a billion dollars. Mick looked perplexed. Then Tony and Amana burst out laughing. Mick got it and started laughing, too.

"So you want to buy me out," Mick began. "How about if I just give it to you?" "That'll work." Tony chuckled. "No, what we really wanted to do was thank you for saving me from jail in Tennessee, and for putting our kids through college."

"How did I do that?" Mick asked, feigning ignorance. "You know what you did," Tony answered. "I'm not exactly sure how you managed to produce the knife that saved me but I knew for sure you were behind it." Tony paused. Mick still listened looking non-committed.

Tony went on. "I understand that the hiker who actually found the knife was the morning drive time jock on one of your stations in Cookeville, and he was just promoted to station manager at one of your stations in Tampa." Mick spoke up, "Well, he always wanted to move closer to his parents in Sarasota." "And it doesn't hurt any that he's not in Tennessee anymore, either," Tony suggested. "Why, whatever do you mean?" Mick laughed.

Tony continued. "It was also interesting that the prosecutor was running in the primary for the U.S. Senate against Bobby Stafford, a former Big Signal employee. I wouldn't be surprised if Stafford's contributor list contained the names of a large number of Big Signal employees, would I?" "Probably not," Mick admitted. Then smiled.

Against his better judgment he decided to break with his usual "close to the vest" approach. "Do you know how expensive 51 senators cost these days?" he asked Tony, as if Tony would have any idea. "No," Tony answered, all ears. "Millions. And then more millions," Mick told him. "It got so it was far cheaper to grow our own than buy them on the open market." Tony was only surprised by his candor, not by the truth.

He also knew why Mick needed to "buy" 51 senators. Big Signal existed because of the deregulation of radio. Congress mandated it and Congress could change it. Big Signal's very existence depended on Congress continuing to tolerate this incredible concentration of power in Mick Randall's hands.

Because Congress wrote the rules they could reverse themselves and force divestiture almost overnight. If that happened radio station prices would plummet, and Big Signal had paid a premium for virtually every station it owned knowing it would make its high cost back by charging higher advertising rates when it controlled the market. If Congress didn't remain hospitable to Big Signal's interests their stock price would collapse, and Mick would be lucky to be a millionaire instead of a billionaire.

Mick continued to spill the beans. "Our sources told us that the prosecutor actually found the real knife and destroyed it or hid it so he could prosecute you and make headlines. If the knife had been found your entire story would have been corroborated and there would have been no case, no reason to go to trial, no media coverage. Things being slow in Cookeville, your case was the biggest thing he was going to get for free publicity. We had to short circuit that as quickly and quietly as possible."

"I wondered why he got so flustered and almost popped a blood vessel when the knife appeared. You mean he actually had the knife and withheld it so he could prosecute me?" "Yes. You just happened to get caught in the wheels of politics," Mick offered. Tony whistled. Amana got angry. So angry, in fact, that she couldn't speak. Tony thought it was probably a good thing that the prosecutor was several hundred miles away, given the look on Amana's face.

"That's great!" Tony exclaimed. "The guy gets trumped, and he can't say a thing or he goes to jail himself. He must have realized you were playing hardball then." "Well, it worked. He basically dropped out after that. Not officially, but we knocked the wind out of his sails and he basically gave up. He knew he couldn't compete after that," Mick finished the thought. "One down, 50 to go."

The table was quiet for a minute. Amana finally calmed down enough to speak. Tony let her talk while he chowed down on Jambalaya. Mick was enjoying blackened mahi mahi with andouille sausage and green peppers.

Amana was thinking about what she would like to do to the prosecutor but instead she stuck with what they had come to tell Randall. "Mick, Tony and I just want to thank you for saving him, and for the settlement that pays for the kids' college. And if I can get my husband to stop picking up hitchhikers you'll never have to do it again," she said, getting in a dig at Tony. Tony let it pass. "We wanted to say thanks even though we can never repay you," she finished.

Then Tony added, "And even though we know you don't have any material need in the world we have been including you in our evening prayers every night since. We are praying that your wealth won't keep you from believing and being saved," Tony concluded, getting in a dig of his own on Mick.

"Well, thanks, I think." Mick responded, not knowing how to take being prayed for. "But you know it really didn't have anything to do with saving you. We had to stop that prosecutor from getting any more publicity. Saving you was just a bonus. Getting Dineen was a hat trick." Tony and Amana looked at each other, a little appalled.

Mick went on. "By the way, did you know that since your incident with Dineen, radio listenership went up 10% nationwide? And since it was sweeps month we'll be billing 10% more across the board for over 2000 stations? We'll make billions extra, straight to the bottom line."

"Well, that's all well and good, but why offer me a settlement?" Tony asked. Mick answered, "Legal dug up everything they possibly could on you, and they determined that there was no way to portray you as a public figure. Which meant you had a strong suit for slander against Big Signal and every other media outlet in the land for the way they portrayed you. And all the print media libeled you, too. We could see trucks of money pulling up to your door. So we determined to settle right away. I make it a point to settle early rather than late. It's cheaper and there's more control," Randall said, matter of factly. It was almost as if Mick was telling Tony he was a fool for settling for so little when he had helped make so much money for Big Signal and had such a good case.

Changing the subject, Mick told Tony, "You know, when you take the ripple effect, the boost to the economy overall from your little stunt was probably enough to push the whole country out of a recession. You made us billions and saved the economy. You're a hero!"

"I understand," Tony said. "You know, Mick, the truth is we don't care what happens to you, either. We only pray for our own sake. It's just a bonus if you get saved," Tony said, facetiously, comparing Mick's actions to his and Amana's. It took a minute for this to register with Mick. Sometimes talking with Mirakul was like getting a view into a weird parallel universe. It was an interesting sight but he didn't want to go there.

"Let me ask you this," Tony said. "What would you do if you lost all your money and your stations, and then you lost your health so you couldn't start over ?" "Not gonna happen," Mick shot back. "Well, what if it did?" Tony asked. "I don't think about it just like I'm not thinking about it now," Mick responded. "Well, my gift to you is that you should," Tony said. "Consider it a settlement."

Mick thought about this sidearm comment for a second. He just wasn't spiritual. Material things were what he could see and feel and own and manipulate. Spiritual things held little interest for him. "O.K.," he said. "I'll think about it." Tony figured he was just being polite. Pushing it any further wouldn't do any good.

"But tell me this," Mick asked him. "Why did you settle for such a small amount?" "Because that's all we needed," Tony told him. Mick puzzled over this for a second, thinking how foolish it sounded to him. He missed the utterly sublime wisdom of what Tony had just said.

The idea that Tony and Amana would only take what they needed meant that they relied on the providence of God and had no avarice. It meant that they realized wealth was a trap that could corrupt their souls and the souls of their children and descendants. But when a poor man speaks wisely no attention is paid to him. All this went right over Mick's head while he thought about how stupid Tony had been not to go after damages from everyone and get rich when he could. Mick was thinking, "That's why Tony is a loser. No killer instinct."

Mick let Tony pick up the tab. Tony left a nice tip and, with Amana in tow, bid farewell to Mick. "Hey, I'll get those former ministers on the radio!" Mick yelled, as Tony and Amana walked off. Tony just waved. Mick sat there for a second thinking about how Tony would never amount to anything. Then he remembered something. He pulled out his cell phone and dialed his office. Lunch was over. Time to get back to work. Mick dug in like a starving man.

As Tony and Amana drove away Tony felt sad. Why couldn't he say the right things to get through to Mick? Tony thought about the warnings to the rich in the *Bible*. Why was it always the "other guy" that God's admonitions were for, never us?

If Tony pointed out to someone that refusing to believe in the Real Presence of Jesus in the Eucharist was just like the many disciples who left Jesus in the Gospel of John because he told them they had to "eat his flesh and drink his blood," they would say that was for someone else, not them. Or if Jesus said that divorce and remarriage was adultery, that was for someone else, too, not them. And the list went on and on.

Everybody wanted to be saved but not change what they did. Tony wondered if he was doing the same thing somewhere in his life. "I sure hope not," he muttered. "Hope not what?" Amana asked. "That you ever leave me," he answered her, changing the subject of his thoughts. "Of course not," she said.

Northern Kentucky faded behind them as they crossed the "Big Mac" Bridge over the Ohio and headed north on I-71 for Akron. Amana put her hand on Tony's thigh and gave him a slow series of pats. "You did the best you could. Maybe he'll come around some day." "Maybe," Tony said. Tony didn't know he would have other opportunities with Mick in the future. "Let's go home," he said wearily. No one on the highway knew that one of the richest couples in the land was passing by, because it wasn't measured in dollars.

Meanwhile, headed up Vine St. in his blood-red Maserati, Mick was embroiled on his cell phone with a prima donna jock who was threatening to leave and go to work for a competitor. The last time this had happened Mick bought the other station the night before the jock moved. When the guy woke up, he still worked for Randall. Didn't any of these guys learn?

Mick Randall was so busy busting this guy's chops that he didn't notice that the lights had changed at McMicken. A Patanzaro Family produce truck that had just left Findlay Market rolled through the intersection. Mick was only doing about 40 mph. It wouldn't have been so bad if it hadn't been for the truck's forward motion climbing over the top of the sports car.

None of the bystanders knew who Mick was, although he was obviously rich. One of the local homeless reached into the car under the guise of checking Mick's pulse and deftly palmed his Rolex watch. But just as he began to pull his arm out there was a growl as Mick grabbed him with his other hand and dug his nails into the man's arm. Mick wasn't going down without a fight. The man screamed and dropped the watch. He yanked his arm out and yelled, "He's alive. Somebody call 911!" Then he took off.

North America didn't know it yet but Big Signal was about to become a champion of the handicapped. Mick would never walk again but he wasn't about to curl up and die.

Once again God was about to show that the kingdom of his Son was now, however subtle that might be. He would use the actions of the amoral, the evil and the ignorant to further the work of the kingdom in spite of themselves.

For two thousand years mankind had gradually come out from under the cloud of despair and selfishness that prevailed

among the Gentiles in the Old Testament. Even the Jews, who
were the only ones with hope in Old Testament times, had a
different expectation for what they were getting in a messiah.
Now virtually all of humanity, from its most important heads
of state on down, had learned that they had to couch their
actions in terms of doing good because of this pervasiveness
of Christ. His influence wasn't necessarily recognized nor was
he acknowledged by all as savior but Christ was the
underlying revelation that made mankind want to appear good
rather than evil.

In Old Testament times there was no such compulsion. But
God had rewritten his word on mankind's hearts when he sent
his only Son. Goodness was slowly, inexorably winning, no
matter how bad things looked from time to time. It was only
in the blackest of hearts that the spark of desire for goodness
had been extinguished. In fact, the devil was recasting evil
with lots of half-truths to make it appear to be "good" because
he couldn't trick people otherwise anymore. Evil was
definitely out of style.

It would not be long after his accident that Mick Randall
would inadvertently take on the work of the Lord, as he
struggled to maintain his empire against the vultures of the
entertainment industry. Whether Mick would ultimately end in
good or evil no one knew except God. The cosmic jury was
still out. The trial had entered a new phase. Stay tuned. Don't
touch that dial.

Back on I-71, and unaware of the crushing accident that would
change Mick Randall's life, Amana had started singing
"Country Roads." Tony joined in on harmony. Smiles slowly
returned to their faces. Singing together always made them
smile. "Hey, remember when we drove back from the Braun
show with Tony from the *Lettermen* and we sang three part all

the way home?" he asked Amana. Amana nodded. "That was one of the best times we ever had in the business," Tony said. "That's because it wasn't business. It was pleasure," Amana told him.

"I like singing with you," Tony told her. Amana smiled. "Wanta grow old with me?" she asked him. "Sure, if I can't stay young!" Tony answered. "Tell me you'll still be singing with me when we get old and gray," she implored him. "Of course," he said. "I'll just turn off my hearing aid." Amana slugged him in the arm. And they both laughed.

After they tired of singing Amana asked, "Shall we say our rosary?" "Sure," Tony answered. And he reached up to the mirror and grabbed his new "Blue Army" standard issue plastic rosary. It looked exactly like a million other ones, including the one that had saved his life three times before it broke.

Then he and Amana began, "In the name of the Father, and of the Son and of the Holy Spirit. Amen... I believe in God, the Father almighty, creator of heaven and earth, and in Jesus Christ, his only Son, our Lord, who was conceived by the Holy Spirit, born of the Virgin Mary..."

About the Rosary

From the earliest days of the Christian church monks had hand-written copies of the scriptures to read that would become the *Bible* in the late 300's A.D. A monastic tradition developed very early of praying all 150 *Psalms* every day called the *Daily Office* or the *Liturgy of the Hours*. Lay people wanted to be able to pray this devotion, too, but most Christians could not read or write nor could they memorize all the *Psalms*. Gradually, a "people's prayer" developed utilizing a few simple prayers that could be memorized. Various ways of counting the 150 prayers were used, pouches of pebbles, groups of small sticks, etc. This first form of devotional prayer included several prayers that would become part of the rosary. Around 800 A.D. Irish peasants began to tie knots in a string and pray 150 *Pater Nosters* (*The Lord's Prayer or "Our Father"*) or *Ave Marias* (*The Hail Mary*). Eventually these two prayers were combined and the rosary as we know it today came into wide use when St. Dominic began promoting it in 1214. It became universally accepted by all Christians. Soon objects were invented that could be strung together to make a circle. The Old English word for "prayers" was "bedes," so the objects became rosary "beads."

For the last 800 years the rosary has consisted of these prayers: the *Apostle's Creed* - the earliest digest of what the Apostles taught and that all Christians professed belief in, the *Our Father* and *Hail Mary* - both from Luke's *Gospel*, and the *Glory Be* - the great acclamation prayer of praise for the Holy Trinity. Because of great devotion to Mary, our spiritual Mother, 150 *Hail Marys* were substituted for the 150 *Psalms* and then separated into groups of ten with an *Our Father* in front of each group and a *Glory Be* after. Each of these groups (or *decades*) was prayed while meditating on the 15 "mysteries" that tell the story of the birth, death and resurrection of Jesus (along with his mother, Mary, who represents all of us through the *Incarnation*).

These "mysteries" were broken down into three sets - 5 *Joyful*, 5 *Sorrowful* and 5 *Glorious*, one set of which was prayed each day in rotation. This allowed for a smaller set of beads. All this could be memorized and meditated upon by anyone regardless of their education. It was a kind of little catechism for everyman. When the full cycle of all 15 "mysteries" was finished this "spiritual bouquet of roses" or *rosary* became a crown of prayer to the Lord in honor of Mary. It was never the "vain repetition" that Jesus warned against in the Gospel. It was always just the opposite.

Even in the turmoil of the 16th century, teachings about Mary's place of honor in the Church were never disputed. The rosary didn't become controversial until the late 19th century when some people began to portray it as "Mary worship." Although the rosary is a "spiritual bouquet of roses" that honors Mary ("*All generations will call me blessed*" - Luke 1:48) it is first and foremost a *meditation on the life of Christ*, not a prayer to, or worship of Mary. The rosary centers our attention on the life of Christ and what he has done for us. The grace of this daily prayer strengthens our faith in Jesus, our Lord and Savior. In the history of Christianity it is actually abnormal *not* to practice some form of this daily prayer. But the devil wants to tear down Mary to discredit her son, our Savior, and divide Christians. If you would like to counteract this and foster Christian unity, praying the rosary is one way to do it. This ancient prayer belongs to *all* Christians!

Many sites on the internet offer free rosaries (keyword: *Free Rosary*), or you can visit any Catholic church and in the vestibule there will usually be rosaries hanging up that anyone is welcome to have. Take some and spread them around to other Christians! They come in assorted colors and sizes, and they're way cooler on your car mirror than air fresheners or fuzzy dice.

Addendum

On October 16, 2002, Pope John Paul II proclaimed the year from October, 2002 to October, 2003 the "Year of the Rosary" for all "the various Christian communities." He also made history by suggesting an additional set of mysteries of the rosary - the *Mysteries of Light* or the *Luminous Mysteries*. This new set of 5 mysteries highlights the **public ministry of Jesus**. Chronologically these mysteries fit between the last *Joyful* mystery, *The Finding of the Child Jesus in the Temple*, and the first *Sorrowful* mystery, *The Agony in the Garden*.

The five *Luminous Mysteries* are:

1. *The Baptism in the Jordan* (Mt 3:17, etc.)
2. *The Wedding Feast at Cana* (Jn 2:1-12)
3. *The Proclamation of the Kingdom* (Mk 1:15)
4. *The Transfiguration* (Lk 9:35, etc.)
5. *The Institution of the Eucharist* (Jn 13:1)

This is the most significant addition to the rosary in 800 years! But it is profoundly logical. These mysteries have always been part of the story of Christ. Now they help make the rosary what the Pope calls "a compendium of the Gospels" for all Christians to contemplate in their prayer life. His encyclical encourages <u>all</u> Christians to include the rosary, and particularly these additional *Luminous Mysteries,* in their daily prayers. Perhaps this will be a turning point for the cause of Christian Unity. It's a great time to be alive!

You'll be hearing more about this over the next 800 years.

Also by Mike Mergler and his group *Fortunate Son*:

Long Night's Journey Into Day
- the world's first rock 'n' roll "faith witness."

This non-fiction story is the spiritual journey of a Hollywood songwriter and rock concert promoter from a decadent life to the saving graces of our Lord, Jesus.

Told in both written word and song, it includes a book and 2 CD's with 24 original "classic rock" style songs, one for each chapter of the book.

Overall, this album is a phenomenal work. I highly recommend it to all Christians...I think it is a tremendous blessing to hear the testimony of one who has walked the walk.
- James Branum - EXITZINE (www.exitzine.com)

(the songs are) ...catchy, meaningful, energetic, and sometimes downright moving. Like all good pop music, if you listen to it 3 times, you'll want to listen to it 300 times.
- Bud Macfarlane, Jr. - novelist and founder of St. Jude Media and the Mary Foundation

Suggested List Price is $24.95 for the complete set. But you can order your copy today at the special price of **only $10** each U.S. ($12 Canada and $20 International). Plus, we pay shipping and handling! All funds must be check or money order only, in US Dollars and drawn on a US bank, or you can order by credit card online at our website:

www.stmichaelrecords.com

MUSIC ORDER FORM

Please send me *Long Night's Journey Into Day* - the world's first rock 'n' roll "faith witness!"

US Customers _____copies @ $10 each = $_____
Canadian   _____copies @ $12 each = $_____
International   _____copies @ $20 each = $_____

Total Enclosed: $_____
Payable to: **St. Michael Records, Inc.**

(US bank check, money order or cash only. All funds in US $$$. NO credit cards. NO foreign checks or foreign money orders.)

Send order to:

Name: _____
Address: _____
          _____
City: _____State/Prov:_____
Country: _____Zip:_____

Special Instructions:

Mail your order to:
St. Michael Records, Inc.
PO Box 2912
Dayton, Ohio 45410-2912
All orders shipped within 24 hours.
Or visit our website at: www.stmichaelrecords.com